MW00903355

Climb to Victory
Over Breast Cancer

Jayashree Thatte Bhat

DIAMOND BOOKS

www.diamondbook.in

Publisher	:	**Diamond Pocket Books (P) Ltd.**
		X-30, Okhla Industrial Area, Phase-II
		New Delhi-110020
Phone	:	011-40712200
E-mail	:	sales@dpb.in
Website	:	www.dpb.in
Edition	:	2023
Printed by	:	Mercury Super Prints, Shahdara, Delhi - 110032

Climb to Victory Over Breast Cancer

Author : *Jayashree Thatte Bhat*

'Nothing in life is to be feared; it is only to be understood.'

— *Madame Marie Curie*

Acknowledgement

With a heartfelt prayer to the Almighty God, I express my extreme gratitude to all the Oncology Researchers and Scientists, and literally hundreds of women in Canada and India, for their help and support for this work.

I extend my sincere thanks to Diamond Pocket Books (P) Limited, New Delhi, India, for showing complete faith in my work and publishing this informative book for my readers.

I dedicate this book to:

All the Scientists, Medical Researchers and Healthcare workers
The world over
For their devoted, tireless work with intense passion;
Because of them
We're Almost There
In defeating Breast Cancer!

Contents

As the Climb begins...

There is a large community center in one corner of the city which is quite popular among all the citizens of the city. It has many unusual facilities, such as a swimming pool, games room, weights room and a small gymnasium, on its main floor. As you go upstairs to the second floor, there are four rooms of medium size that are ideal for holding group meetings or small parties. The rooms are available to anyone, any group or association on rent as long as the person who books them is a member of the community. The rent for these rooms is very reasonable; so most of the communities and associations, especially the non-profit organizations of the city, rent these rooms for holding their meetings. The center has a small parking lot for a few cars and provides free parking. In addition, its location near a major train station also becomes its asset for its popularity.

Right now, there is a meeting going on in one of these rooms. It seems like an unusual meeting; for, the chairs are arranged in a circle instead of facing the small stage in the room and there is no public announcement system set up. There are only seven chairs and except for one, all are occupied by women. It looks odd at a glance to see that no one is talking and all are just quietly glancing at the empty chair. From time to time, each woman is dabbing her eyes with a tissue paper. They all look quite sad. Just then, one of them gets up from her chair, and after blowing her nose and clearing her throat, starts speaking.

"One day, our chairs will also remain unoccupied like that one..."

The speaker, Anila Joshi, a woman in her fifties or so, is addressing the remaining women. They start listening to her intently. "We all know we have a disease that will end our lives, perhaps sooner than we expect. As breast cancer patients, we all know the bitter reality, but we are not going to just sit and shed tears, or feel sad and just keep looking at that empty chair."

She says after surveying the situation.

"Instead we are going to hold the occupant of that empty chair as an example to follow. You all know who sat in that chair with us until last month, right?"

Everyone nods.

"Her chair may be empty today but remember, her life never was so. Not even after she discovered she was a victim of breast cancer in its final stage. It was remarkable that her joyful bearing remained so till the end. We are going to remember that spirit of hers at all times. She was such a tremendous source of strength to me when I myself underwent mastectomy..." Anila waits for a few seconds. She takes a deep breath and continues. "You all know that I had to have my left breast removed when cancerous lumps were detected in it, right?" All of them nod again. "When I was lying on the hospital bed, completely depressed and feeling helpless, she visited me regularly and brought magazines and interesting books for me to read. Sometimes she read some passages from them to me; sometimes she brought poetry books and recited a few of the poems to me. She knew that poetry was something of my great interest."

Then Anila glances at another woman who looks of about forty years of age and says, "Tanuja, she was not an accomplished singer like you are, but when she recited those poems, the whole inner meaning of the poems seemed to come to the surface. That was so beautiful." Anila sighs and becomes abruptly quiet for a moment. Everyone in the room sighs too and there is a complete silence again for a few moments.

"I tried everything medically possible for her but just could not save her." Dr. Sudha Sant, a reputed breast cancer specialist of the city in her forties, breaks the silence. Her voice seems heavy with sorrow.

"When she came to me, her cancer had already gone to its terminal stage. In the X-ray, it showed that both her lungs were cancer invaded. It was just too late to do anything." She adds.

"But did she not have any tumors or lumps or anything in her breasts?" One of the women inquires.

"Of course she did. Her right breast was filled with lumps, one of them the size of a small lemon, I would say."

"Then how is it that she did not notice them earlier? Say, while changing clothes or in shower? Mine was only of a small pea size when I discovered it." Malti Patel, a woman who looked to be in her late fifties or early sixties, asks.

"That's true, but Malti, if you remember, your daughter forced you to go to your gynecologist for some other problem and that's when your gynecologist felt a lump in your breast. Thankfully she referred you to me immediately. When I examined you and looked at your mammogram, that's when your lump was detected, although it was still quite small, like a pea as you said. When we found out that it was malignant, we immediately started your treatment. It was in the very early stage and needed only a lumpectomy. That's why your breast was saved, and so were you my dear, right?"

Malti whole heartedly nods with a big sigh of relief that is also mixed with sad memories of her lost friend.

"Poor thing!" Dr. Sudha Sant continues. "She never realized that she had breast cancer. It would have been possible to do something to save her had she come to me for examination early." Dr. Sudha Sant says. "Particularly, as you all know by now, in cancer cases, *time is very important*. Time is the essence. The earlier it is discovered, the better it is. Early discovery followed by immediate treatment is what is needed. If you delay any one of these two, there is no pardon. The demon is sure to get you."

All of them look at the empty chair, for the demon had taken their friend's life. No one says anything for a long while. There is a brief and uneasy silence spread in the room.

"We are not here to lament but to recall and appreciate how courageously she spent her year after her cancer was detected." Anila once again takes charge of the proceedings.

"If that is so, then get that damn empty chair out of sight. It is so very depressing to even look at it." A much younger looking woman, perhaps in her late twenties or early thirties, very graceful with a shapely body, grabs the chair and starts pushing it to a faraway wall. The whole place reverberates with a loud noise coupled with the tic-tock sound of her high heeled shoes. For a moment everybody is speechless and just stares simultaneously at the young woman as she is pushing the chair. The young woman returns to her own chair, readjusts it and asks her neighbor to shift her chair a bit.

"What? Umm…what? What's it you want?" The neighbor, Kiran, another relatively young woman, also in her late twenties or early thirties, looks a bit confused.

"I said adjust your chair so that six of us will form a proper circle. Right now, it looks a bit crooked." Kiran gets up and follows the instruction.

"Are you settled now, Sheila? And you, Kiran?" Anila looks at both of them with a smile and adds, "Sheila, you are absolutely right. Good you removed that empty chair from our sight. It did emit some 'vibes' of depression, especially for all of us who are victims of breast cancer, isn't it?"

"Well, except me, I suppose." Says, Dr. Sudha.

"That's right Dr. Sudha. You are the cancer specialist here. As a matter of fact you are the one who has called this meeting today. Shall we proceed with the agenda of this meeting now?"

"Yes, yes." All the women agree to proceed with the meeting.

"Ladies," Dr. Sudha starts talking, "this meeting is specially called for a novel idea, an idea for developing a formal support group, associated with all major cancer centers of the city for breast cancer victims." Dr. Sudha gets ready to chair the meeting of that day and it progresses as per the agenda.

Dr. Sudha clears her throat and starts talking, "Ladies, first of all, thank you all for coming to this meeting today despite such a short notice. The reason why I have called this meeting today is to give you all a brief background; in one of my casual meetings with Anila, I mentioned to her the idea of forming a Breast Cancer Support group. To my utter surprise, Anila just took to that idea like wild fire. In theory, it is not a new idea. What we term as 'group therapy' is being practiced in many other countries today. So, a formal Support group as such is nothing new. It is just that such concept does not exist in India and perhaps in many other countries with older cultures. Women discussing openly about their own health problems especially breast cancer, is still a big taboo here, isn't it?" Dr. Sudha briefly looks at everyone and sees them nodding.

"But that is not the situation in many Western countries. When I was in Canada on a two-year research fellowship in

Oncology, I came across many Cancer Centers there, which offer group therapy to women who are breast cancer patients. This service is offered to all of them in addition to their medical treatment. I was so impressed with their work that right then and there, I took a decision that after getting back to India, I should start a similar project, based on the same concept for women with breast cancer. As a doctor, especially as a breast cancer specialist, I felt that this was my calling. And when I mentioned this to Anila, she just loved the idea." Dr. Sudha briefly looks at Anila and smiles.

"As you all know, she is a very well recognized social worker, and also a breast cancer survivor, herself gone through mastectomy. I thought she might be the best candidate for discussing this idea with you all in detail. And that is the purpose of this meeting, my dear ladies. Her role here will be what we can call, a 'patient representative'. How do you like that?"

Everyone claps at Dr. Sudha's suggestion. They unanimously declare Anila as the 'patient representative'.

"Thank you ladies," Anila says with a smile and modesty.

"As a doctor and a breast cancer specialist, I shall help you. I'll also send all my other patients to this group for support, including those in the future..." Dr. Sudha says.

"And I feel confident that all the patients will gladly join this group on Dr. Sudha's recommendation. We are indeed fortunate that we are starting such a project together as a 'group therapy' under Dr. Sudha's guidance for supporting breast cancer patients," Anila says.

There is again a light applause from the rest of the women in the room.

Dr. Sudha looks quite pleased with their response. She starts talking again to the group. "It is better not to think of what a woman goes through when one or both of her breasts are required to be removed in a mastectomy procedure. By now, I know each one of you very well and you all as a group provide an excellent sample for me and many other researchers like myself to know what any woman goes through mentally and emotionally during such times." She looks at her audience. Each woman is listening to her intently.

"We have had many interactions between us and I know personally each one of you and your case-histories. I have seen and met your family members and I have seen their reactions and responses to your disease, especially your husbands and children. However, during all our interactions, I always felt that you were not opening up completely. I felt that you were a bit detached from me. Then I realized that that could be because I was your doctor and not a friend or a fellow patient. Judging from this experience, I came to a conclusion that there must be a different way of communication, some other channel to establish some kind of bond between two women patients suffering from the same disease; so that there could be a distinct openness between them. The more I thought about it, the more I was determined to bring this idea of 'group therapy' for support into practice. The first name to come to my mind was of Anila." Dr. Sudha looks in the direction of Anila and smiles again.

"Anila was my very first patient on my return from Canada. It was a couple of years ago. When was it, Anila?"

"Exactly two years ago. I remember even the day, date and time." These words from Anila amuse everyone there.

"As I said earlier, I had a two-year research fellowship at a renowned Cancer Center in Canada." Dr. Sudha starts talking again.

"I spent those years in cancer research with some top caliber scientists there. I thought that the Center was an extraordinary place. Every possible advanced research tool was available there. For me it was like entering a wonderland. What impressed me the most, however, was its method of giving *moral support* to the patients. In every Cancer Center in Canada, I came to know that a small portion of the Center is dedicated completely to the activity of giving moral support to the patients, thereby the 'support activity' becoming an important and integral part of the cancer center; perhaps as important as the Center's research and treatment wings. Such activities also offer awareness, education and counseling on all aspects of the disease to the patients and even their families."

All the women are listening to Dr. Sudha with utmost attention.

"There are qualified psychotherapists, psychologists and psychiatrists among the counselors. There are many survivors of breast cancer as well, like our Anila, who are working there as patient advocates and patient representatives, most of the times, on volunteer basis."

Dr. Sudha looks at Anila with gratitude to signal her genuine appreciation. "These women volunteers, or patient representatives, share their experiences. They talk to women who are newly diagnosed with the disease and give them courage. For the awareness and educational activities, there are various workshops conducted on various topics relating to breast cancer and all other forms of cancer. I have seen doctors, scientists and researchers, meeting regularly with these social workers and psychologists, to discuss each other's work; this to me was very impressive. Another amazing thing that I noticed there was …"

Dr. Sudha cleared her throat and continued, "Adjacent to my research lab, there were two rooms of moderate size; one was decorated with Indian décor and the other with décor from the Far East. Yoga classes were regularly arranged in the room with Indian décor. People in the center seem to firmly believe that the practice of Yoga offers peace of mind to the patients. In the other room, I saw that emphasis was on relaxation techniques practiced in the Far Eastern countries. I would say that this part of the center was specifically designed for only moral support and had gained being an essential part of the main Cancer Center. This was a 'cultural exchange' in the truest sense of the word between Canada and the Far Eastern countries, such as ours." Dr. Sudha looks around to see how her idea is received by her listeners.

All the listeners look fully engrossed in Dr. Sudha's speech. At the same time, however, they also look absolutely still, almost like statues, as though only their bodies are there, but mentally, they all have drifted somewhere else. Could it be possible that while listening to Dr. Sudha, they all have gone into their own past, visualizing the events when their breast cancer was diagnosed for the very first time? Perhaps, yes! Definitely yes!

Looking at them, it seems that those days are unfolding before each woman's mental eyes, almost like a movie. Each one of those five women; Anila, Tanuja, Malti, Kiran, and Sheila sitting there today, is a breast cancer survivor, each one with her own distinct story, situation, and uphill battle with breast cancer, while gaining strength to reach the summit of recovery!

Anila

Nainum Chhindanti Shastrani
Nainum Dahati Pavaka...

Atman(soul) cannot be destroyed by a weapon, nor can it be burnt. It has no end. It is immortal!

Vasansi Jeernani Yatha Vihaya
Navani Grunhyati Naroprani...[1]

Just as a human being changes his or her clothes, so does the *Atman* change the attire; and the attire of the Atman is the physical body of human beings. The physical body is temporary, it is fleeting and transient!

Dr. Manav Joshi was reading aloud his favorite book on the Hindu philosophy, and the sound of his reading was ringing in the veranda. Day and night, he was seen sitting in his armchair, reading aloud, sometimes even in the wee hours of the morning. This had become his routine for the last two years; get up in the morning, read for a few hours, take a shower, have something to eat and read again, take a nap in the afternoon and then after having a cup of tea, read aloud a few lines from this book again. His evenings were also occupied by reading some similar books on Hindu philosophy, and that continued till he would be tired and ready to sleep at night. He had made this routine very rigid and unfriendly, with absolutely no room for anyone or anything else, not even for a conversation with his wife Anila.

Anila was almost staring at him while he was reading the philosophy book. Sitting on an armchair in that position, holding the book that way with both hands and looking into it, he seemed like a stranger to her. 'Who is this man?' she thought to herself. 'It wasn't so just a couple of years ago. He was an enthusiastic member of the society then. He was a loving husband, a very

---

[1] These are lines from the *Bhagvat Geeta.*

romantic at that; a caring father to our only daughter, Mala. We three used to have so much fun together…' Anila's thoughts started flowing back into the past.

Manav loved playing badminton and was a member of a near-by sport club. He was a very popular professor of English literature in the college. The English course he taught was regarded as one of the best courses in the college. Students lined up for his classes. Those who couldn't get admitted to it, felt disappointed.

Even at his home, there used to be a continuous flow of people. Their house was a place where everyone was welcome with open arms. When his students and friends visited him, he would spend hours with them talking and laughing. When Anila's friends and colleagues would come, it was Manav who would spend more time with them. Mala's friends loved him too. Many among them would say to her, 'you are so lucky Mala; your dad is like a *friend* to you. Ours is so strict…' Mala would laugh at their comment.

Anila looked at him again. He was still reading his book aloud.

'Is he reading it for the sake of reading?' she wondered, for his voice was completely arid. She remembered, when he read poetry, there was so much passion in it; she loved his passionate voice that she was grown familiar to over the years. 'Where is it now?' she questioned; 'this voice has no life in it', she concluded.

"What happened? Why did he change so suddenly? Why did he stop talking to people, mixing with the people, going to places, even going to the sports-club? He hasn't played badminton, a sport that he likes so much, in months. He hasn't touched his badminton racket; he hasn't even touched *me* in the last two years. For some unknown reason, he picked up those philosophy books and since then, he hardly talks to me, his dear wife, Annie…"

Anila looked at him again. Sitting on that armchair, he was looking like an old man, who had lost interest in everything in life. She just shook her head lightly with frustration and went into the kitchen. From the kitchen window, she could clearly hear that dry, life-less voice of his. She tried hard and then, she started hearing the same, passiona.e tone in his voice. As she heard that voice longer, she started feeling the same familiar passionate tone reverberating in her kitchen, except it had acquired a touch of melancholy in it. She sat on the kitchen chair and started listening to it intently. The sounds of his passionate voice took her straight back into her beautiful past.

A young man by name Manav Joshi had recently joined the community college staff as an instructor in the department of English. It was the month of June and the semester had just begun after the summer holidays. This young instructor entered the class with his briefcase. It was his first time teaching a class. The students looked at him with a keen eye and after assessing this young man cruelly, started leaving the classroom. He didn't seem to care though. He opened his briefcase and pulled out a book. It was a poetry book. The very first poem was a sonnet by John Milton, titled 'Paradise Lost'.

When I consider how
My light is spent...

Manav Joshi, after introducing himself to the class, started reading aloud from the book. His deep, passionate voice filled with emotions expressed in the poem captured some ears and the students stopped going outside. One by one, they all came back and took their seats and started listening to him. In a few minutes he got them fully engrossed in the emotion and passion of that sonnet.

...They also serve
Who only stand and wait...

He finished the last line of that sonnet and looked around. Students were motionless, listening to his superb teaching without a word, as though they themselves were 'lost' in Milton's 'Paradise'! He closed the book and with a smile on his face, reminded them about the period being over. The students almost applauded his teaching. They all went towards him and started talking to him. The way he taught that sonnet that day made some students feel as though their instructor himself had been blind like John Milton. The immortal sweetness of Milton's poetry was delivered to them by Manav Joshi with no reservations that day. The students got hooked up to his teaching forever, and neither he nor the college administration staff ever looked back. Manav Joshi was a hit as an English professor, especially for English poetry, for the years to come.

Anila was in the class that day. She was a first year student taking English Literature as her optional subject. She was listening to his teaching, like everyone else, with an intent ear. Like everyone else, he had impressed her too, except he had done a little more to her than to others. He had touched her heart, she felt. She waited until everyone left the classroom. He was busy collecting his books and papers and putting them neatly in his briefcase.

"Are you new in this college?" She mustered her courage and walked towards him.

"Yes." He smiled at her and closed the briefcase.

"I liked your teaching very much."

"Thank you, thank you very much. This was my very first time teaching a class of this size in a college." He smiled again at her and started walking towards the door.

"I would say it was a total success…" Anila complimented him again. He just nodded with a smile and continued walking.

"I am a first year student here, planning to achieve a degree in Social Work …" In an attempt to continue the talk with him, she also started walking with him and volunteered some information about herself.

"Oh? But then, you are here in English Lit…" He asked, exactly as per her expectation.

"I decided to try out English Lit. as an optional subject, so I attended this class today."

"So? What's the outcome now?"

"Well, it is definitely going to be my option now."

"Good. I am happy to hear that." He looked at her.

"Perhaps I might take it as my Secondary subject…" She said innocently.

"I never imagined English Lit. would be a secondary subject for anyone…" He emphasized the word 'secondary' and gave her a mischievous smile.

'Oh God, he is funny too…!' She thought when she saw his smile.

"Where did you go for your college education?" She asked him.

"I went to a community col'ege in New Delhi for my undergraduate degree. Then, I finished my both Graduate and Doctorate programs at the Delhi University."

"Wow! You have a Ph.D. in English Lit."

This was more of a question to him. He just nodded and said, "Please, do register in my class. I hope to see you there every day." He sounded quite earnest when he said this. He then gave her a long look, a look that seemed like an hour long to her, and then started walking rather fast. She stood still for a moment. A funny kind of tingling shiver went through her entire body in that second when she saw him look at her with that gaze. 'Yes, Manav, yes. Believe me; you'll see me every day from now onwards...', she said to herself and started walking towards the cafeteria. She had to share this beautiful incident with her dear friends, who were waiting for her there.

"I am so glad you are taking my course." Manav said to Anila the very next day after the class was dismissed.

"You don't even know my name." She said.

"I know. It's Anila, right?" He asked.

"How do you know that?" She was genuinely surprised.

"I have my own ways of finding out, especially about things or people I like." He said with his typical mischievous looking smile. She blushed at which he gave out a loud laughter.

And the rest was history. She didn't have to learn Milton's 'Paradise Regained' as she had gained it already.

Manav and Anila started meeting frequently outside the college environment. The more they met each other, the more they felt that they were 'made for each other', and fell in love with each other. Anila finished her Bachelor's degree in Social Work and started working in a nearby rehabilitation center in guidance counseling. Manav was very nicely settled in the college, extremely popular with both the students and the teaching staff. On one fine day, they both tied the knot. The entire college staff was invited for the wedding. They set up their home in a very close vicinity of the college.

Many of Manav's senior students would come to his home for guidance. At times, even at home, it would seem as if he was conducting a college class for English right there. He had no problem helping anyone at any time, especially if the questions were about something in English poetry. That was his love and passion. Robert Frost, William Wordsworth, H.W. Longfellow, John Milton, were Manav's favorite poets. And Lord Byron! When he taught Byron, one would feel as though the Goddess of Poetry had blessed Manav with her whole heart. Anila had no qualms about his students coming to their abode either. Many of them would come frequently, feeling quite free in their house. Many times, if she had some time, she herself would sit through Manav's teaching and would really enjoy it. Many times, she would serve the students hot steaming coffee. They all would then discuss jointly about some poet over a hot cup of coffee. On such occasions, there was never any time limit, nor there remained any distance between the teacher and his students.

Manav loved his wife and her healthy attitude of supporting his passion of teaching. To show his appreciation, many times, he would go outside late in the night and get her a string of fresh Jasmine flowers that she so dearly loved. Many of his students had noticed this. They had also noticed that huge mirror hung on a wall adjacent to their double bed in their bedroom, when they visited their home for the first time.

'There is a huge mirror besides his double bed, did you notice it?' Someone would start the topic.

'No wonder he can explain Lord Byron's poetry so well...' some other student would answer.

'Our Prof is a romantic soul...' a third student would say.

'Not just him. You need two to tango...' a girl would say.

'What do you mean?'

'His wife must be a romantic soul too. Know what I mean...' the girl would give her opinion like an expert.

'Did you see anything else interesting in the bedroom?' someone would inquire.

'Who do you think I am, an intruder or a spy or something…?'

'No, no. just asked. You are a senior and go there frequently, that's why I asked…'

'Hum, let me think…'

'I noticed many dried up strings of jasmine flowers hung on one side of the bed…' someone would report.

'Really?' the girls' eyes would become saucer sized after hearing that.

'Oh, what a romantic couple…' All the girls unanimously muse over the idea and release a big sigh. Their gasp would be very clearly audible.

A discussion such as this one was quite common among Manav's students. And it was true. Manav and Anila had a wonderful relationship and a very romantic one too. Once in a while, when she would stand in front of her huge mirror to get ready for work, he would come from behind and embrace her; then looking at her image in the mirror, he would say to her, 'you are really the sunshine of my life, Annie!' That was his pet name for her. She loved it too. Looking at her, he would recite a few lines of one of his favorite poets,

> *'…Shall I compare thee*
> *To a Summer's day*
> *Thou art more lovely*
> *And more temperate…'*

She would be totally lost in his recitation of some such remarkable, classic poem in his voice that was full of passion, but then, "okay, Dr. Manav Joshi. Enough of Shakespeare now, I've got to go to work…" She would come out of her own *trans*, trying to free herself from his strong hold. However, she would give up her attempt rather quickly and very much willingly.

The birth of their daughter was almost like a cherry on the top! They named her Mala, a beautiful and imaginative combination of their own two names. Anila left her fulltime job to care for their daughter, but Manav's teaching at the college continued, and he flourished in his career, gradually assuming the Dean's position of the Arts faculty at the college. After Mala started full time school, Anila joined workforce on a part time basis and started going to a nearby hospital in a patient-rehabilitation program as a group therapy helper.

Before long, Mala grew up to be a well-groomed, bright young woman, and after completing her high school successfully, was ready to go the college. Everyone thought that she would choose her father's college but she chose the one a little far away from their city and got an admission there. It was time for her to leave home. The Joshi couple had organized a big party for her send-off to the college. Many of their colleagues from work as well as most her own friends were invited to the party. The party was arranged in one of the halls on the college campus. Manav left a little early to oversee all the arrangements. Mala was getting ready in her room with a few of her friends around. A lot of laughing and giggling was going on in her room. Anila was getting ready in her room next door. Just then Manav walked in.

"What happened? Did you forget something?" Anila asked him, she was busy tying her hair in a bun.

"Yes, a very important thing." He said, looking at her intently.

"What?" Anila was standing in front of her huge mirror trying to finish tying her hair. She was wearing a beautiful blue silk sari and a long pearl necklace that was dangling on her bosom freely. With her both hands raised above her head, she looked like she had assumed one of those famous dancing poses of the old Ajanta sculptures.

Manav came from behind and hugged her tightly and started kissing her passionately.

"This, this is what I had forgotten." He said and continued kissing her beautiful neck.

"Manav, Manav stop it. The girls are right next door getting ready…" Anila resisted a bit.

"I know that. But I wanted to do this, one last time before we send our daughter to the college, Annie, before we become empty-nesters. That's why I rushed home." He said.

"Why, wouldn't an empty nest be completely free?" She teased him.

"Yes, but that's no fun. Playing hooky to our grown up daughter and caressing you has been more fun to me. There is a different kind of thrill in it."

"Silly you, that's so childish…"

"May be, but so what? And that's exactly what I want to do right now, one last time…" He gave her that all too familiar mischievous smile.

"You are one crazy man, I tell you." She laughed.

He held her face and turned it towards him. He looked at her again very intently. Clad in a deep-blue silk sari and a pearl necklace, she looked like a star studded night to him. He started reciting,

> *"She walks in beauty, like the night*
> *Of cloudless chimes and starry skies;*
> *And all that's best of dark and bright*
> *Meet in her aspect and her eyes…"*

For a brief moment, she also got carried away, especially with that passionate voice of his and the way he recited those lines to her. But she didn't let him finish the poem. Instead, she shook him gently holding his shoulders. "Manav, wake up buddy, wake up from your childish antics. We have planned a huge party for our daughter, and we are the hosts, remember?"

He laughed and left the room murmuring softly a line from Lord Byron's poems.

Lately, this had become Anila's favorite pastime. When Manav read passages from those philosophy books aloud in his dry, emotionless voice, she would imagine the sound of his passionate, familiar voice in its place, which would invariably take her into their past, a lovely past that she had enjoyed together with him, for more than twenty years. Alas, that past had become her *treasured past* now, perhaps with no guarantees in the future!

Why not? What changed that? What happened, really? Even when she was diagnosed with breast cancer, he kept his 'self' intact. He was scared at the beginning when it was newly diagnosed, no doubt, but then he soon collected himself and took care of everything. He was her friend, her consoler, even her nurse looking after her wonderfully. Then what happened suddenly, that he changed so much, to this extent? Anila drifted into the past again. She could clearly picture the days when her disease was diagnosed.

"Annie, you look quite tired these days…" Manav said to her one day after she got back from work.

"Hum. May be I'm entering menopause, or may be, I'm missing our daughter very much …" Anila warded off his comment with a shrug. Mala had left home for college in another city for quite some time now.

"May be so. But just to be sure that there is no other problem, get yourself checked by a doctor, dear." He said.

With her increasing feeling of tiredness, Manav insisted her to see a doctor. One day Anila returned from work with a tremendous fear and worry on her face.

"Why do you look like this Annie?" Manav inquired the moment he saw her.

"Just back from a doctor's clinic," she said.

"And?"

"He has ordered a whole bunch of blood tests for me and, and ..." she couldn't complete her sentence.

"And, and what?"

"He is sending me to a breast cancer specialist." She broke down crying.

"What, a breast cancer specialist?"

She just nodded.

"Why, why does he suspect that?" Manav's body developed a mild tremor on hearing that. "Did he examine your breasts?"

She nodded again.

"And?"

"And he said he felt a few lumps in my left breast. Since they are rooted deep inside, I couldn't feel them at all. But the doctor did. Initially he thought that it could be just a *fibroadenoma*[2]. I used to get it once in a while when I was much younger." She said after the first crying spell was over.

"May be, he just wants to rule out anything extreme like cancer, that's all. I'm sure those lumps are just some benign lumps, like what you said, a fibroadenoma or some such things." He collected himself right away and consoled her. He then added, "We'll take the appointment of the specialist right away. Don't worry my sweet Annie ..." He dialed the telephone number and took the first available appointment of Dr. Sudha.

The day of her appointment dawned.

---

[2] Details given at the end of the book.

"Manav, my left eye is twitching since this morning." Anila said to him as she was getting ready for the appointment.

"So, what does that mean?" He said while getting ready.

"That means something really bad is going to happen today. I am feeling scared."

"Don't be silly. These are all stupid superstitions, only the uneducated and irrational people believe in all that. Nothing bad is going to happen today, okay? There is nothing to fear." He assured her and started reciting,

> *"Fear no more the heat O' the Sun,*
> *Nor the furious winter's rages..."*

"Manav, for crying out loud, will you stop this? Will you keep your Shakespeare aside for a few moments?" She seriously yelled at him and he stopped right away. He could see that she was scared.

They were sitting in Dr. Sudha's clinic. Anila's examination was finished and so were the blood tests and other relevant tests. The doctor had ordered 'stat' results of all tests, therefore the test results were back. As was feared by Anila, the lumps detected in her left breast, unfortunately, were not just fibroadenoma, but were found to be *malignant.*

"It is a little unusual that a woman has more than one malignant lump in her breast at the same time, Mrs. Joshi. I have found that very rarely in my medical practice." Dr. Sudha turned towards Anila and Manav, and said in a very serious tone. Anila almost froze listening to the diagnosis; and Manav, having lost his balance completely, blurted out foolishly, "Oh my God, that means her days are numbered now, isn't it?" Clearly he himself had gone in a terrible shock after listening to Anila's diagnosis and had no control over what he was saying.

"What are you talking, Mr. Joshi?" Dr. Sudha stopped him right away from making such an erroneous comment. "I can understand that you have faced a sudden blow after listening to your wife's diagnosis and that is why you are in a confused state of mind. But there is no such thing as her days being numbered, okay?" Dr. Sudha was very firm about what she said. She was not pleased at all with his remark. She continued, "Mr. Joshi, you are a professor in a college, I'm surprised at your insensitivity of saying such depressing things in front of the patient." Dr. Sudha looked genuinely disturbed with what Manav blurted out.

She then turned to Anila and said, "Mrs. Joshi, you don't worry; the mainstays of breast cancer treatment are very many, like surgery, radiation, chemotherapy, hormone therapy, and targeted therapy. Researchers around the world are working to find better ways to prevent, detect, and treat breast cancer, and to improve the quality of life of patients as well as survivors. Scientists are studying novel treatments and drugs, along with new combinations of existing treatments."

Then she added further, "Women with early-stage breast cancer may be treated with removal of the entire breast, called mastectomy or only the removal of the lump with cancer and a portion of the surrounding tissue, called lumpectomy. It is a breast-conserving therapy, generally known as BCT; it is usually, followed by treatment with radiation. In your case, however, although cancer is detected at an early stage, you have multiple lumps. Therefore, you will have to undergo an immediate mastectomy; that means we will have to remove your entire left breast immediately. Mrs. Joshi, more women, particularly young women, are electing to have a mastectomy; it seems to offer them peace of mind. I would go one step further and remove some of your lymph nodes as well from the armpit. That way we'll eradicate the cancer completely and give no chance for its further growth in any other tissues of the body such as liver or lungs." After explaining everything to the couple, Dr. Sudha gave them an idea about what she intended to do next.

The first shock was slowly wearing out; Anila and Manav both seemed fairly quiet while listening to her.

"Mr. and Mrs. Joshi, quite honestly I am a bit surprised at your reaction to the diagnosis." Dr. Sudha looked surprised. "After the diagnosis of breast cancer, almost all my patients cry loudly or yell hysterically, a few of them even faint; some husbands faint too, some freeze completely for a long time, and some start doubting my medical prowess and take their case elsewhere, a few have even challenged my diagnosis and threatened to filing a court case against me. You have done none of this. I really admire your strength and your 'sangfroid'!" Dr. Sudha must have barely finished her complementing the two for their bravado when Anila tried to stand up but started shaking with an intense tremor. Manav tried to hold her but his hands were shaking badly too.

"Let me help you both." Dr. Sudha got up from her chair and moved towards Anila to help her stand up. And she noticed that Anila was not only shaking violently but her sari was completely drenched in her own urine. She looked at Manav to say something, but she noticed that Manav's pants were just as much drenched in his own urine, as Anila's sari was in hers!

Tanuja

A very small bungalow, like an English cottage, is built in the middle of a small sized lot. It has everything in small proportion; a small yard in the back, a small yard in the front and a small patio at the entrance to the bungalow. A beautiful flower garden blooms in the front yard and the back yard has a small vegetable garden. The patio has four earthen pots, each one containing a rose bush, in its four corners. A single seater swing hangs on four brass links in the center of the patio. The swing has a bright red colored, velvet cushion placed in it. The four rose bushes, when in full bloom, brings a special decorative look to the patio and enhance the whole ambiance of the entrance area.

The bungalow has two rooms in the front area and three in the back. Of the three rooms in the back, there is the master bedroom, another bedroom for the children, and the third room is a kitchen with a small dining table in one of the corners. All these rooms look quite simple with modest furniture and equipment.

Of the two rooms in the front, one room is a living room, which has four comfortable looking chairs with a coffee table in the center, nothing special or an expensive look about this furniture. A small show case with a glass door displays many pictures of the family. The second room, which is by far the largest room in the house, is decorated artistically and shows beautiful taste of the owners of this bungalow. This room is the music room! Old, authentic and very expensive looking musical instruments, such as two Tamburas, three Tabla sets, three Harmoniums and one Sarangi, are neatly kept on an equally beautiful, thick Persian carpet that is laid on the floor of this music room.

All these instruments look shiny and spotless clean. That is because, it is a regular routine of the lady of this house to dust and clean all these instruments every single morning. She enters this room every morning only after taking her bath. After cleaning the instruments, she worships them and then lights an incense stick in the room. She then sits on the carpeted floor with her eyes closed and hands in a *Namaste* position until the incense stick burns out. On occasional mornings, if she cannot follow this routine, for whatever reason, her husband completes the routine himself. One can feel an air of sanctity in that room.

As can be easily guessed, from the artistic décor and the beautiful music room with its valuable contents, this house belongs to two musicians, Tanuja and Ajoy Bose. Tanuja is one of the leading singers of the country and her husband, Ajoy, is a renowned Tabla player. They have custom made this house for their comfort and convenience, and for their two daughters, Sangeeta and Shruti.

Tanuja and Ajoy have already started giving training to their two daughters in classical vocal music, although they are quite young in age. Sangeeta is just about twelve years old and Shruti, barely nine years. Tanuja teaches them the notes and nuances of various *Ragas* and Ajoy teaches them the intricacies of various Talas.

Right now, the whole family is in the music room and the girls' music training is in session. Tanuja is teaching them the notes of Raga Bageshri, and Ajoy is accompanying them on his Tabla.

"Repeat after me now, girls, *dha ni sa ma* ..." Tanuja starts singing.

"...*dha ni sa ma* ..." Sangeeta is playing the Tambura and both the girls try to copy her.

"... *ma ga re sa*..." Tanuja sings and the girls repeat after her.

"... *ga ma dha ni*..." Tanuja sings again and the girls repeat after her.

And, almost as a rule, the notes of that *Raga* sung in Tanuja's melodious flawless voice took Ajoy back into their past. 'She had sung the very same *Raga* when I first laid my eyes on her', Ajoy thought to himself.

That was many, many years ago, in a conference in Kolkata.

A huge, prestigious conference on classical music of India is going on for three days in Kolkata. Most of the stalwarts of music have gathered for this conference. It is an honor to be invited for this conference and even more so, if requested to present your music in this conference.

One of the oldest and very-well recognized vocalists, Guru Mathurabai, is invited to present her classical music for the conference. She is sitting on the stage with all her paraphernalia, which includes her many senior disciples as well. They are all sitting behind her. Guru Mathurabai starts singing one of the most favorite *Ragas* of all times, *Raga Bageshri*, and within minutes, the effect of her singing makes the whole atmosphere come to a standstill. The audience is completely spell-bound. Just then she gestures to one of her senior disciples to join her in singing. The senior disciple joins her in singing and after a few minutes, the entire audience is swinging at the beat of her singing. This disciple is a young woman barely in her late twenties, named Tanuja. Her pleasant face, demure look and the way she is dressed up for this occasion, all impress the audience. Her Guru gives her a look of pride and appreciation for her singing and gestures her to complete the musical piece. Tanuja captures the attention of the entire conference.

A young man named Ajoy is also attending the same music conference. He is extremely fond of playing Tabla and has been taking lessons from a renowned Guru of Tabla. Just as everyone, he is also taken aback by Tanuja's singing and her melodious voice.

Guru Mathurabai's performance comes to an end and in a thunder of applause she takes a bow from her connoisseurs. As she descends the stage, she is surrounded by the audience and is completely hidden in their gathering. All her disciples also descend the stage after their Guru, each one carrying something, like a musical instrument or bouquets of flowers or candles, in their hands. Tanuja descends down carefully with a delicate musical instrument, a Tambura in one hand. Seeing her, Ajoy hurries towards her, offers to take the Tambura in his hand and starts complimenting her for her singing.

"What a voice, simply heavenly." He says.

"It's God's grace." She says politely and declines his offer of carrying the instrument.

"And, what a singing caliber? Simply amazing…" He persists.

"It's my Guru's grace." She says again very politely and starts walking towards a room that is specially assigned to her Guru for the evening.

"And, that song you presented in it, oh simply heavenly!"

"It's called *Bandish,* not song…" She corrects him and smiles at him.

"May I know your name please?" He feels amused by her brevity.

"Tanuja." She just utters her name and continues walking.

"Mine is Ajoy." He tries to introduce himself to her but she just smiles at him and enters the room disappearing completely from his sight. He feels frustrated. He stands there for a few minutes with a hope that she might come outside but instead, he sees her Guru enter the room. He gives up and turns back to leave. Just then, his own Guru of Tabla comes there and asks him, "Have you met Guru Mathurabai in person?" Ajoy shakes his head.

"In that case, come inside with me, I'll introduce you to her." Ajoy is hesitant but in that split moment remembers that Tanuja is Guru Mathurabai's disciple. He readily agrees and follows his own Guru to Guru Mathurabai's room.

"Oh, please come in, come in…" Mathurabai welcomes Ajoy's Guru with a big smile.

"What a performance? Mathurabai, I say you created history today, really. That Raga you presented, as though it was created only for you. Simply fantastic." Ajoy's Guru is showering compliments on Mathurabai liberally.

"Thank you, thank you, *ji*! It's after all He who gets me singing…" Mathurabai looks up to the sky, indicating God and gives a hearty laugh.

"And you are training your disciples also very well, I must say. That young woman, who joined you later in the singing, she very expertly complimented your singing with hers. That's wonderful." Mathurabai thanks him again and calls Tanuja outside. She then tells her to bow down and touch his feet with respect. As she does so, he says, "my heartfelt blessings to you my dear girl. Mathurabai, she will carry your torch much further. And this is my disciple, Ajoy. He has been learning playing Tabla from me for quite a few years now. A very dedicated disciple and quite promising too." It is Ajoy's turn now to bow down and touch Mathurabai's feet. She blesses him and the two Gurus start talking with each other about music and also many other things besides music.

"Thank you, my dear God!" Ajoy looks at the ceiling and purposely says it a little loudly while smiling at Tanuja.

"What's that for?"

"Well, you were avoiding me earlier, but God brought me straight to you, right here inside this private room." They both laugh and a link is established between them.

This incident took place a good fifteen years ago. What started as a simple relationship between a singer and her connoisseur transpired into 'love' and within a year, Tanuja and Ajoy tied a knot.

Ajoy's prowess in Tabla was also getting recognized by the listeners and that complimented Tanuja's singing career. In the last ten years or so, not a single performance took place where she didn't take Ajoy's accompaniment on Tabla. A special chemistry was created between Tanuja's singing and Ajoy's playing Tabla and people just loved this chemistry. This 'duo' had become immensely popular with all the music connoisseurs, especially with the younger crowd, in the entire country. They were performing in most of the major and prestigious music conferences and music gatherings of the country. People would buy expensive tickets and go to the concerts mainly to hear this 'duo' perform; they would get back more than their money's worth for these concerts. Every music concert of Tanuja and Ajoy was a success. Their performances seemed like a miracle to the listeners. Their musical prowess was considered to be one of a kind, their concert an unbelievable event, every time. 'Two stars are born', people would say. The stars in the sky were smiling on them and so was the Goddess of music, showering her grace on them!

Three years into the marriage, Tanuja and Ajoy gave birth to a beautiful baby girl. They named her Sangeeta, a name that stands for music itself in Sanskrit. Three more years, and they received another beautiful gift from God, their younger daughter. They named her Shruti, a term in Sanskrit, on which the entire classical music of India is based. Tanuja and Ajoy took their daughters to every place they performed. The girls, although quite young in age, would sit quietly through the concerts, intently listening to their parents perform, which in turn also became a topic for admiration for the connoisseurs. Their music, together with their family life, flourished over the years, as though everything was made in heaven. Tanuja and Ajoy were riding a high tide!

"Ajoy, are you ready now?" Tanuja looked at him and asked. "The girls are ready now for your Tabla, dear." She said.

She looked at him and knew instantly that with his eyes closed, he was totally lost in something, something of the past, of course.

And she could guess what it was.

"Earth calling Ajoy' 'Earth calling Ajoy…" Ajoy heard Tanuja's voice calling his name and the girls giggling. He came out of his 'trance'. Giving Tanuja a sheepish smile, he pulled the Tabla set in front of him and got ready for playing. Tanuja just smiled at him and turned her attention towards her daughters.

"Now I will start teaching you a new song in *Raga Bageshri*, Okay?" Tanuja told her daughters and gestured Ajoy to start playing Tabla.

"In vocal music, a lyrical content is also very important, which should complement the Raga as well." Tanuja was teaching them the basics of *Khyal* singing.

"What do we call a song in *Raga* music?" She quizzed her daughters before starting the song.

"*Bandish.*" The girls simultaneously answered.

Feeling satisfied with their answer, she started singing a well-known *Bandish* in *Raga Bageshri*,

"…*kaun karat tori binati piyarava*…"

"...*kaun karat tori binati piyarava*..." The girls started repeating after her and Ajoy slowly joined them by playing his Tabla. That was his favorite Bandish.

"...*Jabasay gaye moray*..." Just as Tanuja tried to reach the lines of the *Bandish* in the higher octave, she started to cough mildly.

"Mummy, I will get a glass of water for you." Little Shruti quickly got up and ran into the kitchen to get her mother a glass of water. Tanuja closed her eyes, bent her head down and cupped her mouth with her hand; while Ajoy moved closer to her and started stroking her back gently.

Every stroke was reminding him again and again of that black day he had been trying so hard to forget. How many days has it been now; or has it been a year already?

The same prestigious conference of classical music was organized, this time in Mumbai. There was only a week remaining before its commencement date. Tanuja and Ajoy were very happy to receive the invitation to perform in it. Thousands of music lovers were expected to attend this conference. Tanuja was preparing for her performance and so was Ajoy since he was accompanying her on Tabla.

She started practicing a composition in pentatonic scale; as she was deeply engrossed in improvising, she felt a funny twitch in her throat and she busted out in a coughing spell. It didn't sound like a simple cough. *A cough like this for a vocalist?* She asked for a glass of water to Ajoy. After taking a few sips, she felt a bit better, so they ignored it and she went ahead with her singing. Nothing extraordinary, nothing unusual either, they thought. It was forgotten already.

The day of the performance approached and the whole family got ready for travel. They arrived at the Mumbai airport and headed straight to the conference hall. Just as they reached there, many people surrounded them with a lot of enthusiasm. The organizers escorted Tanuja and Ajoy to the stage and were seated among the music dignitaries. Their daughters were seated in front of the stage along with the audience, from where they could conveniently see their parents.

Tanuja started presenting her music that she had prepared for this conference so diligently. Ajoy joined her with his Tabla in front of him. All the accompanying instruments joined her too. The way she was improvising, the listeners felt as though the notes of her music were brought straight from the heavens. The intricate designs and the fine ornamentation she created with those notes were as if she was unfolding one treasure after another, each one priceless before the next. It was simply a fantastic presentation.

There were long periods of applause intermittently that were exciting to the organizers of the conference. She came almost towards the end of her performance when she felt the same kind of twitch in her throat that she had encountered earlier in the week at home. That twitch was followed by a spell of cough. She stopped momentarily and gestured Ajoy to pass a glass of water to her. He did. She sipped some water but it didn't help. She coughed again. She took a few more sips of water. Still it didn't help. She finished the whole glass of water and yet her coughing continued with increased intensity. One of the organizers rushed to get more water for the singer. Just then she coughed really loudly and with that coughing spell, fell down on the stage, totally unconscious, with her mouth open, with a tiny stream of blood oozing out of her mouth.

"Oh my good God!" Ajoy said loudly, pushed away the Tabla and rushed to his wife's side. He picked up his wife's body delicately and started walking to the exit door. His exclamation was clearly heard through the microphone. Therefore, people started running towards the stage. Seeing him carry his wife's body like this, they became curious and wanted to know, 'what was going on?'

Their two daughters saw the whole thing and started crying. There was immense fear spread on their faces. In those few moments, many of the organizers rushed to the stage. Someone called an ambulance for Tanuja. Some of them wanted to help Ajoy carry her, but Ajoy was not in this world. He was too engrossed in his grief and extreme worry, and totally confused about his wife's medical condition. What happened there in those few moments to his wife was a puzzle to him.

Just then the ambulance arrived. With its siren going at full blast, there was one big chaos. Someone advised Ajoy to make use of the ambulance. He darted towards the ambulance. All this time he held Tanuja's body in his arms without letting anyone, even the ambulance drivers, touch her.

The ambulance rushed to a nearby hospital. Series of medical examinations, blood tests and X-ray tests took place in those few hours. What came out of all that was a dark, shattering Truth!

"Cancer? My wife has cancer?" Ajoy was sounding too excited with shattered nerves. He could not believe what the doctor in the hospital told him.

"Yes, Sir. I'm sorry to inform you but all the tests that we did for your wife strongly point only to one disease, and that is cancer. I am not a cancer specialist, so I sent all the records to a cancer specialist. The specialist suspected lung cancer but then his report indicated that it could very well be Metastatic cancer to the lungs, meaning that cancer from another region of the body has spread to the lungs, since she coughed a lot as you informed us, and vomited blood."

Ajoy was practically frozen while listening to the doctor.

"Then after examining her thoroughly, I felt tiny lumps in her both breasts, perhaps they could be malignant and that cancer could have gone from her breasts to her lungs." The doctor continued.

"I really can't say anything definitely right now, but my guess is that she could be suffering from breast cancer..." The doctor was almost apologetic to inform him about Tanuja's disease.

"B r e..., B r e..., B r e a s t C a n c e r?" Ajoy had a hard time repeating it. The doctor just nodded and said, "I have requested the cancer specialist to come here; she is actually on her way."

"But then, the blo...blo..blood, why did she vo...vo...vomit blood?" The words could barely come out of Ajoy. He started stammering badly.

"Again, it is my strong suspicion that she has breast cancer. The cancer specialist will explain it better to you, Sir."

'Tanuja could have breast cancer! Really?' Ajoy wondered. 'Yes, really, Tanuja does have breast cancer!' The thought resounded over and over again in his head. He froze and his whole body became stiff. The doctor slowly walked him to a nearby chair, seated him and left the room, leaving him alone with his wife lying on a table, covered in a hospital gown, unconscious.

There was some noise in the corridors outside. A senior doctor, the hospital administrator and a couple of nurses walked in the room.

"Mr. Bose, you heard what our doctor in the emergency room suspected, right?" The senior doctor walked towards Ajoy and almost startled him in his frozen state. "He is a very bright young doctor of our hospital and therefore we feel that his suspicion could be right. However, we have contacted one of the finest and renowned breast cancer specialists of the country and she is on her way here." He assured him. Ajoy just gave him a cold look. His mind was still in a frozen state.

"How are you doing, Mr. Bose?" The doctor seemed genuine. Ajoy just shook his head. "Please don't worry. Our hospital administrator will book a private room for your wife, and we will do everything within our capacity to make sure she is taken care of absolutely wonderfully. After all, she is the nightingale of our country, isn't she?" Ajoy nodded. The doctor was obviously aware of Tanuja's profession and musical prowess. He then told the hospital administrator who came in with him, to arrange a private room for Tanuja and instructed the nurses to move her there immediately. Then he gently put his hand on Ajoy's back and said, "Have courage, Mr. Bose, everything will be alright," and left the room.

Just then, Dr. Sudha arrived there.

One look at Dr. Sudha, and Ajoy felt as if all his emotions were gathered together at once.

"My wife can't have breast cancer, madam, she has been perfectly alright, except she had flu-like symptoms with a persistent cough many time. She is a classical vocalist, therefore, her shortness of breath and difficulty in breathing would be obvious to me; but that certainly doesn't mean that she has breast cancer, isn't it doctor?"

Dr. Sudha had a hard time looking at his naïve face; how would she answer his innocent question.

"I know who she is, Mr. Bose; you first calm down and listen to me with patience. The resident doctor thoroughly checked your wife, and he felt lumps in her breasts and noticed remarkable thickening in her breasts and underarms. I saw all her reports before I came here in this room. You see, when the breast cancer has metastasized to the lungs, the patient may not notice any symptoms right away. The first symptoms are likely to feel a little like cold or flu, as you said. But, persistent cough, shortness of breath, difficulty in breathing, wheezing, and coughing up blood clearly point to the breast cancer spreading to the lungs. This is

Climb to Victory Over Breast Cancer

what we term breast cancer with *lung metastases*. I looked at the tumor cells under a microscope, and I clearly saw that they are cancerous breast cells. We will double check all this with the *fine needle biopsy*[3] to confirm that, of course. The tiny stream of blood that oozed out of her mouth could be the result of the same, now spreading in her lungs. " The doctor tried to explain to Ajoy everything in simple language.

Ajoy, still in a frozen state, just stared at the doctor with a blank gaze. The doctor gave him a compassionate look and gently left the room, with a promise to see him very soon.

As Ajoy's mind started coming out of its frozen state and as he started overcoming the original shock slowly, he started thinking of not just Tanuja but also about his young daughters. Those long hours had passed in extreme agony and worry for him. Where were the girls? Who was with them in this new city? They must be scared to see their mother faint like that in the middle of her concert, and to see their father carry her in his arms and leave them in such a rush in an ambulance. They must be scared to see people make one big clamor like that.

He looked at Tanuja. She was lying on the table in front of him, still partly unconscious. He walked towards her and gently caressed her face with his hand. A tiny line of dried up blood was still visible on one side of her mouth. He touched that line of dried up blood with his finger and just as he did so, he could not control his emotions any more. He broke down completely and started crying profusely. He was still crying when the hospital administrator and a nurse came into the room, ready to wheel away Tanuja to another room.

A private room had been arranged to start proper medical treatment for her. The nightingale of the country was a victim of breast cancer!

---

[3] Details given at the end of the book.

Malti

"*Ma*, please come with me, at least see how you feel…" Kirti nagged and implored her mother; she was not going to listen to any of her mother's excuses today.

"Don't be silly Kirti, there is no way I'm ever going to see a psychotherapist, Okay?" The mother retorted.

"*Ma* please, just once, let us visit her. I heard she is really very good." Kirti begged her mother again.

"That's not going to help me Kirti. You know that, nothing is going to ever help me…"

"*Ma*, please don't talk like that. Why don't we go out somewhere, anywhere you like, perhaps just for coffee, and then on our way home, drop in to see this psychotherapist, literally for fifteen minutes. No more…" Kirti was relentless.

"Well, okay… we'll do that since you insist so much." The mother gave in.

Kirti immediately ran inside to book an appointment on the telephone with the psychotherapist for her mother, 'only for fifteen minutes' as the mother agreed. Kirti and her mother, Malti Patel, were sitting on the patio in the backyard of their huge bungalow having their morning tea.

It was a daily routine for Malti and her husband Manubhai, for more than thirty years, to have their morning tea on the patio. There was a beautiful set of four wicker chairs and a table neatly arranged on the patio. The maid would bring a tray holding two fine China tea cups and plates, spoons and forks and lay them on the table. Just as Malti would come outside and sit on her favorite wicker chair facing the lawns of the huge backyard, the maid would bring another tray with a tea pot filled with hot tea, some biscuits and cut-up fruits. Shortly after that, Manubhai, still in his pajamas and an elegant gown over it, would join Malti on the patio. Malti would pour some tea in his cup and hand it to him. She would then pour some tea in another cup for herself. They both would slowly sip the hot tea, enjoying its flavor in each other's company and getting ready to start their busy day.

However, Malti's routine of having her morning tea on the patio had stopped altogether. Not only that, she gave up her morning tea altogether and hardly went on the patio that she so loved. It was at Kirti's insistence that Malti had agreed to join her on the patio for the morning tea that day.

"Oh my god, some of the trees have grown so much taller since I was a child." Kirti exclaimed while looking at the well-manicured lawns and the bushes and trees while sipping her tea. "*Ma*, it's so beautiful here in the mornings, isn't it?"

"Hum." Malti said absent mindedly.

"In Mumbai, you hardly see a tree. We call it a concrete jungle, hardly any tree in sight." Kirti said.

"Hum." Malti said. She looked like her attention was drifted somewhere else.

"And such lawns and beautiful bushes, you have to drive for hours, to some far away park to see them." Kirti said.

"Hum." Malti responded while staring in a blank space.

"Even the air smells so fresh. And the peace, oh, it's so quiet and peaceful here *Ma*, there is hardly any sound heard here." Kirti went on chirping about how she felt at the moment, but all Malti responded to everything she said was with just a 'Hum'.

"I go to my Mumbai apartment and there's a constant noise of some kind or other, coming from somewhere, round the clock." Kirti turned to talk about her apartment, on which her mother's response was just a 'Hum', again.

"*Ma*, I don't think you heard anything that I said; why aren't you saying something, anything?" Kirti complained about her mother's lack of response.

"I know you are sitting with me for the morning tea because I forced you. I know you stopped having your morning tea altogether. I also know that you hardly come on the patio; but *Ma*, how long are you going to mourn Daddy's death? How long are you going to feel sorry? I know his was a sudden demise but..." As Kirti started talking about her father, Malti turned her face towards her, but with a blank look. Slowly the sound of Kirti's talking started becoming fainter and fainter, as if Malti was slowly moving away from her daughter, away from all the surrounding, away from it all, into the past; her own past with Manubhai, her dear and loving husband of almost thirty five years.

She glanced at the bungalow that was dead silent since Manubhai's passing away. But, as Kirti's voice became fainter, there were sounds emerging from the bungalow, slowly becoming louder. She started hearing those sounds, sounds of life, her life when the bungalow was full with people. She felt the bungalow becoming alive again, with those all too familiar voices and sounds.

"Malti, where's my towel..." She heard Manubhai yelling from the shower.

"Here it is dear." She rushed to the shower to hand him a towel.

"Malti, have you finished all the preparations for my *pooja*?" She heard her mother-in-law asking her. It was her routine to do a two-hour long pooja every morning and needed a lot of things prepared for it.

"Yes, yes, *Ba*, it will be ready in a couple of minutes, okay?" She gently told her.

"*Ma*, may I wear your blue sari today?" She heard Kirti yelling from her bedroom. She wanted to wear her mother's sari for the college day celebration.

"Yes, but make sure you don't put too many pins on the sari." She told her.

"*Ma*, I can't find my tennis racket?" She heard Anand, her youngest child and son, hollering all the way from the front door. His birth had brought a lot of joy to the family as he was the one to carry the family name,

"Anand, it's right there, look carefully." She told her son lovingly.

"*Ma*, can I skip school today? I have got really bad stomach cramps." She heard Aarti complain about her stomach cramps. Aarti never had any liking for school and gave every reason possible to skip it. After entering puberty, *pms* was one more addition to her list of excuses for skipping school.

"Aarti honey, you need not skip school for the whole day. I'll give you a pill and that should take care of your stomach cramps in a couple of hours, okay?" She rushed to get a pill for Aarti's pms problem.

"Madam, there is a call for you…" She saw her servant standing in the doorway, politely holding a hand telephone receiver.

"Who is it from?" She asked him.

"A lady from your Ladies Club, madam…"

"Okay, let me talk to her." Malti took the receiver from the servant's hand and started talking.

"Hello, yes, I do remember the Ladies club meeting this afternoon. What time is it at? Yes, yes, I'll be there. Oh, by the way, do you need a ride? Okay then, I'll pick you up, I'll ring you up just before leaving my house, be ready…" Malti hung up the telephone.

"Madam, the cook says she doesn't have enough vegetables to cook for the dinner …" She saw her maid approaching her with the cook's complaint.

"Then you go to the market and get them soon. You know I make sure everyone eats plenty of veggies at dinner time, right?" Malti took some money out of her purse and gave it to the maid to get vegetables from the market.

"*Ma*, how do I look in your sari? I took some matching jewelry from your closet too." Kirti was modeling her attire to her mother. Malti looked at her daughter; Kirti's face was beaming with happiness.

"You look lovely dear..." Malti said while admiring her daughter in her sari. Kirti said 'bye' to her mother as she left for the college celebration.

And as Malti saw Kirti leave the house, so did she see that reverie of her past vanish away into the thin air. All those voices and sounds of life were also silenced completely. Instead, she heard Kirti calling her name.

"*Ma, Ma,* are you okay? Are you listening to me?" Kirti was gently holding her shoulders and shaking her. Malti gave her a blank look.

"*Ma,* I took an appointment with Shantabai for you early this afternoon." Kirti told her mother.

"Shantabai? Who's she?" Malti came out of her blank state of mind and asked in confusion.

"That's the name of this psychotherapist. Perhaps that's her professional name, I don't know that." Kirti told her. "You were getting that illusion again, weren't you *Ma*? You were thinking of Daddy and all of us still living at home, isn't it *Ma*?" Malti just nodded and kept quiet.

"We have to go and see that psychotherapist; it will be really good for you. Now, let us go inside, enough of sitting out here on the patio. You always think of Daddy too much when we sit here." Kirti led her mother inside to her own bedroom.

Kirti was right actually. Every time Malti sat outside at Kirti's insistence, she was lost in that illusion of her past. What

Kirti didn't know was that she got the glimpses of that illusion even when she was inside the house, anywhere, in the living room, dining room, family room, her bedroom, especially in her bedroom. Her life had been totally entwined with her husband's life for more than thirty five years, and with his sudden demise, it had become completely vacant. It seemed impossible for her to live without him, to live in his absence.

It was as if he had taken away with him the very essence of her life, and there was no use of her living anymore.

Kirti took her mother to Shantabai, the psychotherapist, as per the appointment that afternoon. Her clinic was in a little brick house with a small garden and a white fence all around it. There was a little gate in the front portion of the fence and a brick walkway that led to a few steps in the front.

Kirti and Malti climbed up the steps to the front door and rang the doorbell. The receptionist opened the door, requested them to take off their footwear in the front area and led them to a sitting room. After seating them with a polite gesture, she went inside to inform Shantabai. Despite the afternoon Sun, the room seemed a little dark. The walls and ceiling were all painted in deep blue color, and drapes of thick material of the same color were hanging at the windows. There was no furniture in the room, just a thick Persian rug with a few bulky looking cushions neatly laid on it. People were expected to use those cushions for sitting. There was a beautiful statue of Buddha on a tall pedestal in one corner of the room with a spot light focusing on Buddha's face. That was the only light in the room, the rest of the room was fairly dark. Instead of sitting on the rug and waiting, Malti and Kirti walked closer to the statue and started looking at it intently. With the spot light, the divine expressions of Buddha's face had become even more prominent, adding tranquility to the entire room.

"The statue looks so peaceful, isn't it?" Shantabai entered the room.

"Yes, it certainly does…" Kirti flustered a bit but collected herself very quickly. She and Malti looked at Shantabai. She was a tall woman with a nice brown complexion. Her long hair was let loose on her back. She was wearing a light yellow sari and a matching yellow blouse with long sleeves. 'She looks like a daffodil…' Malti thought to herself. Shantabai had a very pleasant countenance that was encouraging to both Malti and Kirti.

"Can you sit on the floor? Otherwise I can get a couple of chairs for you." Shantabai's voice was quite deep, its depth sounding very sweet.

"Yes, we can sit on the floor, no need to get chairs." Kirti said and all three of them sat on the rug using cushions. Shantabai sat in a lotus position and looked very comfortable in that pose.

"I understand your father is one of the leading astrologers of the country." Kirti tried to start the conversation with Shantabai.

"Yes, he is." Shantabai said.

"Do you practice astrology?" Kirti asked her.

"No, I don't, but my father has passed some of his knowledge to me over the years. So I do know a little bit of that science too." Shantabai responded pleasantly.

"Would you like to talk to my mother?" Kirti asked.

"Is it for astrology?" Shantabai asked Kirti.

"Uhh…not exactly." Kirti was not explicit about their intentions for seeing Shantabai.

"As I said earlier, I do not practice astrology. I am a psychotherapist by profession. Would you like to see me for psychotherapy?" Shantabai made it quite clear about what she does, and what she *does not* do.

"My mother is feeling too depressed lately, so I thought I should bring her here to meet you." Kirti said.

"I hope, not for some entertainment with her astrology reading..." Shantabai stressed the word 'entertainment' and sounded slightly irritated.

"Oh no, no. Please, I didn't mean it that way at all..." Kirti felt embarrassed.

"That's okay, don't worry about it. A lot of people assume that being a daughter of a famous astrologer, I'm also an astrologer. Many people look at the science of astrology more as an activity for a good 'pastime'. They don't realize that it is a totally separate branch of science. My father always tells me, it can be a powerful tool that can be used in many areas of psychology, but I don't apply it in my psychology consultation. In my many years of practice as a psychotherapist, I have come to believe that astrology can provide a good base for starting some valuable conversations with the patients. Personally, it helps me connect with my patients quickly and positively. But I do not conduct my medical and scientific techniques of psychotherapy based on that science. Would that be okay with you ladies?" Shantabai intently looked at both the ladies. She wanted to know if after hearing this, they would still be interested in her professional services.

'This lady is quite forthright, and firmly believes in her own profession and convictions...' Malti was looking at Shantabai all the while she was talking, and thinking to herself, 'she is a trained psychotherapist. She must be quite good at it; otherwise she could have easily ridden on her famous father's name for her personal gains.' Malti became interested in her.

As Malti was assessing Shantabai, Shantabai was assessing Malti. 'She looks lost in her thoughts, as if she is somewhere else. She seems to believe in astrology more than anything else right now. Perhaps, I should start with astrology, to get her attention and to connect with her...'

"I am going to draw an astrological chart for you first, before I start any of the medical techniques for therapy. Can you please tell me your date and time of birth?" Shantabai looked at Malti and asked her.

"It's August 31ˢᵗ, 1940, time is um …" It was Kirti who answered instead of Malti.

"And, the time of birth?" Shantabai asked again. She was almost sure that the daughter may not have this answer. As guessed correctly, Kirti looked at her mother for answering this question.

"…it's 4.am …" Malti gave the information in a very nervous sounding voice.

Shantabai smiled, feeling happy that her strategy of getting Malti say something, anything at all, worked for the time being. She jotted Malti's time of birth and then quickly and skillfully drew some kind of a horoscope chart on a pad of papers.

"You are a woman of tremendous energy. You try to achieve forty eight hours of work in twenty four hours, isn't it?" Shantabai looked at Malti and asked her. Her hand writing and her skillful drawing the chart impressed Kirti and Malti. They looked at her while she looked like she was studying the chart intently for a minute or so. Her conclusion of Malti's personality impressed Malti even more.

"Shantabai, you are one hundred percent right. *Ma* does do a lot of work in a short time. What she achieves in mere half a day, many women can't even think of doing it in two days." Kirti said.

"You mean, I *did do* a lot of work…" Malti corrected Kirti that gave a mild surprise to both Kirti and Shantabai.

"What do you mean, *Ma*?" Kirti asked.

"I mean, I *did, as in the past,* do a lot of work. I used to be busy all twenty four hours back then, but not anymore. Now, my all twenty four hours are free. No, not just free, they are *empty*! They are completely empty. I have nothing to do, no one to look after. My life is totally hollow, just plain meaningless and empty. Nobody needs me any more..." Malti stressed the word 'empty' over and over again.

"Why do you call your life *empty*?" Shantabai asked her gently.

"Because, it is so. My daughters got married and moved away. My only son wanted to go to the foreign land, so I let him. He is so well settled there, there's no chance of him ever coming back to India now. And my dear Manubhai..." With those words, Malti started getting that blank look on her face again. 'She is slipping into somewhere else...' Shantabai knew right away. And so did Kirti.

"I can very clearly see that you have been suffering from some depressing situation for the past few years. Is it true?" Shantabai asked Malti but she didn't say anything. She had already dipped into the past, her own 'la la' land.

"Actually it's the last two years that she has lost complete interest in everything, I mean everything. She doesn't want to go anywhere or meet anyone, to wear any nice clothes or anything. All she wants to do is sit in her own bedroom and stare at the ceiling. She doesn't even as much go in the yard or the garden or even onto the patio that she loved so much. We have a beautiful house, and a beautiful garden around the house but she doesn't care anymore." Kirti answered on Malti's behalf.

"Kirti, did your father pass away suddenly and unexpectedly?" Shantabai asked Kirti, and Kirti just nodded to her.

"And what was his name?"

"Manubhai, Manubhai Patel. People called him '*motabhai*', elder brother, with love and respect." Kirti said.

With the mention of that special name, Malti felt a slight jerk that brought her back to the present instantly.

"Yes, my Manubhai left me suddenly, and so unexpectedly, you have no idea. How I felt when that happened, and how I feel now, only God knows." Malti looked at the sky once and then looking at Shantabai, started talking directly to her. And that's exactly what Shantabai wanted; Malti to open up and talk!

"It was almost midnight." Malti was telling Shantabai, "Manubhai came into the bedroom after finishing his work. He was a renowned lawyer of the town and was very busy. We started our life together with nothing, you know, absolutely nothing. When we met, he was still doing his Articling. Nobody called him *motabhai* then. But he was bright, he wanted to start his own practice and I supported him completely, mentally and financially too. I was working in a small office as a clerk. After marriage, we moved into a very small apartment, with hardly any furniture or other luxury things. But we worked hard, especially my Manubhai worked his way through the Law firm and in just twenty years, we built a huge bungalow on acreage. We had many servants and a social status that anyone would envy. He helped a lot of people who had no money to pay their fees, you know. That's when people started referring to my Manubhai as 'motabhai', out of love and respect." Shantabai looked at Malti as she was telling her about her own past. There was definitely an expression of pride in Malti's eyes about her husband.

Malti continued talking, "we had three beautiful children, all bright and lovely like my Manubhai. As Manubhai became more and more successful in his law practice, I left my work, and started concentrating totally on my children. His old mother was also living with us. Our house was full, my *life* was full! Just taking care of all of them, and especially my Manubhai, was a twenty four hour job for me. I had to actually squeeze out time for getting involved socially in the ladies club and all that. Can you imagine? Life was simply fantastic then, not empty like today…" Malti gave out a long sigh. Shantabai was listening quietly, and so was Kirti.

"Slowly one after another, all my children left home. Kirti and Aarti got married and settled far away from here. Anand left for Canada, only to visit us once in every two or three years. Manubhai's mother passed away. All of a sudden, there was no one in the house…" Malti took a big breath and continued, "… but I had my Manubhai. I started focusing completely on him and believe me; he alone kept me quite busy. As it was, he was dependent on me; after our children left home, he became totally dependent on me. He just couldn't do anything without me. He relied on me for literally everything, so much so, you have no idea. Right from putting paste on his toothbrush and giving him towel after his shower in the morning to laying his night pajamas on our bed, I took care of him. Taking the morning tea on the patio, sending hot lunch to his office, planning and serving a beautiful four course meal in the evening, I personally looked after everything. So many times, he brought his colleagues and even his clients for dinner to our home at a short notice, but that didn't make me nervous or angry or flustered, I would have the dinner ready with no problem at all."

Malti took a few seconds break and continued again, "and then that black night fell. It was almost midnight when Manubhai walked into the bedroom after finishing his work. He was working on some complicated case, he told me. He hadn't had his dinner yet, so I prepared a light meal and took it to our bedroom for him to eat before he goes to sleep. I was serving him the food when he felt he was sweating. He requested me to turn the fan on full strength. I did. But he was still sweating…" Malti gasped a bit but continued, "…he asked for a glass of water, so I poured some water in a glass and tried to hold the glass to his mouth. He was breathing very heavily. I tried to open the buttons of his shirt. He looked very, very uncomfortable. I tried to force some water in his mouth, with the hope that that would make him feel better, but that water didn't enter his mouth, it just rolled down his chin. That's because, Shantabai, the messenger of death had taken my Manubhai away from me at that moment on that black night..." Malti cupped her face partially and started crying. Kirti quickly pulled out a handkerchief from her purse and gave it to her mother.

"I got a call in the middle of that night by our maid." Kirti started telling Shantabai about what had happened on that night. "She was screaming and crying on the telephone. I couldn't understand what she was saying; all I could get was that she wanted me to come home immediately. I knew something was drastically wrong there; 'where is *Ma*?' I asked her but she just kept on crying. I knew I needed to go there as soon as possible. I picked up my purse, and my husband and I got into the car; we drove there as fast as we could. The drive from Mumbai is good two hours long, but honestly, I don't even remember now how we drove that night. When we reached home, we were told by the servants that they heard a very loud scream from the bedroom upstairs, so they all ran towards it. They described to me what they saw, Shantabai. According to their description, the ceiling fan was on at full strength, water and food was spilt all over the floor of the bedroom, Daddy was lying on the bed with his mouth open, dribbling some foam from one side, and *Ma* was lying on him, unconscious." Kirti looked like she was about to cry too, but she managed to control herself, and continued.

"When did this happen? Why did you not call the ambulance right away?" I yelled at the servants, but they all stayed quiet. Quickly, I called the ambulance to take both of them to the hospital. We rushed to the hospital. All I remember now is that Daddy was in one room, covered from head to toe in a white sheet, and *Ma* in the adjacent room, looking unconscious. She was under heavy sedation, I was told. 'How is my father?' I asked the nurses, they just shook their heads and looked at the sky. Shantabai, our father was gone. I was told that a massive heart attack of barely a few seconds took his life. All I did was to scream and bury myself in my husband's arms and cry my heart out." Kirti broke down.

Shantabai got up, got two glasses of water and passed them to the two ladies. Sipping some water made them feel a little refreshed. "Are you okay now, ladies?" She asked them.

Malti finished her glass of water. She sniffled a few times and started talking again.

"Ever since then, my life has become one big empty hole. Kids came, stayed with me for a few days, then left. I realized that they have their own lives to live. But then, it's also true that no one needs me anymore. And that huge empty house, it looks like it is going to swallow me one day." Malti started crying again.

"As you said, Mrs. Patel, you have suffered a big shock two years ago, right?"

"Yes, it was about my Manubhai…" Malti said.

"Mrs. Patel, is there anything else you are suffering from recently? Anything that you are suffering from, *today?*" Shantabai asked Malti gently.

"Today?" Malti said with a slight surprise in her voice.

"Yes."

"Well, that's what it is, Shantabai, *Ma*'s extreme boredom with life is what the suffering she is having today." Kirti said.

"Okay then. If there is nothing else, I will start working on her case to cater to her needs of feeling 'empty' and depressed. Now, before I start working on your case, I must ask you, how is your general health?"

"My g e n e r a l   h e a l t h ..." Malti faltered and kept quiet suddenly. Her stammering almost gave it away that she was not well.

"You are obviously having some health issues, isn't it?" Shantabai asked her.

"Did my chart tell you that?" Malti asked her.

"Perhaps yes, perhaps no. I told you earlier, I do not read peoples' horoscopes or birth charts although I am good at drawing them skillfully. But I am extremely good in my own profession, which is psychology; and that tells me clearly that you definitely have a physical health problem right now, and not just mental depression." Shantabai was serious.

"But, I don't want to live anyway, so why bother going to a doctor? I have no purpose in life; nobody needs me anymore, so where is the point in checking my health issues?"

"In that case, you don't need to see a psychotherapist either, isn't it? Psychotherapy is for people who want to get better and live well." Shantabai closed her chart and started getting up slowly.

"No, no, please sit. I have not been frank with you Shantabai." Malti said.

Shantabai sat again in her lotus position and started listening to her.

"I went in excessive depression after my Manubhai left me." Malti said.

"It was hard to recognize *Ma* just a year after Daddy died. She was looking so ghastly, my beautiful mother looking almost like a ghost. I couldn't see that. So my sister and I insisted *Ma* see our family doctor soon, before she goes in some permanent kind of depression stage." Kirti said.

"And then?"

"We took her to our doctor. After examining her thoroughly, our family doctor advised us to take her to see Dr. Sudha…"

"Dr. Sudha? Isn't she the renowned breast cancer specialist?" Shantabai looked surprised and worried.

"Yes. Shantabai, she's the breast cancer specialist. I couldn't believe my ears first, 'did I hear correctly?' I had doubts. But when our family doctor insisted that *Ma* should see a good breast cancer specialist, that's when I knew she meant it. So I took her to Dr. Sudha. To our total dismay, *Ma* has been diagnosed with breast cancer. Our family doctor had found a small lump in her left breast. After the fine needle biopsy, Dr. Sudha confirmed that the lump is malignant…"

"Oh God, no, and…?" Shantabai said

"And what? *Ma* does not want to do anything about it." Kirti said with total despair. She and Shantabai both looked at Malti to see her reaction, but Malti looked like she was already lost in her own thoughts again. At this moment, she was thinking of her visit to Dr. Sudha.

"Soon after all my children left home, Manubhai, that's my husband, and I became the empty nesters. Just about that time, *Ba*, that's Manubhai's mother, also passed away. My children and *Ba* kept me very, very busy, for almost twenty hours of the day, you see." Malti was lying down on the examination table in Dr. Sudha's office.

Kirti was with her too. It was at the insistence of Kirti and her family doctor that Malti had agreed to go and see Dr. Sudha, the breast cancer specialist.

"I see." Dr. Sudha was carefully examining Malti and keeping her mind engaged by asking questions about her lifestyle. "Why were you so busy when they were around?"

"Oh, that's because they were totally dependent on me for practically everything and for all their needs. My children needed me in their studies too. Kirti, that's my daughter sitting outside in the waiting room, had a habit of reading her schoolbooks aloud and would insist that I sit in her vicinity somewhere. She needed me for doing all her studies. Aarti, that's my younger daughter, didn't like schoolwork at all, so I had to literally push her to complete the high school graduation. So, she needed me for pushing her like this. Anand, that's our youngest child and son, he is very bright like his father, but seemed bored with his studies. So I had to nag and nag him constantly to study. He needed me even to complete his schoolwork and homework. And *Ba*, oh she was quite old and she needed me literally every step of the way..."

"Hum and what about your husband?" Dr. Sudha was examining Malti's right breast.

"Oh my Manubhai, doctor, he was a very successful lawyer, all self-made too, you see."

"You must have helped him a lot in his early years then?" Dr. Sudha had moved on to Malti's left breast.

"Yes, doctor. Financially, too."

"Oh?" Dr. Sudha was examining Malti's left breast very carefully.

"Yes. I had to work full time to support my family income in those early years of our life. Afterwards, of course my Manubhai's law practice flourished so much that there was no need for my full time work, so I gave it up, but by then, my three children were there, they kept me on my toes with their constant needs and demands."

"Hum..." Dr. Sudha's face looked a bit serious as she pulled the gown over Malti's bare chest.

"What? What is it doctor?" Malti got up and sat on the table, looking worried.

"Mrs. Patel, you know why you are referred to me by your family doctor, right?" Dr. Sudha was washing her hands.

"Yes, yes, I know."

"Your family doctor felt a tiny but significant lump in your left breast and wants me to give you a thorough examination on that lump."

"What's that?" Malti's face was almost warped with worry.

"Call your daughter inside. I'll explain that to both of you together." Dr. Sudha said.

Kirti came inside and sat on a chair. She also looked extremely worried.

"Mrs. Patel, I am going to do a fine needle biopsy on the tiny lump I felt in your left breast. We need to do this small procedure to rule out or confirm…"

"To rule out or confirm what?" Kirti and Malti both asked simultaneously.

"That the lump is not malignant." Dr. Sudha looked at them and said it in a serious voice.

"What's that?" Malti asked innocently as Kirti just looked at her in horror.

"That's cancer, Mrs. Patel. We just want to rule out or confirm cancer in your left breast…" Dr. Sudha said.

"Cancer? I could have cancer? That can't be true, doctor, no, that can't be…" Malti said. Kirti was still in a shock.

"Well, I hope so, that's exactly why I want to do a quick biopsy on that lump, okay?" Dr. Sudha said.

"Is that a complicated procedure doctor?" Kirti finally pulled her courage and asked.

"No, not really. I usually do it right here in my clinic. It's done under local anesthesia. The advantage is that the results help us rule out all the doubts and suspicions of any complications such as cancer." Then Dr. Sudha explained what a fine needle biopsy entailed to both the ladies and immediately carried it out.

"Come and see me tomorrow to discuss the results." Dr. Sudha said as Malti left the clinic in total confusion.

And the confusion was over very shortly, within twenty four hours!

"Well, all the doubts and suspicions are over now." Malti and Kirti were sitting in Dr. Sudha's clinic exactly forty eight hours after their first visit to her.

"Mrs. Patel, I am sorry to tell you that the lump in your left breast is found to be malignant. The result of the tests confirmed that you have a cancerous lump in your left breast." Dr. Sudha informed Malti and Kirti.

Malti had developed breast cancer!

"So, mother has cancer?" Kirti managed to utter those words; her throat had gone completely dry.

"Yes dear, I'm sorry. But don't worry about it. Your mother has a tiny lump that can be removed relatively easily, without losing her breast. She is very lucky that it was detected so early in the stage. I'll carry out the breast conserving therapy, as it is called by all doctors. Surgical removal of the lump is usually referred to as lumpectomy. Breast conservation therapy is used for patients, such as your mother, who are a little older and diagnosed with early-stage invasive breast cancer. Also, it is usually of stage I or stage II in the classification system. It is a safe method in patients with early stage of breast cancer and is being used more and more in the treatment of breast cancer."

"I have breast cancer?" Malti finally seemed to get what was being discussed between Kirti and Dr. Sudha. They both looked at her questioningly.

"But mother is so very healthy, and she has no family history, then how is it possible mother developing this disease, doctor?" Kirti pulled herself from the deep shock and collected herself.

"What you said about your mother's health or lack of family history must all be true. I can't deny it, but then it could also be possible that she got this disease due to some other reasons..." Dr. Sudha said.

"Such as what, doctor?"

"Such as stress, perhaps."

"Really?"

"Yes, really. As a matter of fact, it's my strong suspicion that developing this disease in your mother's case could be because of her mental stress and depression. The sudden passing away of your father was a very traumatic event in your mother's life, which could have caused her excessive stress and mental depression. It's a long-standing belief among doctors and scientists that there could be a link between stress and breast cancer. If someone is excessively stressed or depressed, they could suppress their immune system with it, and that may affect the hormonal balance in the breast, which could be the link between stress and breast cancer. And one more thing about your mother's case..."

"What is that?" Kirti looked worried.

"Her one word 'need', resounding in her conversation, gave it away too. The entire time I was examining her, she was telling me how everyone 'needed' her constantly. And now, how her 'being needed' state is completely over, especially after your father expired. According to her, this situation of 'not being needed by anybody' has culminated into her thinking that her life is totally meaningless; this feeling obviously has caused excessive depression in her mind. This depression could be the root cause of stress in your mother's case, resulting in her getting breast cancer." Kirti was listening to the doctor very intently, and so was Malti.

"But doctor…" Malti was about to say something but suddenly kept quiet.

"Of course, let me also tell you that breast cancer is an extremely complex disease and it's very difficult to pin-point any one single risk factor, like stress, being responsible for developing the disease. In your mother's case, it is a well-founded guess, that's all." Dr. Sudha said.

"But doctor…" Malti tried again to interrupt the doctor but Dr. Sudha continued her explanation to Kirti.

"There is nothing to worry, the breast conserving therapy is very safe and at the same time, a very effective treatment for non-hereditary or sporadic forms of early breast cancer. That's what your mother seems to have."

"But doctor…" Malti finally got her chance to interrupt the conversation; and just as Dr. Sudha finished her explanation to Kirti, she pushed her chair back and standing up, said,

"It really doesn't matter now. As I told you, nobody needs me, and since nobody needs me, I don't want to continue living this meaningless, un-needed life anyway."

And before even the doctor or her daughter could say anything to her, Malti went out the door, and walked towards the car, ready to leave.

"Mrs. Patel, Mrs. Patel…" Malti heard someone calling her name. She opened her eyes. Shantabai was calling her name and Kirti was standing beside her, staring at her.

"Mrs. Patel, you must get that malignant lump out immediately. Don't you understand that? You are a smart woman, and surely you understand that the sooner it is out…"

Shantabai couldn't complete what she intended to say because Malti interrupted her.

"…better are the chances of surviving, I know that. But Shantabai, like I said earlier, no one needs me. And since nobody needs me, why bother living? I don't want to live a meaningless, *un-needed* life." As if resolved to a final decision, Malti got up and started getting ready to leave.

"*Ma*, wait." Kirti said in a firm voice. "This is exactly what you said when we visited Dr. Sudha's clinic, and without a moment's wait, you just left. Now you are doing the very same thing again, but this time, I'm not going to let you just leave like that…" Kirti got up, held Malti's hand firmly and rooting firmly her own two feet in the thick carpet, started talking to Shantabai.

"Shantabai, the doctor has told us that *Ma*'s breast cancer is a result of her excessive stress and depression that has arisen from this miserable attitude of hers. She is continuously weaving this ridiculous idea in her mind that nobody needs her and she keeps calling her life a futile, useless existence. Fortunately, right now there is only one tiny lump in her left breast, and it is at stage I according to the doctor. If she gets that lump out by doing immediate lumpectomy procedure, and then followed by a good and regular medical treatment for only a few days, she should be just fine. Shantabai, I have been nagging *Ma* to go through this surgery. It's not a big, complicated one, but she just does not listen to me at all." Kirti sounded frustrated.

"Shantabai…" Kirti continued, "Dr. Sudha has also suggested a regular treatment by a psychotherapist after the surgery, that's when she suggested your name to us. Then I thought, why not come here immediately, *before* the surgery? Perhaps *Ma* would listen to you, a professional psychotherapist. Actually, that's why we are here today." Kirti took a deep breath.

"I am so glad you both finally told me honestly and frankly what the real problem is, and why you are here today. There is a serious health problem with you Mrs. Patel, and that is, you have breast cancer." Shantabai got up too.

She put her hand on Malti's shoulders and said in a very gentle voice,

"Malti, may I call you by your given name?"

Malti just nodded.

Shantabai said, "Malti, you are not the only one in this situation; as in, where you feel nobody needs you, or your life is one big empty hole. I have come across many, many women who go through such situations and have the very same feelings, especially after menopause. Their children grow and leave home, husbands are still quite busy and tied up in their work, and older people who live with them and depend on their help are dead and gone. Life suddenly seems hollow. The days seem longer with not much to do. Naturally these women start to feel that no one needs them anymore. Around the same time, menopause sets in. It creates a doubt in their minds about their 'womanhood' and that becomes an additional stress. All this culminates into excessive stress or excessive depression or a combination of both. I see that's exactly what has happened to you, my dear." Shantabai sounded so loving; her deep, sweet voice was touching Malti's heart.

"We all very well know that our body is very closely associated with our mind. All the feelings, problems, stresses that occur in our mind affect the body directly. That is not good for the body. It gets affected, and when the body gets affected, sometimes, a deadly disease such as breast cancer, can originate from it and overpower our health."

Shantabai took a few breaths and continued.

"In the case of breast cancer, along with medicines and other medical treatment, women should also consider psychotherapy for controlling it. It can soothe them and it can also release some stress. It can help them get over the fear of this disease as well. Psychotherapy is an excellent tool that focuses on mind, which in turn, helps the body. Malti, do you get it now?" Shantabai had a very sweet smile on her face. With that smile, she looked so kind.

"Malti, come and see me regularly after you see Dr. Sudha. Do not postpone your visit to her anymore." Shantabai gave a light hug to Malti. With that gentle and almost loving hug, Malti did feel a little relaxed and a little relieved of her stress.

"Shantabai, could she come to you a few times before she sees Dr. Sudha please?" Kirti asked Shantabai.

"Oh sure, if you think that might be necessary. Take my appointment next week again and make it for two hours. I have a feeling that we will need that much time." Kirti and Malti both nodded.

"And I repeat, go and see Dr. Sudha as soon as possible. Don't postpone that anymore…" Shantabai smiled at Malti.

Kirti and Malti left Shantabai's place after expressing their heartfelt gratitude.

"Kirti, I'm glad you insisted on me seeing this lady. I think she'll be a big help to me in many ways; and not just for dealing with my breast cancer, but for *everything else*." Malti gave her daughter a meaningful look when she said, 'everything else'. Her eyes were filled with tears of some relief!

Kiran

"Kittu, Kittu, look at the sky, sweetheart…" The little toddler, barely a year old, started looking at the sky.

"Say now, '*twinkle twinkle little star*'…" Kittu started clapping his tiny hands with joy.

Kiran was standing by the window, trying to entertain Kittu perched in her arms. Little Kittu had become the sole purpose in this world for his mother, Kiran. Though he was ceremoniously named Krishnadev, Kiran lovingly shortened it to Kittu.

"Kiran, we have given him such a fine name, Krishnadev, that of a great king, and you have corrupted it by shortening it to Kittu. What a pity!" Kiran's mother-in-law, *Amma*, often joined Kiran with a smile during such moments.

"Let it be so, *Amma*! Kittu is not such a bad name either. I like it."

"But, the poor child will forever be known by that silly name."

"That's okay, *Amma*." Kiran was still playing with her son.

"Look at me. I always address Rangraj as Rangraj, never Raj or Raju or any such short form." *Amma* said.

"That was fine in a small village like yours *Amma*. But now we live in a metropolis like Mumbai. We have to be among all sorts of people here. Krishnadev is too long a name. I don't think children in the school would be able to properly pronounce that name. Kittu is a nice, convenient short form." Kiran said and then added, "*Amma*, you know that everyone here calls Rangraj, Raj, even at the bank, right? It's the very same thing with Kittu's name, too." *Amma* quietly nodded at her explanation.

"*Amma*, do you think Kittu was Lord Krishna's pet name?" Kiran thought *Amma* was a bit disappointed after this conversation.

"Yes, yes, Lord Krishna was also 'Kittu' to his mother Yashoda…" *Amma* laughed and while nodding heartily, concurred with her. That made Kiran feel better. Such was the relationship between those two women, a very friendly and loving one.

Rangraj Rao, Kiran's husband, was employed as an accountant at the local bank and was recently transferred to Mumbai on a senior post. He moved to the city with his mother and made Mumbai his home place. Kiran was working as a Cashier in the same branch of the bank where Raj got his transfer. When those two met at some bank function, some 'strange' chemistry developed between them.

Raj took Kiran home to meet Amma one day, after the bank closed. *Amma* liked Kiran, especially her coyness and decent manners. And shortly afterwards, on one auspicious day, they tied the knot in an impressive ceremony and began their married life. How the first two or three dreamy years flew by, neither of them realized. And then they thought of starting a family. *Amma* had been long waiting for such a welcome decision.

One day, *Amma* saw Raj enter home with a big box of sweets in his hands.

"*Amma*, you are soon going to be a grandmother."

He put two pieces of sweets in her mouth, saying 'One, if it's a granddaughter and another, if it's a grandson,' and started laughing. He looked so very happy.

After the full term, a baby boy was born and the entire household was overjoyed. The news was too exciting for everybody. Especially for the old woman, *Amma*!

After the untimely passing of her husband, *Amma* had raised her son all by herself. It was a trying time for her, especially in the little town where she had lived. There was nobody to help her. But, Raj was a good son, he graduated from the high school and then from the local community college with good grades and landed on a job with the local bank as a teller. After successfully passing the bank examinations, he got promoted to be an accountant. After Raj's wedding, this moment of becoming a grandmother to Raj's baby boy proved to be the epitome of her joy. This little prince, with his recent arrival into this world, marked the continuity of Raj's father in her mind.

The baby was named Krishnadev, with a shortened form, Kittu. Day by day, Kittu was making progress and his every new step was so very gleefully being noted. 'Kittu balances his head, Kittu recognizes this and recognizes that, now Kittu can turn on his sides, now Kittu can sit up without a support, and so on'. It was Kittu, Kittu and Kittu all along. Kittu was the one around whom the whole world revolved. That is how at least his mother and grandmother thought and behaved.

The period of six months flew by as if it was only a brief moment. Kiran rejoined her duty at the bank. *Amma*, who loved the child more than she loved her own self, was available at home to take care of Kittu. Therefore, Kiran took the decision of joining her work at the bank. She weaned her baby boy immediately, and fortunately, her son got used to the ready-made milk formula for the babies.

Kittu was soon going to be a one year old. It was unbelievable how fast the months had passed. Kiran had been working at the bank already for almost six months since her maternity leave ended. Lately, and strangely, she started feeling some lumps that seemed like milk-accumulations she had experienced during her weaning times in her breasts. 'It has been over six months now? Why do I feel these lumps in my breast?' She wondered.

The observations and the thought began to worry Kiran. It even showed on her face; *Amma* was the first one to notice it.

"You don't look so cheerful now a days, Kiran. What's the matter?" *Amma* asked Kiran one evening after her return from work.

"Oh nothing, nothing at all. I think it must be the work pressure at the bank. It gets very tiring. I am also feeling a bit stressed out these days due to work, that is all."

"No. I don't agree. You are not the same old Kiran any longer. What's the matter?"

"Nothing at all, *Amma*. Honestly." Kiran's dry and cold response did not satisfy *Amma*. 'There must be more to it', she thought. She moved closer to Kiran and patting gently on her back, said, "Kiran look into my eyes. I am Raj's mother. And since your marriage, I am your mother too. Mothers know intuitively what the daughters feel. Tell me the truth. Tell me what bothers you?"

Amma's words, drenched with love and concern and even more so, her loving touch made Kiran breakdown. She started sobbing uncontrollably.

'This is not the time to ask her what was wrong,' *Amma* knew. She let the reassuring touch of her hands on Kiran's shoulders do the talking. Kiran sobbed and cried and *Amma* stood there by her side in silence that seemed like an endless period of time. When the eyes had run dry, Kiran dried her nose with her sari and asked, "Where is Kittu? Is he sleeping?"

"Yes. I put him to bed before you returned home. He won't wake up at least for a couple of hours now."

"*Amma*…" *Amma* was standing right there next to her. "*Amma*. I am going to die soon." Kiran said.

"Oh my god, oh no! What an evil thought." *Amma* was shocked beyond imagination on hearing those scary words. How would she ward off this evil thought, she quickly joined her hands in a prayer to the Lord.

"It is true. I am going to die. Really! Very Soon…"

"Speak no evil, my girl. Think of good and speak of good. I beseech you in the name of Lord Krishna. Tell me what's on your mind, Rani." *Amma* had hard time controlling herself, but she managed it.

Kiran held her by the hand and led her to an inner room. Seating her there in a chair and herself sitting at her feet on the ground, Kiran said, "*Amma*, listen to me carefully. I am saying this for the very first time to anybody. A woman would tell this perhaps only to her mother, but you are my mother, in fact even more than that. You have given me immense love all through my married life, and that is why, I want to tell you what's on my mind before I tell anyone else. *Amma, Amma…*" She stumbled at the words a little bit. *Amma* looked confused and very tense.

"*Amma*, I feel some small lumps in my right breast. I feel them every time I take my bath. I am very scared of them. In the beginning I thought they must be lumps of un-suckled milk like those infamous milk-accumulations some women get after weaning the baby. But now it is nearly six months since I stopped breast feeding Kittu and those lumps are still there. *Amma*, I am terribly scared. Would these lumps be that of cancer?" The word 'cancer' sent a shiver through *Amma*'s spine. She did not hear a word after that one.

Cancer! The deadly disease. And breast cancer at that. That was even worse. She lost all her courage and finally, she broke down too. With no strength in her legs, she continued sitting on the chair helplessly and crying along with Kiran. For how long they had been sitting like that could not be guessed. When Raj returned home from work late in the evening, and saw them seated motionless like statues, he got truly scared.

Climb to Victory Over Breast Cancer

"Rani, *Amma*, what's the matter? Is Kittu alright? Is everything alright?" His questions shook them out of their trance. Kiran once again burst into tears. That scared Raj even more. He rushed to their room. Kittu was sleeping soundly in the cradle. He felt relieved.

What could be the matter then? He had no clue whatsoever. He was speechless. It was *Amma* who broke the silence. "Rangraj, Rani is unwell. Take her to a doctor. Right now…"

Amma sounded like she was giving orders. It was unusual. And that confused him even more.

"What's the matter?"

"Take her now. Take her to a women's specialist. A good lady doctor. I have heard someone mention the name of Dr. Sudha. She is known to be some specialist. Take Kiran to her. Go to this doctor right now, without wasting any time." *Amma* said in the same tone, a bit of an authoritative one, again.

"I will. I will. Right away, *Amma*, but please, will some body tell me, what's the matter with Rani, what's all this rush?" Raj got into a real panic.

"You first take her to Dr. Sudha's clinic, get her examined and come home only after the doctor has examined her thoroughly." *Amma*'s authoritative voice continued.

Raj did not stretch the issue. Kiran got up and got ready to go and Raj took her straight to that famous lady doctor, Dr. Sudha without wasting even a minute, as his mother had ordered.

They reached Dr. Sudha's clinic. In the outer room of the clinic, the receptionist was making the patients comfortable and taking down the details of each one systematically.

It was Kiran's turn.

"Name?"

"Kiran Rao." Raj responded for Kiran.

"Age?"

"Twenty eight."

"Other details please."

"She is my wife. I am Rangraj Rao. Kiran works as a cashier with the bank. We have a son. Krishnadev is his name. He will be one year old in another fifteen days."

"Other family members?"

"One. Besides we three, there is my mother living with us."

The receptionist took it down pretty fast and neatly.

"Please be seated. You may have to wait for a while as there is no appointment in your name." She said.

"That's alright, we knew that." Raj said.

"It could be just half an hour or as late as two or three hours."

"That's okay. Actually, I realize we are here without a prior appointment, and yet you have accommodated us. Thank you."

"You are welcome! Please take seats in the waiting room. Be comfortable. I will call you as soon as there is an opening." The receptionist said with a smile and started attending to another patient.

It was the tradition of the clinic to examine, as far as possible, all the patients. Although this was not a walk-in clinic, Dr. Sudha did not like any of her patients being turned away just because he or she didn't have an appointment, especially if the patient looked like being in an urgent need of help. When the receptionist came and told them it was Kiran's turn, Raj gently held her hand and led her in to the doctor's room.

This was Dr. Sudha's patient examination room. The atmosphere there was purposely made pleasant. In one corner of the room, a large bronze idol of Goddess Durga was placed on a pedestal. There was a garland of fresh flowers hanging from the idol's neck. A soothing, melodic tune was being played on the stereo in the background. The lighting in the room was just adequate, not too bright nor too dim. The fragrance of the flowers, the quiet music and mild lighting in the room all together would make the patient feel at ease. In the center of the room, there was a red mahogany table with a huge leather chair on one side, for Dr. Sudha, and four smaller chairs on the other side for patients. Away from the table and adjacent to the far wall was the examination table. Neatly hanging on that wall were charts and pictures of female anatomy. It was quite a queer sight to see one wall displaying charts of delicate female organs, which directly faced across the room, the huge idol of Goddess Durga, a female symbol of human strength!

"Now, what can I do for you, Kiran Rao?" Dr. Sudha asked Raj and Kiran while signaling them to take seats. She started looking up the history sheets that the receptionist had filled up for Kiran.

Sensing the reassurance that showed on the loving countenance of Dr. Sudha, Kiran in spite of the fear of possibly being a candidate of cancer victim, felt a bit relaxed. She joined her hands in a greeting to the doctor and sat down in one of the chairs opposite to her. After she sat down, Raj greeted the doctor and sat down too.

"To tell you honestly, I don't know why we are here. It may seem stupid but it is true. When I returned from my office, I found my mother and Kiran both crying uncontrollably. I have brought her here because my mother bid me to do so. Other than that, I really have no idea why we are here. My wife hasn't told me anything either." Dr. Sudha seemed quite amused at the honest reply of the husband.

"That's fine. What I would like to do is a thorough physical examination of your wife. Would you please go outside and take a seat in the next room?"

"Oh Yes." Raj said and left the place dutifully. Dr. Sudha asked Kiran to take off all her clothes and wear just a thin cotton gown to facilitate a thorough examination.

"Kiran, please cooperate with me. Will you please answer my questions honestly, without hiding anything?"

Kiran nodded.

"You had a baby recently, right?"

"Yes"

"Any complication? Any problems with the delivery?"

"No. Nothing whatsoever."

"Did you breastfeed the baby?"

"Yes. I did."

"For how long?"

"About sixteen months during my maternity leave. But then I had to wean him, as there was no option after I joined work."

"How long since you stopped breast feeding?"

"Say about six months,"

"Do you have your periods now?"

"Yes"

"Any complications in that?" Kiran just shook her head.

Dr. Sudha was questioning her and simultaneously examining Kiran's ears, nose, throat and also taking the measurement of her pulse rate, blood pressure, body temperature and all that.

"Did you have any fever any time?"

"No. Not at all"

"Any Infection?"

"No"

"Any problems in your sexual activity?"

Kiran shook her head to indicate a big no.

"Good! Now take the gown off so that I can examine your stomach, chest and the back."

The words 'examination of chest' almost brought tears in her eyes. Dr. Sudha's experienced eyes did not miss that detail.

She said, "Come on young girl, tell me the whole thing."

"Doctor, I stopped breast feeding my baby a good six months ago. I find some lumps in my right breast. I don't really know if they are of un-suckled milk or of something different, something more dangerous..." Every part of her body trembled as she said this.

"Oh, I see..." Dr. Sudha had finished examining Kiran's abdomen and the back and was about to turn to her breasts.

"Does it pain?" Dr. Sudha asked Kiran while gently pressing her left breast.

"No."

"Here?" It was the right breast this time.

"No. Here neither."

"I do feel two lumps in your right breast. I see the reddishness on the skin there. Since when has it been so.?"

"Reddish skin? I never noticed that."

"Did you not see yourself in the mirror?"

"No."

Dr. Sudha once again examined the right breast very carefully.

"I feel two lumps in this breast. Good that you discovered them now. I think it is early enough. Now let us do it this way, let us do the biopsy right here in my clinic."

"My God! What is a biopsy, Doctor? Doctor please, please get Raj in here. I need him."

Kiran was terribly frightened. The nurse called Raj and led him into the room.

"Mr. Rao. Please listen to this very carefully. I feel two lumps in your wife's right breast. I have also observed that the skin around it is reddish. That is not a good sign. I have a doubt that these lumps may not be ordinary. We'll have to confirm what it is. Therefore, I recommend immediate biopsy. We will do it right here in my clinic. Technically it is called a *fine needle aspiration*. In this procedure, I will draw out some cells from the lumps in her breast, Of course, that will be done under local anesthesia, and send the sample to the pathologist. The advantage of this kind of biopsy is that the results will be available soon and we can rule out all the doubts and suspicions of any complications such as cancer."

"Cancer…? Did you say cancer?" Raj broke into heavy sweating; what was this horrible thing he was hearing 'out of nowhere'?

When he left the house to take Kiran to this doctor, he did not even have a clue as to why he was bringing her here. It was clearly at the insistence of his mother that he had brought Kiran to this clinic. It was then that it dawned upon him why he saw Kiran and Amma crying uncontrollably on his return from the office.

"Doctor, why do you suspect that this could be cancer?"

"I said 'rule out all suspicions of any complications such as cancer'. I will not be able to tell you anything definitely unless

I have the biopsy report in hand. My suspicion arose because those lumps are not painful, and she said she did not suffer from high fever in past six months after she stopped breastfeeding her child. Obviously, there had been no infection of any kind. That rules out what we call *lactation mastitis*. And still we see those lumps present. Also the skin surrounding them is reddish. These indications make me suspect something like that." As Dr. Sudha was talking, Raj was getting more and more nervous.

"Yet, as I said, unless I have the biopsy report in hand, I cannot tell any which way about this. Don't worry, your wife is only twenty eight years of age, so in my judgment, there is nothing to worry. It would be an exceptional case if her report tells something different. Only in very rare cases that women under thirty become cancer affected. That is why I am recommending a biopsy immediately."

Raj didn't look calm at all; he was still sweating profusely.

"Mr. Rao, I have noted Kiran's family history; and there seems to be no case of cancer in her family. She is a woman of only twenty eight years of age, therefore, suffering from breast cancer seems unimaginable to me." Dr. Sudha tried to console Raj.

"Doctor, is it possible that you do the biopsy tomorrow? Tomorrow afternoon? I must see my mother and my son before anything else…Please." Kiran requested the doctor.

The earnestness in her voice made Dr. Sudha give the suggestion another thought.

"Kiran, biopsy is not a major operation or any such thing as you might fear. It is done right here. Within minutes. Almost like taking a sample of blood. The advantage is, we can have those results in hand in a couple of days or so. Once the results are out, you both can have some peace of mind. We can then give a good thought as to what could be done with those lumps. But this confirmation is a must for me to have, to advice you in the right way. You need not take the decision in a hurry because you have been fortunate in detecting the lumps quite early..." Dr. Sudha sounded quite reassuring to both of them.

"Fortunately for you, your mother-in-law told your husband to bring you to me, a breast cancer specialist. There is something of suspicion, obviously, even to her, don't you see it? An early biopsy will settle the issue right away. It is in your interest Kiran."

Both, Kiran and Raj saw the point, so they agreed.

"Mr. Rao, I always recommend a husband or a close relative of the patient be present during this procedure. It helps the patient feel secured and better prepared for the test." The doctor then requested the nurse to keep all the equipment ready for a fine needle biopsy.

Accordingly, the nurse brought all the equipment systematically arranged in a tray, and the brief procedure was carried out.

"That's it. It was pretty fast, wasn't it? Kiran, put on your clothes now, and book an appointment with my receptionist to see me in a couple of days. By then the pathologist's report would be here. We will discuss everything then, alright?" Dr. Sudha said.

Kiran and Raj returned home after sincerely thanking the doctor.

Amma was standing at the door waiting for Kiran and Raj to return, with Kittu in her arms. As soon as he saw his mother come to the door, the little boy nearly jumped at her.

"Oh my darling son," Kiran said. As she caught him in the mid-air, his head struck her right breast. Kiran faintly sighed on the impact.

"What's the matter? Did it hurt?" Raj asked her.

"Not much. May be the effect of anesthesia is receding." Kiran answered.

"What is receding, you said?" *Amma* was shocked at the utterance of the word, anesthesia.

"I will tell you everything, *Amma...*" And then Raj described in detail all that had taken place in the clinic.

The wait of next forty eight hours was of nothing but full of anxiety, making all three of them extremely uneasy. Only Kittu was blissfully unaware of the tension prevailing there. Kiran had taken a couple of days off from work, so he was happy to have his mother home with him the whole time.

"Come in please. Be seated." The nurse led Kiran, Raj and *Amma* into the doctor's room and indicated towards the chairs. Dr. Sudha was studying Kiran's file. The pathologist's report was in the file.

"Good morning, Doctor." Raj greeted the doctor as he took his seat. "I have got my mother also with me. She insisted on joining us."

"Very good. She is welcome. That way, she will be able to get all the information first hand. I encourage family members to be present with the patient." Dr. Sudha looked quite serious as she spoke. It alarmed Raj a bit but he did not let it show on his face. Kiran and *Amma* were looking quite nervous.

Dr. Sudha held a sheet of paper in hand, cleared her throat and began to speak, "Kiran, I have your biopsy report here."

"And ?" Kiran could not hide her anxiousness.

"As I told you the other day, a Fine needle biopsy report is considered to be conclusive. Particularly when it is positive..."

"Oh my God! Do you mean..." Raj looked pale as a paper.

"I am very sorry to tell you Kiran, the report indicates that the lump that was tested from your breast is flooded with cancer cells. I'm very, very sorry. You have developed breast cancer. It is confirmed." Dr. Sudha could not look into Kiran's eyes while talking. It must have pained her too to break the news to this family.

"O my God! Cancer! That means I am going to die. No escape from it. It's a sure thing. No. Oh No. My little Kittu... Kittu...my baby..." Kiran let out a weak cry and fell unconscious in the chair.

Raj and *Amma* froze completely. Without any movement, they stayed still and stiff in their chairs. The doctor called in a nurse in a hurry. The nurse rushed in.

"Get me some ammonia, cotton balls and a glass of water." Nurse quickly got everything and held a cotton ball soaked in ammonia near Kiran's nose to regain her consciousness. With that strong smell, she soon regained her consciousness. The nurse handed Kiran a glass of water and gestured her to drink it. The nurse, then, went near Raj and *Amma* and gave them a light jerk on their shoulders and wrists. The jerk helped them come out of their frozen state, but they seemed as if they had lost all the strength from their bodies

"Would you please lie down on that table for a while?" The nurse took the empty glass from Kiran's hands and asked her most courteously.

"No," was Kiran's curt response. The nurse just looked at the doctor and left the room.

"Doctor, did you say Kiran has breast cancer?" Raj had somehow managed to gather strength to ask Dr. Sudha; *Amma* was still in a semi-frozen state, not able to respond in anyway.

"Yes. I am sorry."

"That means I am going to die. Isn't it doctor?" Kiran asked. Dr. Sudha gave a fleeting glance in her direction. Before she could respond to her question, Kiran fired away, "and before I die, you would chop off my right breast. Isn't it?"

Again, before even Dr. Sudha could respond to her question, Kiran said, "and Doctor, you will cut my breast off; de-shape me and then leave me to rot and die. Is it not?" Kiran had almost become hysterical and Dr. Sudha, who only a couple of days ago looked so calm and compassionate, kept staring at Kiran vacantly. She was shocked to see this young, fragile woman yell and talk like this.

"Rani..." Raj lovingly pulled Kiran in his arms. Resting her head on his chest, Kiran started sobbing hard. "Rani, calm down. Calm down honey…"

Then he turned to the doctor and said, "Doctor, doctor please explain to us everything in detail. Please don't give us this shocking news and then stay quiet." Raj himself sounded like he was on the verge of crying. Amma was holding Kiran's one hand tightly, partly to give her some support and partly to have some for her own self.

"Mr. Rao, quite frankly, I was taken aback by your wife's reaction. I'm sorry but I didn't mean to stay quiet as you thought. When I saw your wife's biopsy report last evening, even I was quite upset. Quite honestly, I did not know how I would explain this to you this morning. I have been in this profession long enough to see such cases. I thought I knew everything that is required of me to know in this profession. But ever since I read your wife's report, I have become quite restless myself." Dr. Sudha looked genuinely upset.

"Why so, Madam? It is nothing new for you in your medical practice." Raj asked.

"You are right. It is not. I'm a breast cancer specialist and my practice is treating breast cancer. But what I have seen with your wife still made me restless."

"Why doctor, what do you mean exactly?" Raj was visibly nervous.

"Mr. Rao, your wife is suffering from a relatively rare kind of breast cancer. It is a special kind of advanced cancer and regarded as a serious one. It is called *Inflammatory Breast cancer*.[4]"

Whatever control Raj had exercised over himself up until that moment, was lost completely at the mention of the words 'advanced cancer'. His darling wife had fallen prey to one of the most dreaded diseases; and he had absolutely no defense against it. He did not have even the slightest idea of any such disease just two days earlier, and today? The news was being hammered into his head so suddenly out of nowhere. The deadly disease was going to kill his wife and ruin his family life. And that bright little son of his? The death of his mother could devastate him permanently, who knows?

'Oh my Lord!' Raj uttered these words, drew Kiran even closer to his chest and began to cry profusely. The uncontrollable flow of tears down his cheeks was dampening her thick hair. Though *Amma* could not understand much of what the doctor had said, she could sense the seriousness of the situation. She too started crying ceaselessly and drying her tears with her sari from time to time. Dr. Sudha left the room for giving them some privacy.

How long those three were sitting there in that state of mind could not be guessed. All three had their eyes red and swollen due to incessant crying. Dr. Sudha returned shortly afterwards

---

[4] Details given at the end of the book.

and requested the receptionist to get cups of hot coffee for all of them. She also told her to reschedule all other appointments for the morning.

"*Amma*, Mr. and Mrs. Rao, let us have some coffee. I know it is a very trying time for you, but what can we do about it? It has happened already and we have to face the situation. Please have some hot coffee, it might help ease your tension. You will feel a bit better. Let us see what can be done from here on. Let us plan."

The nurse brought in four cups of coffee and put them on the table. Dr. Sudha passed the cups to Raj, Kiran and *Amma*. They all refused; Dr. Sudha looked at them, they were looking like three robots sitting in front of her, totally motionless and emotionless.

"Mr. and Mrs. Rao, I need to summarize what I told you all earlier. Kiran, you are suffering from inflammatory breast cancer. The lumps you found in your breast after you stopped breastfeeding your child were not the lumps of un-drawn milk as you believed but they were lumps of cancer. It is unfortunate that you did not notice the skin of your breast around the lumps that had become reddish. The exact sequence would be that it was *your breast-skin that was the first to be affected by the cancer*. Over a period of time, it invaded the cells in your breast and formed a couple of lumps there. You detected the lumps, but unfortunately, the redness of the skin slipped your notice completely."

Dr. Sudha stopped for a while to see their reaction to what she was saying. They still looked the very same, completely devoid of any reaction or feeling.

"Believe it or not, it is seldom that one comes across this kind of cancer. It is very, very rare; perhaps, only about one percent among the breast cancer patients!" Dr. Sudha continued her explanation.

"And it was only our Kiran who was chosen to be the one. What justice of the Lord is this?" *Amma* broke the silence.

"What next? What do we do now?" Raj somehow managed to come out of his frozen state and asked the doctor.

"What do you mean, 'what do we do now '? The procedure of mastectomy of course! The removal of the affected breast! We must go for the surgery immediately. No time left now. Immediately after the operation, we must opt for the radiation, followed by the chemotherapy."

"Removal of what?" Suddenly Kiran blurted out loudly.

"Removal of your affected breast, the right breast, of course!" Dr. Sudha was a bit shocked to hear Kiran's loud voice.

"Doctor, what are you trying to tell us, that there isn't any other option? No option at all?" Kiran was really loud.

The doctor shook her head.

"No. No. Doctor, I don't want that." Kiran said in a dry voice that was filled with utter conviction. Dr. Sudha, including Raj and Amma, wondered if this was the same woman who was crying endlessly, and looking helpless, only moments ago.

"Dr. Sudha, what's the survival rate among those who have this rare disease, after surgery and all that?" Kiran asked again. It was really a daring question. There was a certain determination in her voice. It startled all of them.

"I can comment on it only on the available statistics." Dr. Sudha said.

"Let us have it. Doctor, I can take it." Kiran assured the doctor.

"This type of cancer is known to be the 'aggressive' type. The survivor of this cancer lasts for about a year or two, occasionally three years!" Dr. Sudha said, almost in an apologetic tone when she informed Kiran.

"And for those two or three years, the patient's life would be filled with all kinds of treatments and chemo and what have you, isn't it?" Kiran confronted the doctor without mincing words.

"Well, yes, you can say that. However, the present technology does suggest that the survival can be extended to more than one year." Dr. Sudha tried to put all the information in perspective.

"Is it guaranteed?" Kiran's voice had gone up by one more level.

"Well, no. There are no guarantees, my dear, but..." Dr. Sudha was about to say something when Kiran interrupted her, saying, 'let's go,' and abruptly got up from her chair.

"Let us go, Raj. Get up *Amma*. Let us go. Whatever we were required to do here is done already. Thank you very much, doctor. Honestly, I cannot thank you enough for all that you did for us." Kiran said with total dryness that was clearly evident in her voice and on her face.

"When do we start the treatment?" Dr. Sudha asked. The unexpected change of stance taken by Kiran had caught her quite unaware.

"*Never.* The treatment would never happen. It's all over." Kiran picked up her purse, ready for leaving the place.

"Please listen. Kiran, listen to me..." Dr. Sudha tried to say something but Kiran interrupted her again.

"No, I won't listen to you. In that treatment, first you will remove my breast. May be both breasts to avoid any future problems, who knows? Then with radiation, you will subject my body to another kind of harshness. Then you will subject me to drink doses of that horrible poison under the name, 'chemo therapy', in the hope that something better might evolve and keep me alive for a few more months. And all this for what? Just to live for an additional year or two? May be three years, tops! No thanks. I do not wish to live like this. I have no desire to present my body to you for its dissection or to de-shape it permanently."

"Don't take such an extreme view about the treatment, Kiran." Dr. Sudha was trying to calm her down.

"It is not an extreme view. I am saying all this, based on what you just told me. Doctor, I love my breasts tremendously. I am proud of them. They have given immense pleasure to my husband all along. They have fed milk to my child for six whole months. I would say my milk is still flowing in his veins. I do not want to lose my breast under the name of 'treatment', okay?"

Kiran got up to go. *Amma* and Raj got up too.

"Doctor, you have been very kind to me. I have seen the expressions on your face when you told us about the pathologist's report. You seemed genuinely disturbed by it. That look on your face alone told me a lot about you. You are a kind person and I thank you genuinely for your compassion. But Doctor, whatever time is left of my life now, I would rather spend it with my family, in *my style,* and in the way *I* want than in this treatment. In that little time I do not want to make innumerable visits to various doctors and hospitals, and suffer the nauseating smells of the medicines. This is my final decision. Let me spend these last few months of my life with dignity. And more importantly, in the way that *I want.*"

"Mr. Rao, please talk to your wife, put some sense in her head. Advise her. Discuss with her the benefits of my treatment after she has calmed down from this extreme emotional shock. I see her outburst as a natural reaction to finding out about her disease. Mr. Rao, I have seen many patients turning hysteric on being told that they are cancer positive. But later, when they calm down, they do realize the gravity of the situation and take a rational decision with my advice. Your wife's reaction is quite understandable. Don't be disturbed by it. Don't worry about it, but do call me when you have taken the right decision, decision of immediate treatment, that is, without wasting any precious time. We can start it right away. There is no point in trying to convince her right now, for right now, she is extremely emotional." Dr. Sudha gave a heartfelt advice to Raj. She could see that this young family had just suffered a thousand volts jolt with the news.

Raj didn't know what to say to the doctor or how to react to Kiran's sudden outburst. He was even more confused than before. He barely managed to thank Dr. Sudha for her help and advice, and the three of them left her room.

No one uttered a single word in the taxi on their way home. One could have easily taken them all to be deaf and mute.

Sheila

"Sheila, just a couple more photos…"

"Ohff, oh! No, no. I am really tired. Please, let us do that tomorrow."

"Oh pretty please, just two more photos and the whole session would be complete, I promise."

"Oh well, okay…" With reluctance Sheila agreed to the photographer's requests. He took a couple of her shots and then started wrapping up his equipment.

This incident took place one afternoon in a huge and an elegant photo studio. The photographer was one of the top and the most coveted photographers of the country. But then, Sheila was also one of the most desired and coveted models of the country. For lingerie, she was the top model, she *still* is, and wanted by all photographers, including the important ones as this photographer.

Sheila, a young woman with a gorgeous body and an absolutely perfect figure, also has a sweet looking, oval shaped face with two beautiful big eyes to go with that body! No wonder she has captured the entire Lounge Wear industry as a model. No matter how the clothes are, when she wears them, they look just perfect. And that helps the clothes industry sell their products in millions all across the country. Sheila as a model has become their trump card for selling their clothes, especially for their lingerie.

A tall body with long, slender limbs and a very narrow waist line, Sheila really can boast about her perfect figure. And the epitome of her figure is her beautiful, shapely, big breasts! As if a skillful sculptor has poured his heart and soul in carving them and then placed them precisely, with a perfect angle, above her slender waist.

Climb to Victory Over Breast Cancer

The truth is that a skillful sculptor *did* carve them and *did* place them neatly on her slender torso, almost fifteen years ago. Those breasts were the reason she got into a modeling career; and just as she entered the modeling career, she almost immediately shot up to being one of the most sought after models of the country. That career gave her a life of luxury she could never have dreamt of earlier. Whenever there were new and aspiring young women entering the field of modeling, Sheila very easily overtook them, mainly because of her figure with those 'out of this world' breasts!

Sheila need not worry about her modeling career and thereby, a life of plenty of money and luxury, as long as her breasts remain the same beautiful way. And *they will*, because they have been *'man-made'* and designed especially for her! Her beautiful breasts have given her security of a modeling career, and of life as well. Yes, those breasts have given Sheila a guarantee of cancer-free life!

It all started almost fifteen years ago, in a tiny village near the town of Burrelpur in North India. Sheila was a schoolgirl of about twelve years of age. Her real name, as per the registration in the school, was Shailender Singh. Youngest of three daughters in the family, her older two sisters, Baljeet and Daljeet, were much too older. They were in their late twenties.

"Shailu, get me my *kurta*…" Baljeet would yell from the bathroom and little Shailu, as Shailender was called at home, had to run and get it for her.

"Shailu, go in the kitchen and make me a cup of tea, I am very tired now…" Daljeet would order her as soon as she would come home from work, and of course, Shailu had to go to the kitchen and make her a fresh cup of tea. Both the sisters would give a lot of small chores to their younger sister and Shailu had no choice but to do the chores.

"Shailu, get me a glass of water, I am thirsty…' her father, *Papaji*, would ask for a glass of water almost every hour on the hour and she had no choice but to get it for him. *Papaji* would keep asking for many different things to be done for him practically for the whole day, and as she was the only one around, she had no choice but to do them for him. She many times felt that he was constantly bossing her around without uttering a single loving word. What she detested even more was, when the Sun would come up and the day would get hotter, *Papaji* would take off his shirt and continuously scratch his hairy stomach and chest, his equally hairy back, and sometimes with one hand raised, scratch the armpit with the other. At such times, she would avoid to even go near him. A young girl of pre-puberty years, she had developed nausea for him. When no one was watching, she would sit in her favorite place in the backyard and cry silently for hours, wishing every moment that her mother was alive, although she didn't remember how she was, for she passed away when Shailu was too young.

She didn't remember how her mother looked but heard the village folks saying that she had inherited her mother's good looks with a light complexion and beautiful big eyes. She never heard anything about her mother's passing away, not even from her sisters, except when people would say, 'he is in a shock due to sudden death of his wife'. She didn't quite comprehend fully what they said; all she had seen ever since she was a very young girl her father sitting around the house whole day doing absolutely nothing except ordering her relentlessly, and her two older sisters leaving for work at the crack of the dawn, doing a lot of manual chores for people to bring home money for the livelihood of the family.

Shailender was sent to a nearby village school when she became almost eight years of age, but she had no interest in learning anything. The school was one of the most primitive schools with no facilities that would attract little girls and boys and encourage them to learn and study. She barely managed to finish four grades and was able to do some reading and writing, when one day she was sent home by the school head for family emergency.

Her eldest sister, Baljeet, while finishing her daily chores, was found to vomit some blood and after a few hours, died. The whole thing was so sudden that it gave no time for anyone to take her to the Burrelpur hospital that was about seventy miles away. *Papaji* was completely motionless, just staring at her dead body, and repeating, 'that's exactly how she died'. He meant his wife. Villagers took the dead body and cremated in the village crematorium. He didn't even go there. The family observed the mourning period and then everyone got back into their routine, *Papaji* becoming even more depressed looking and much more difficult to handle since that day.

Shailender started going back to the school, a place that had become her solace, to free herself from the depressing environment of home, especially from Papaji, at least for a few hours of the day. She was barely in the middle school when she was called by the school head one day to be sent home, when exactly the same calamity befell the family one more time. This time it was Daljeet's turn to get intensely sick. With the previous experience in memory, a few of the neighbors got together and admitted Daljeet to a hospital in a nearby town. But that small town hospital had very limited equipment for a proper diagnosis of Daljeet's disease. Daljeet died with no cause known to the local doctors or nurses. She too, in short, had left the world suddenly and unexpectedly.

The family saw three deaths, one after another in a short span of time. All three were women, two among them, quite young. Nobody knew why it happened. Was it a curse of some sort? *Papaji* became completely neurotic, and Shailender even more averse to go near him. She quit school altogether and started wandering all over the village during school hours; but who would have noticed that? There was no one to question her for any of her actions, or take care of her. She started detesting everything about her home. A young girl, having just entered her teenage, she occasionally visited her friends' homes, but that was never a happy visit as it would generate an intense feeling of jealousy in her, especially when she would see their mothers making hot meals for them and taking care of their needs. She felt extremely lonely in this vast world.

And one day, as Shailender was wandering through the meadows, she was located by the school peon and taken to the school office. Scared like anything, she started shivering with fear. What had she done?

"Come in…" the school head said. An elderly lady was sitting and talking with the school head when Shailender was brought into the office.

"Come, come, and sit down." The school head gestured her in a kind voice. Shailender got the mat from the corner, laid it on the floor and sat down. No student was allowed to sit on a chair in the school. Besides, both chairs in the office were occupied.

"Meet our guest, Usha *ji* Pundit. She is new in town, and has come to our school all the way from New Delhi." The school head said.

Shailender looked at the guest. A lady in her fifties or so, she had a very kind face. She felt a little at ease.

"*Namaste.*" Shailender politely greeted the lady.

"*Namaste.* And what is your name?"

"Shailender, Shailender Singh." Shailender told her name in a very low and polite tone.

"Shailender, how old are you?" The lady asked with a smile. Her disarming smile made Shailender feel further relaxed.

"Thirteen years." Shailender answered politely to this 'kind-looking' lady.

"Usha *ji*, please tell her yourself why you are here today." The school head said.

"Well, okay. Listen, the Central government of India, that's at New Delhi, you know that, right?"

Shailender just nodded.

"Good. They have made some kind of an arrangement with all the state governments of the country to inculcate literacy, and if possible, promote education up to high school graduation for everybody, especially for girls and young women, free of cost. This is a major project and the government of your state is also participating in the project. With big cities and urban centers, we have had no problem. Most of the people are literate; many go to schools and complete their high school education. It is in the small villages, such as this one, where it poses a real problem, and a real challenge, I might add." Shailender was listening to her intently.

"We are trying to meet that challenge by taking one village at a time. We are taking up that project starting right here, with your village."

The school head looked very pleased listening to Usha *ji*.

"When do you think this project would start here?" She asked with enthusiasm.

"Oh, it would be starting next month."

The school head looked happy. And so was Shailender, she nodded with a smile and a nod to express that she was able to understand what the new lady said.

"Usha *ji*, it is commendable that you have dedicated your whole life to this cause; inculcating literacy among the villagers, especially women of India." The school head looked at Usha *ji* with great admiration and respect.

Usha *ji*, accepting the compliment turned to Shailender and said, "Shailender, I am told that you were a bright student, and you were just a couple of years away from completing your middle school when you quit school a few months ago, for no obvious reason, is that right?"

Shailender nodded and looked down.

"Would you join my project, then?" She asked.

Shailender looked up and nodded again.

"First, you will have to finish the middle school right here, and then judging from your progress, I will arrange for you to go to the town of Burrelpur to complete your high school graduation. That means you will have to be away from your home for three years. Is that okay with you?"

This was Shailender's big opportunity to get away from her miserable home environment, especially from *Papaji*. She nodded vigorously as a firm 'yes' to her question.

"You said she has an old father at home. I think we need to take his permission for his daughter to be a part of this project, isn't it?" Usha *ji* turned to the school head and asked.

"No, no, you don't need his permission. Please don't talk to him; I do want to learn…" Shailender blurted out rather loudly that startled both those ladies in the room.

"Calm down Shailender, there's no need to get excited. I'll talk to your father and get his permission for you to enroll in this project, okay?" The school head assured her and then looked at Usha *ji* with meaningful eyes.

Climb to Victory Over Breast Cancer

'These two women look like they will definitely help me,' Shailender assessed the situation and felt relaxed.

"If I finish the middle school successfully, then I will get to go to Burrelpur, right?" She looked at the ladies and asked bravely.

"Yes." Both of them answered simultaneously. "You will go to Burrelpur."

There was a faint smile, this time of satisfaction, on Shailender's face. And not surprisingly, even on the face of her school head.

"Okay, you can go now. But don't go back wandering on the meadows now, go to your old class room. I'll send a chit with the peon and the teacher will allow you in the class." The school head gestured her to leave.

Shailender picked up the mat, put it neatly in the corner and left the office room with a big smile on her face, darting straight to her old class room. She joined the project and worked diligently for the whole year, finishing her Middle school successfully in just one year.

Usha *didi* had grown to be fond of this young girl over the year. She had even started addressing her by her family pet name, Shailu. During that year, Shailu would come to her house every single day after school for studying. Once in a while, during the year, Shailender would pick up some of the magazines that were regularly delivered to Usha didi's place, and look very intently at the advertisement inside, especially if they were done by young beautiful women's pictures, women with shiny long hair and straight white teeth.

"Are these women real" She would ask Usha didi sometimes.

"Yes, I guess so. Why?" Usha didi would ask her.

"They look so beautiful, with perfect bodies and all that. And their hair and teeth, they are so beautiful; they seem out of this world. Is that possible?" She would ask her Usha didi innocently.

"Yes. These women are called models." Usha didi would answer.

"What?"

"Models. I am sure these young women take extra care of their bodies and their hair and teeth too. As I understand, they eat very little and exercise a lot, to maintain their beautiful, shapely bodies." Usha didi would explain to her, amused a little with Shailender's innocence.

'I wish I could be a model,' Shailender was fascinated by these models.

"Usha didi, now that the project in our village is completed, where will you go?" Shailender asked her.

"Back to my place of permanent residence, of course!"

"Where is that?"

"Mumbai. But, why do you ask?"

"Usha didi, I don't want to go to Burrelpur." Shailender said in a low, sad voice.

"What?" Shailender gave Usha didi a mild shock.

"I said, I don't want to go to Burrelpur."

"I heard that. Why not? I thought you always wanted to get away from here. Besides, you did very well in the middle school, so finishing high school education will be very good for you. I shall recommend appointing you as a school teacher when you come back here."

"I don't want to go to Burrelpur and I don't want to come back here after I finish high school."

"Then what do you want to do?"

"I want to come with you to Mumbai."

"What?" Shailender gave Usha didi another mild shock.

"That's silly, and you know that. What will you do there? And what about High school?" Usha didi tried to collect from the shock.

"I can do my High school studies in Mumbai too. Could I stay with you? I promise that I will study very hard there."

"I'm not sure what you have in mind. I don't even know what you are talking about right now? Taking you with me to Mumbai will be very difficult for me."

"Oh please, please take me with you. Please allow me to stay with you, and in return, I'll do all your household chores. I'll be like your maid, a live-in-maid. And just like the models in those magazines, I will eat very little, so you need not worry about my food either…"

"Shailu, Shailender, what are you saying? Do you think my difficulty is because I can't give you food?"

"Usha didi, in this last year, I hardly stayed at home. After school hours, I was in your house most of the evenings, going home just to sleep at night, sometimes not even that. You made arrangements for me for many nights to sleep in your home, remember? The warmth I had in your home and the genuine affection and love I received from you, I have never ever experienced that in my entire life. I have absolutely no attachment to my home, or to that man who is my father, only biologically at that."

Usha didi was listening to her and looking at her with a big surprise spread on her face. She was clearly taken aback by what Shailender said. She also noticed that Shailender's mannerism and bearing had improved by manifold in this one year, not to mention her language and thought process. The girl had picked up many cultured habits from Usha didi, no doubt.

When Shailender saw that Usha didi did not respond at all to what she just said, say anything, she took that as her indifference and felt dejected. With a sad voice, she said, "I have no one in this world, but who cares? I know if I stay here any longer, I am also going to die …" and started gathering her stuff from Usha didi's house, trying to control her crying.

"Hey, Shailu…" Suddenly being aware of what Shailu just said, Usha didi called out but Shailender continued picking up her stuff one after another without saying a word.

"Stop that and listen to me now. Shailu, I said stop doing that and listen to me, will you?" Shailender momentarily looked at her.

"Listen, I don't have any one in this world either, you know that. You also know that I live alone in Mumbai."

"Then why can't I be your 'someone'?" Shailender interrupted Usha didi. "And if I can be your 'someone', then why can't I live with you there? You always told me you care for me, not a day passed in this year when I felt that you were like a God sent messenger to me, then why are you abandoning me now?"

Usha didi was still feeling a little surprised at the conviction of this young girl of a small village. She laughed mildly at her warped logic and said, "For me, my work is my life."

"But then, I will never interfere with your work Usha didi, I promise." Shailender was determined.

"Well, let me think about all this. This would be a major decision for you, leaving your home and coming with me to a far place like Mumbai; and it is a major decision for me too, believe me." Usha didi said.

Climb to Victory Over Breast Cancer

"Does that mean, it's a 'no'?" Shailender asked her directly.

"No, it means 'I need to think about it'." Usha didi said. Shailender looked completely dejected and on the verge of crying..

"Listen, let me talk to your school head. She is familiar with your village customs and your family situation too. She may talk to your father, and then he may grant you permission to come with me, okay?" Usha didi could not see Shailender's sad face.

"Please do it soon. I can't wait to pack up and leave with you." Shailender said.

"Is that how strongly you feel about leaving this place, and coming with me to Mumbai?" Usha didi asked her with a little surprise in her tone.

Shailender gave her a vigorous nod. Her face seemed like it was brightening up already.

"Okay, if that's the case, then let's decide on that. It's settled. You will come with me and live with me in Mumbai. I'll still talk to your school head though, to get an official permission from your father, okay?" Usha didi said.

The moment Shailender heard that, she dropped everything and ran towards Usha didi, practically fell on her feet and started shedding tears, tears of excessive joy, of course!

Getting an official permission from her father was not too difficult for Usha didi, especially with the help of the school headmistress. Shailender was on her way to Mumbai, just as she had so intensely desired, to be with Usha didi. As an ordinary country girl from a very small village in North India, her life started totally on a new foot with this move, and she settled herself in this huge urban place.

It was almost five years by now that Shailender was living with Usha didi in her Mumbai apartment. She finished her High school education and a two year diploma in teaching kindergarten.

During this time, she did not visit her village even once, nor did she inquire about anyone from there, including her own father. It was like she cut off her roots with that place altogether. To her, Usha didi was her family, her parent, her mentor, her confidante and her Guru, and she had proved herself to be worthy of all that care and affection her Guru showered on her. There never was any regret, in either of their minds, about Shailender leaving her own village and coming to Mumbai with Usha didi.

**

'yeh duniyaa kitani sundar hai....la...la...la...'

Shailender was humming her favorite song from an old Bollywood movie while preparing dinner. Usha didi had been away for a week for attending a conference that was held in another city and was about to return home soon. Shailender was sure that she would be tired from the journey, and so she wanted to serve hot food as soon as Usha didi arrives.

Shailender set up the table for two and was eagerly waiting for Usha didi to come home from the conference, when she saw her walking home with another person, a very smart looking woman in her early thirties or so. They both were talking and laughing, they seemed like they knew each other quite well.

"Shailu, meet my past student and now, a very dear friend, Dr. Sudha."

"*Namaste*" Shailender greeted her and then turned towards Usha didi and said, "Usha didi, the table is already set for you, and I'll place another one for your guest here. Would you both like to have your meals now?"

"That would be wonderful." Usha didi said and then turning towards Dr. Sudha, said, "Get a quick wash and join me for dinner."

After a quick wash, both ladies took their seats at the table and started eating.

"This is really good..." Dr. Sudha said.

"Shailu is a very good cook. She is very bright too." Usha didi said.

"Where did you find her?"

"I had been to a remote village in North India on one of my projects..."

"Your wonderful project of starting schools for the local villagers, right?" Dr. Sudha said.

"That's right. I started a middle school there, that's where I met Shailu. After the middle school years, she just wouldn't stay there with her family, so I brought her here."

"That's wonderful. Shailu, I would say you are one lucky person to live with Usha didi here. She is my mentor, my Guru ....."

"Okay, enough already. Let us eat now." Usha didi interrupted Dr. Sudha. "Why don't you join us too, Shailu?"

"I'll eat a bit later." Shailender said and went inside to get some more food for them. They looked like they were really enjoying it.

"It's really something; we both had our conferences arranged in the same city at the same time, and our living arrangements made in the same hotel, isn't it?" Dr. Sudha said.

"That's because we were meant to meet each other, after so many years. How long has it been Sudha?" Usha didi asked.

"Oh I would say, at least fifteen years, Usha didi. I was barely out of high school at the time."

Dr. Sudha calling her Usha didi caught Shailender's ear. 'Is she also someone like me?' a doubt crossed her mind in that split second. 'May be, may be not' she ignored it.

"Shailu, Sudha was one of my brightest students when I was a school head in one of Mumbai's high schools. She is a doctor now, and a breast cancer specialist, right?" Dr. Sudha just nodded.

"And Shailu must be bright too. Just taste the food she has made…" Dr. Sudha said, while munching on the food.

"But tell me something Sudha; were you not studying the science of genetics a while ago? I remember reading about you getting the top national scholarship in that field."

"You are absolutely right. It's much later that I specialized in the field of Oncology."

"What's that?" Usha didi asked.

"That is science of cancer. I am trying to combine these two areas of bioscience and find a common thread in them."

"How do you mean?"

"It is postulated that there is a 'genetic factor' for breast cancer."

"What's a genetic factor?" Shailu unexpectedly showed interest in their conversation.

"Oh, that deals with the hereditary characters of a human being. To explain in very, very simple terms, the science of genetics says that, since every human being is a product of a man and a woman, the genes of both parents are passed on to the offspring. This is a very simple definition. In one of the papers that I presented, I had quoted one renowned scientist stating that some women had developed breast cancer primarily due to their genetic lineage."

"What does that mean?" Shailender asked.

"That means, those women got this disease because their mothers had some kind of either ovarian cancer or breast cancer. Sometimes, it was their grandmothers or aunts or someone very close in their family, where the genes could be passed on to them, who had cancer. Luckily, the hereditary risk in the general female population is only about seven percent and the percentage of such occurrences is very low, but it still is existent unfortunately."

"Oh, my God!" Usha didi and Shailender both exclaimed at this information.

"You will be surprised to hear but I have read in a few international journals that many cancer centers are opting for 'preventative mastectomy' for a few breast cancer patients now-a-days."

"What does that mean?" Shailender asked again.

"You know what Mastectomy means, right?" Dr. Sudha asked her.

But Shailender shook her head.

"It means removal of one or both breasts by surgery. Preventative mastectomy[5] means removal of one or both breasts without the presence of cancer. This surgery is sometimes chosen as a preventative measure by women who have a strong history of familial breast cancer."

"And how do such women know that they may have breast cancer in future?" Shailender was getting curious about this conversation and that made Usha didi happy but a little curious too.

"They don't know that. Nobody knows what the future holds, right? But, if there is a strong familial background, as I explained before, and especially if there are deaths of women in the families due to such cause, then such women opt for 'preventative mastectomy'. They don't want to take any chances."

---

[5] Details given at the end of the book.

"And what if there are sudden, unexpected deaths of women in the family, actually more than one woman's death in the same family, but nobody knows why these deaths happened, then what should the remaining women of the same family do?" Shailender sounded quite wired up when she asked this question. And her question almost alerted Usha didi.

"Then the remaining women of such family should get themselves checked thoroughly for cancer of female organs, especially breast cancer. And if possible, get the surgery done for 'preventative mastectomy' well ahead of time. It's not wise to take a risk and wait until the onset of the disease, is it?"

"Oh my God, Oh my good God..." Shailender shivered.

Dr. Sudha thought that Shailender was moved by her narration, so she continued.

"One of my colleagues, a surgeon, recently had a case where the patient came to him shortly after her mother died of ovarian cancer. After doing the family research the patient had discovered that her numerous female relatives had died from breast or ovarian cancer. My surgeon friend suggested that this patient also consider getting the genetic testing, to study her risk of breast cancer and also the risk of ovarian cancer. When she was tested, it was learned that in fact she did have a risk of developing breast cancer. She herself was shocked to learn that result."

"And then?"

"The surgeon told her that with screening tests, mammograms, when done regularly, they could find cancers at an early stage and lower the risk of the patients dying from breast cancer. He also told her that with Breast MRIs, which are shown to be better at detecting early-stage cancer in high-risk women, he could detect it much too early. However, detection of a cancer is not the same as prevention of a cancer, even if it is early enough, isn't it?"

"I guess not. So, what did that patient do finally?" Usha didi asked.

"Well, she opted for preventative mastectomy. You see, even if the detection methods have come a long way, preventive surgery is the only way to dramatically reduce the risk of developing breast cancer. Studies have shown that the procedure cuts the risk by nearly 95%. That's very encouraging."

"Did the surgeon cut both her breasts?" Shailender asked.

"Yes, both of them. That's called bilateral mastectomy."

"And how old was this patient, Sudha didi?" Shailender seemed to get emotionally involved in the story. Unknowingly, she had both her hands over her breasts.

"I think she was in her late twenties or so. I am not sure of her age." Dr. Sudha said.

Shailender had become practically mute after hearing all that explanation, but Usha didi and Dr. Sudha did not notice it. They had moved away from this topic to some other one.

"The dinner was simply fabulous Usha didi. It certainly was a treat." Dr. Sudha complimented Shailender too for cooking such good food.

"And you, Sudha," Usha didi started speaking, "the way you narrate your work and describe everything, one would feel as if you are telling a very interesting mystery story or something," She was full of admiration for Dr. Sudha.

"Usha didi, this science is really like one big mystery of life. The more you unravel, the deeper it gets and more complex it seems to become; and the more you search for the treasure, the farther it moves. It seems almost impossible at times to explore and study. Oh, I really get lost in it, as if I am holding a big mystery novel in my hand."

"For you, there is really no difference between the two, isn't it?" Usha didi said with genuine admiration for Dr. Sudha.

"Well, there is, actually. The difference between the two is, there is an end to a mystery novel and invariably, the mystery gets solved; as against that, unfortunately, the end in *this* mystery book remains ever-growing and there is no end to the hunt, if you will, and all this struggle!" Dr. Sudha said and they both laughed heartily.

"It was a lovely evening, indeed." Dr. Sudha got up from the chair and started getting ready to leave. "I think I should leave now."

"We should meet more often than this, don't you think?" Usha didi said.

Dr. Sudha concurred with her and after thanking both the ladies, she left.

Usha didi looked quite tired so she retired to her bedroom. Shailender was still very quiet. Without uttering a single word, she started clearing the table and collecting the dirty dishes and putting them in the sink for washing. While doing that work, she was continuously thinking. Her mouth was shut but her thoughts were racing at a phenomenal speed in her mind.

'Could that be my case too? *Ma* died so suddenly when I was barely three years old. Nobody knew exactly what happened to her and why she died. Could that be some kind of cancer? Baljeet and Daljeet also died so unexpectedly when they were in their twenties. Was that due to some female cancer too? I am approaching my twentieth birthday soon. Would mine be the next turn to die like them?' Shailender shivered vigorously at this thought. She unknowingly increased the speed of her work in the kitchen. After cleaning up everything, she went to her room and lay down on her mattress. She tried to sleep but these thoughts wouldn't stop poking her brains. They had already set in with deep roots by now in her mind.

'What if I have that heredity? Would I get breast cancer? Does that mean I should also cut off my breasts like that patient Dr. Sudha was talking about, to avoid the disease?' She automatically put her hands over her breasts and started stroking them gently. With every stroke, her thoughts became more and more intense and fearful. She tried hard to flick away those thoughts but they kept recurring, over and over again. She took her hands off her chest and put them in a *Namaste* pose, as if praying God above.

She lay awake the whole night in that pose, staring at the ceiling, stiff with fear, while Usha didi was snoring softly in the adjacent room.

Milestones on the Climb...

Anila, Tanuja, Malti and Kiran, each one being a breast cancer survivor with a strong positive attitude, and Sheila, a victim of preventative double mastectomy at a tender age of twenty years, were sitting on the patio of Malti's house. As a 'Core' group for supporting breast cancer patients, they were having their weekly meeting with Dr. Sudha.

"The sessions on basic biology are proving to be very interesting ones. I myself am enjoying teaching them. Let us have them once every two weeks, instead of once a month, Anila." Dr. Sudha suggested and that was noted down by Anila.

"Quite honestly doctor, the information my daughters and their friends are getting from these sessions, Ajoy and I would love to join it too." Tanuja said.

"How do you know what is discussed in those sessions?" Dr. Sudha was surprised to hear Tanuja.

"We make it a point to stand just outside the room and listen to every word you say in that class." Tanuja said and looked at Malti with a meaningful smile.

"You too, Malti?"

"Yes, doctor, me too. I thoroughly enjoy your lecture. It is actually basic biological science about human body that we all should know." Malti said.

"I think it's very valuable information." Tanuja said.

"Well, if you women find it so interesting and informative, then we'll hold such sessions even for the adults. How's that?" Dr. Sudha said.

Every one nodded.

Anila included that point on her agenda sheet. It was to be finalized that there would be a session on basic biology such as the ones they were having for the teenagers, every two weeks, one for the teenagers and one for the adults. Perhaps they would have them conducted regularly in their Support group project in future.

"Ladies, this is the pamphlet I have designed for our workshops." Anila started talking. She was chairing the meeting.

"It covers four major areas."

Then she laid a large piece of paper on the table and everyone started looking at it carefully. The title 'you are invited' was written in a sort of calligraphy.

It was followed by a statement, saying that they were starting a 'Peer Support Group for Cancer Patients and Survivors'.

"I like the title page." Tanuja said.

"What are the four areas, Anila?" Dr. Sudha asked.

"Well, each area is covered by asking a question or two." Anila started explaining.

"The first area starts with two questions.

Question one is, 'are you a cancer survivor?' and the second question is, 'are you presently having cancer treatment?'"

"Isn't this too direct?" Malti asked everybody.

"I think so." Tanuja said.

"Then what shall we say, ladies?" Anila asked them.

"How about, 'do you know someone who has cancer?' This way, cancer patients are invited without asking them a direct question; and if someone knows of a cancer patient, they can also attend our group." Malti suggested.

Everyone agreed. Anila made the necessary changes in her sheet of paper.

"The second area, covered again with a question, is, 'would you like to talk to someone with similar experience?'..." Anila looked at everyone.

"I like this question. It covers the purpose of our support group." Malti said.

"I like it too. It encourages women to share their experiences, if they want to, that is." Tanuja said.

"Yes. That's the real problem we face, isn't it?" Dr. Sudha said. She knew it too well how secretive many women were about their breast cancer because of many different reasons, including a social stigma.

"The third area deals primarily with *'Personal Counseling'*.

Breast cancer patients have unique supportive needs. They need information about their disease as well as the treatment. There are too many misconceptions about various therapies and methodologies that are used in the treatment."

"Excellent, Anila. I like this part very much. Getting *accurate scientific information* about the illness and learning about the benefits and side-effects of the treatment are very important." Dr. Sudha was happy. She knew that with accurate scientific knowledge, awareness about cancer and its treatment would also reach many more people through these sessions.

"Counseling will be given in psychological and social areas as well." Anila continued.

"Dealing with fear, depression or stress is very important, that would give the patients some moral boost with psychological counselling." Malti said.

"And what about social counseling, what's that counseling for?" Tanuja asked Anila.

"Social counseling can help deal with some of the difficult issues, such as talking with family members, children, friends, changes in personal relationships, especially with the husbands or male partners." Anila look ?d at Dr. Sudha and they both knew exactly what she meant.

"Excellent again, Anila." Dr. Sudha exclaimed.

She had seen too many family relationships destroyed because of women in those families developing breast cancer.

"The fourth area is a sad one; it's in the palliative care area…" Anila said and looked around. All the women were quiet.

"This is also a very important area we need to cover." Dr. Sudha started talking when she saw everyone becoming abruptly very quiet.

"Many people begin to grieve at the end of their illness. They develop a sense of mourning for their own death; they become very depressed and sad. At such times, we can provide them with some spiritual guidance and counseling. I'll talk to Shantabai if she can guide us in this respect."

"Oh I believe in spiritual guidance completely. I think some spiritual guidance and counseling is necessary even for those recovering from their illness. It would give them hope in their mental turmoil; and provide some meaning to their life…" Malti said.

This time it was Malti's turn to look at Dr. Sudha and exchange a meaningful look with her.

"Yes, I agree totally. Let us talk to Shantabai for these sessions as well." Dr. Sudha said.

"Excellent work, Anila." Tanuja said and everyone in the meeting agreed

The meeting came to an end. Major decisions were taken and finalized about various sessions to be conducted for the Cancer Support Group. The climb to recovery of breast cancer was gaining strength at every step of the way up; however, the summit was yet quite far!

□

When *Kumbhakarna*[6] wakes up...

"Dr. Sudha, what is cancer?"

A session, conducted specially for teenaged girls, was going on in the living room of Malti's house.

Malti had taken special efforts to make all the necessary arrangement in her house and then had offered her house as a starting place for conducting all the sessions for the support group. Three huge rooms of her house were assigned for these activities. She had rented a dozen chairs and four tables for each room, and had her servants arrange them neatly. Manubhai's old office room and all the bedrooms, except hers, were kept locked. People, especially Malti's coworkers, had full freedom to use the kitchen and dining room. The beautiful patio overlooking the backyard had become their favorite place for conducting weekly meetings with Dr. Sudha. They were all impressed and extremely pleased with Malti's beautiful house and her generosity, not to mention her efficiency in making all these arrangements in the house in such a short time.

Dr. Sudha herself was conducting this session. She had observed in her practice that often mothers found it difficult to talk to their children, especially young girls, about their breast cancer. Torn between their instinct to protect them from fear and the desire to be honest, most mothers avoided the subject

---

[6] This mythological story is given at the end of the book.

Climb to Victory Over Breast Cancer

altogether. A few, who had every desire to reveal their infliction by the disease to their children, were often confused as to how much information should be given to them, so that they would come to terms with their fear and emotions.

Before starting this session, Dr. Sudha hung two huge charts, both of human female bodies, each one on either side of the wall. The middle portion of the same white wall was used as a screen for the slide projector that was kept on a stool a few feet away from it. There were ten girls attending this session. They were sitting on chairs facing the charts and the screen on the wall.

Tanuja's daughters, Sangeeta and Shruti, were among the attendees, and they were instrumental in getting the word around among their friends to attend this session.

"Dr. Sudha, what is cancer?" One girl asked. She had her notebook open and a pen in her hand. So did most of the girls.

"Hum...what is cancer? Let me start with a simple explanation. In a normal process, cells in the body divide or reproduce, as the scientists say, only when new cells are needed. But sometimes some cells continue to divide for no reason and create a mass of tissue. Can anyone guess what this mass of cells is called?" Dr. Sudha asked around.

"A tumor, perhaps?" Someone answered.

"That's good. This mass of cells is called a tumor. These tumors can be benign, meaning non-cancerous, or they can be malignant, meaning cancerous. In breast cancer, as well as in some other cancers, a cell of the tissue becomes abnormal and reproduces without any control or order, forming a malignant tumor." The girls were writing Dr. Sudha's explanation in their notebooks.

"What happens when a tumor starts growing?" Someone asked.

"You know that all cells need food and nourishment to grow and divide, right? But when a few of the cells start growing and dividing without control, as though they are in an 'ON' position all the time, they also start consuming all the available food and nourishment leaving nothing for other normal cells. *These are the cancer cells.* That affects the immune system, as well as the energy levels, thus making the body weak to fight the disease."

"But why do cancer cells grow without any control or order?" A girl, barely in her teens but with a serious face, asked.

"There is no easy answer why cancer cells grow without control. Cancer cells ignore signals that should cause them to stop dividing. Most of the normal and healthy cells have the capacity to reproduce, meaning, a mother cell divides into two daughter cells, the daughter cell in turn divides into two more daughter cells, and this process continues. This is also termed as cell growth."

Dr. Sudha walked to the projector and showed the girls a couple of slides depicting cell growth and division. Then she displayed one more slide where two cells were touching each other. Pointing at this figure, she said,

"Cell growth stops completely when two or more cells come into contact with each other, just like you see here. This is a natural process of *arresting* cell growth. Scientists have termed this entire process, *'Contact Inhibition'.*"

"Contact Inhibition! Oh, does that mean, 'stop, when in contact with the other'?" One girl asked.

Dr. Sudha nodded.

"That's really neat..." some girls remarked and started singing a line from a famous song,[7] making the convenient change to the original song – 'Stop, in the name of touch'!

---

[7] *"Stop! In the Name of Love"* is a famous song recorded by the Supremes in 1965 in the USA.

Dr. Sudha found it amusing to see some girls getting entertained with this hard-core science.

"Unfortunately, cancer cells lose this property and therefore, they grow in such an uncontrolled manner that even when in contact with the neighboring cells, they cannot stop growth. Scientists and cancer specialists use this characteristic property of cells to distinguish between normal cells and cancerous cells. And naturally, cancerous cells are the ones that create tumors." Dr. Sudha explained.

"But Dr. Sudha, you didn't tell us why some cells lose this property and continue to grow without any control or order?" The same girl asked again.

"Yah, obviously some cells don't obey the nature's law, why so?" This girl was sitting next to the previous girl. They both looked serious and also very much interested in Dr. Sudha's explanation.

"This is a good question. 'Why don't some cells obey nature's law?' Do you all know what genetic science is?" Dr. Sudha looked around and saw a few girls nodding and a few shaking their heads.

"Okay, in that case, let me explain in brief. Genetic science, as the name suggests, is the science of genes, it is the study of how living things receive common traits from previous generations through heredity. A gene is a hereditary unit that carries these traits. You all have heard the word DNA, right?" Most of the girls nodded.

"Well, a gene consists of DNA. I'm sure you have learnt in your biology course that it's the DNA that determines the characteristic of a person, right?" Dr. Sudha looked around and saw most of the girls nod again.

"Now, these genes are also the ones that control how the cell functions, such as telling it when to divide and grow, and when to stop growing. All genes work like a clock work in healthy and normal humans. However, when some alteration or change takes place in some of these genes, that's what we call *a mutation;* then the entire natural process can get affected. Most cancer cells are a result of mutated genes. And girls, even these mutated genes can be passed on by heredity from mother or father to the child."

Dr. Sudha looked around. There was a pin-drop silence in the room. All the girls were writing her explanation down very promptly in their notebooks.

Dr. Sudha displayed a new set of slides for the girls and continued, "Cancer is now clearly understood to be a *disease of abnormal gene function.* We now understand that genes serve two major roles in cancer; some cause development of cancer and others stop cancer from developing or growing. Genes that cause cancer are called *Onco*genes. Genes that stop or suppress cancer growth are called *Tumor suppressor* genes. Girls, do you know that we all have Oncogenes in our bodies?"

"What?" The moment girls heard Dr. Sudha say this, they all looked shocked. Some of them dropped their pens in that shock.

"Yes, we all have Oncogenes in our bodies. However, fortunately they are like Kumbhakarna, always in deep sleep."

"Kumbhakarna?" The girls looked amused for, they knew the story of this demon from Ramayana.

"Hum...hum. They are like Kumbhakarna because they are all fast asleep! In a deep, deep sleep! Their demonic action starts only and only if they wake up, and only then they become dangerous. Their 'deep sleep' state is called the 'dormant' state and their wake-up state is called the 'activated' state."

The girls felt amused by Dr. Sudha's analogy of Oncogenes to Kumbhakarna, and her explanation in an entertaining way.

The session was going on for more than an hour, but there was no sign of anyone getting up or leaving. Anila walked in the room to remind Dr. Sudha about their meeting later on. That's when everybody, including Dr. Sudha, realized that the 'class' was over.

"Well, we'll talk about Kumbhakarna in more detail next time…"

Dr. Sudha turned off the slide projector. All the girls gathered around her.

"Kumbhakarna? What were you teaching these girls, Dr. Sudha?" Anila was totally confused with a mythological figure's name in a session that was supposed to be science based.

"See girls, even Anila, who herself is a breast cancer patient, doesn't know what *our* Kumbhakarna is…" Dr. Sudha teased Anila. A few of the girls giggled. Some girls inadvertently looked at Anila's chest, which did not escape Dr. Sudha's quick glance.

'This one part of a female body has gained the maximum importance of being a 'symbol' of femininity everywhere; in literature, arts, lyrics, and even the commercials…' She thought to herself in that fleeting moment and felt a little displeased with it.

"Well, aren't you going to tell me about *your* Kumbhakarna?" Anila said with a questioning face.

"I will, I'll tell you everything, one of these days for sure, how's that?" Dr. Sudha told Anila.

"When would the next session be, Dr. Sudha?" Sangeeta was asking her on behalf of all the girls.

"You could inquire about that to Anila here. They are organizing all these sessions."

Dr. Sudha said and started walking out the door. The girls were dispersed shortly.

◻

Then Rama[8] takes an aim…

"As I said last time, we all have Oncogenes in our bodies, but fortunately for us, they are in a dormant state, sleeping, just like…"

"Kumbhakarna…" some girls sitting in the front row said it immediately.

"That's right, just like Kumbhakarna, they are sleeping. Now we need to know why Oncogenes 'wake up'. Why do they get transformed from their dormant state to the activated state, what is the reason?"

Dr. Sudha looked around the room. It was packed to capacity with people from all ages, men, women and teenagers.

All the chairs from Malti's house were brought in the room and still some people were standing. Anila, Tanuja and Malti were sitting in the front row.

"Detection of Oncogenes has been one of the most important finds for the scientists. Just as finding of DNA and its helical structure turned into a magic wand for the scientists, so did the detection of these cancer causing genes. What makes the Oncogenes get into their activated state is the question. The reasons given are manifold actually. Heredity plays a big role here. Gene function is disturbed with mutation and mutated genes can be passed on from parent to the child."

---

[8] This mythological story is given at the end of the book.

"But why does a gene undergo mutation, doctor?" somebody from the audience asked.

"Honestly speaking, we don't know the exact reason. Some doctors believe that the culprit could be pollution with its chemical carcinogens in the air that we breathe, some believe it's exposure to excessive sunlight which has high doses of UV rays, some say it's smoking, some say it's bad diet habits, all these are considered to be carcinogenic, that is cancer causing. Some even assign it to virus."

"Virus?" People were surprised to hear virus being the plausible cause for gene mutation or Oncogene activation.

"Yes, virus. Virus can cause simple cold and fever, and it can cause cancer too in human bodies." Dr. Sudha saw people had become suddenly very quiet and attentive.

"Virus may not be directly responsible, mind you, but with all the carcinogens I just quoted, they cumulatively affect the general health of the body, which in turn, reduces its resistance. At such times, if the body comes in contact with some virus, its immune system cannot resist the attack, and that can prove to be the reason for the genes to mutate or the Oncogenes to get activated." Dr. Sudha looked at the audience; they were all listening intently to every word she was saying.

"It has been well established for some time now, that cancer, in essence, is a disease of the genes. It could be a multi-genic disease where more than one gene could become dysfunctional and cause cancer in the human body. Any one or more than one of the gene functions, such as gene function of cell growth, gene function of regulation and gene function of maintenance is disturbed or lost due to mutation. Scientists have termed this as a 'multiple hit theory' of cancer!"

Dr. Sudha looked around. There was a complete silence in the room.

She continued,

"There are many types of cancer, at least a hundred of them that have been diagnosed today, but you cannot pin point any one specific reason for any one type of cancer as the sole cause. Breast cancer is one among such cancers, where no single factor can be accounted for the disease. I wish it were so, for, then I could have advised to all my fellow women what to do or what not to do, to avoid breast cancer. But unfortunately my dear people, it is not so!"

"Why only fellow women, Dr. Sudha, we men have breasts too." One among the very few men, who were attending the session, asked. Dr. Sudha smiled at him.

"You are right actually. Men have breasts too, but almost ninety eight percent of breast cancer patients are women. Seldom do you see a man being affected by breast cancer."

"Why so?"

"That is because breast cancer usually develops in the glandular tissue of the breast, specifically in the milk ducts and the milk lobules. These ducts and lobules are located in all parts of the breast tissue, including tissue just under the skin. As this part is rarely present in a man's body, so is the incidence rare for a man getting breast cancer." People, especially men, looked satisfied and almost relieved with Dr. Sudha's explanation.

"Dr. Sudha if the breasts of a woman are removed altogether, the woman should be free of breast cancer permanently, isn't it?" Someone asked.

"Well, yes, but that is an ideal situation. You see, the breast tissue extends from the collarbone to the lower rib margin, and from the middle of the chest, around the side and under the arm. In the breast removal surgery, which is called mastectomy, it is necessary to remove tissue from just beneath the skin down to the chest wall and around the borders of the chest. However, even with very thorough and delicate surgical techniques, it is

Climb to Victory Over Breast Cancer

impossible to remove every milk duct and lobule, given the extent of the breast tissue and the location of these glands just beneath the skin." Dr. Sudha said.

She paced around for a few moments in total silence, letting people absorb the information she had given in her explanation, and then continued further.

"Among many other risks that we talked about earlier, there is an additional risk for women in getting breast cancer. And that is having dysfunction or malfunctioning in their hormone regulation."

Then Dr. Sudha walked to the projector and started showing a few slides with explanation to all the people.

"Here are the pictures of a female body from age ten years to fifty years. Just look at these pictures carefully. You see on the chart - as a female is growing in age, her body is undergoing tremendous hormonal changes. There is some hormonal change in her pre-teen or early teenage, which triggers her menstrual cycle, that means the monthly periods; then when she gets pregnant, her body starts synthesizing another set of hormones, which supports her pregnancy; then when the baby is delivered, she nurses the baby with her milk, which is also a result of some new set of hormones; then when she enters her fourth or fifth decade of life, she undergoes even more hormonal changes during her menopause time and her body ends her menstrual cycle and she stops getting monthly periods, thereby also her ability to reproduce. All this is going on in less than forty years in the female body, with so many hormones playing their specific roles at specific times in her life, for specific reasons."

Dr. Sudha took a brief pause and glanced over the audience. She noticed that practically everyone in the audience, even the men, was listening to her explanation intently. She felt satisfied.

She continued, "Now, just imagine, any one of these hormones that I just mentioned, not functioning at all or over-functioning or functioning at a wrong time, what would happen? Just think."

There was a silence again. One could hear only some faint sound of paper and pen because a few of them were taking down notes from her lecture.

"Dr. Sudha..." One woman from the audience broke the silence, as she was still holding a pen in her hand, As you explained, breast cancer can be a result of many things, such as genetic make-up, faulty hormones or hormonal function, and other exterior risk factors, right?"

Dr. Sudha nodded.

"And when all these factors come together, then the person, I mean the woman, may develop breast cancer, right?"

Dr. Sudha nodded again.

"You also stated that when a woman starts her periods at the right age, that is pre-teen or early teenage, then gets pregnant in relatively younger age, as in before or around thirty years of age, nurses her baby, all this means that her hormones are functioning well so far in her life, right?" Dr. Sudha just nodded.

The woman continued, "That means, so far the possibility of mutation in her cellular function is known not to exist or to stop, right?"

"Um...Hum... go on..." Dr. Sudha said.

"Then, let us say that this woman also stays away from all the external risk factors, such as pollution, excessive sunshine, smoking, bad diet habits and all that; then tell me doctor, can a woman in such situation avoid breast cancer altogether?"

Dr. Sudha was impressed to see that this woman had listened to every word she had explained in the session. She was equally impressed with her question too.

She smiled at her and said,

"Well, yes and no! It is good to follow all these things to keep fit and healthy. I would also say that this is a recommended way to avoid the possibility of getting this disease. Usually most of the women do follow this route, so I would say 'yes'. But…"

"Oh no, the 'big butt'…" Some woman from the audience unknowingly exclaimed softly, but a few people around her heard her and chuckled.

"Yes, the 'big butt' indeed!" Dr. Sudha also heard her and chuckled a bit. Then she said,

"Anyways, as I was saying, the genetic make-up of a person cannot be changed drastically to reduce or rid away the risk of developing cancer. It is very difficult for a doctor to just assess a woman's lifestyle and her situation, and then *predict9* if or when she may develop this disease, although tremendous research is focused on this very issue."

There was a mixture of agreements and disagreements among the listeners. The questioner herself didn't look very satisfied with Dr. Sudha's answer.

"So, there is no specific rule as to when and in what situation a woman may develop this disease then, right?" Some other woman from the audience asked.

Dr. Sudha looked at her and noticed that she was sitting next to Kiran.

"That's right. There isn't any rule or any specific situation assigned as such, for developing this disease." Dr. Sudha looked at Kiran while answering the question.

"Is there any specific age in which a woman may develop this disease, doctor?" The same woman asked again.

---

[9] Breast Cancer can be *predicted* ahead of its diagnosis; read the detail at the end of the book.

"Cancer is believed to be a disease commonly occurring among the older adults now. Accordingly, the highest probability of a woman developing breast cancer is usually around or after menopause, that's around their fifty years of age or after..." Dr. Sudha was explaining, when she heard a loud voice shouting,

"That's a lie, a big fat lie...a total lie..."

Everybody, including Dr. Sudha, was stunned to hear such a loud shout in the middle of a quiet and serious session.

Dr. Sudha looked in the direction of the loud shout. It was none other than Kiran. She was looking at the doctor and retorting at the top of her lungs. Dr. Sudha was shocked, as she never expected such an outburst from Kiran; especially when she herself was a group member, participating in the process of starting a Cancer Support group.

"I am not old, I'm young ..." Kiran turned her face away from Dr. Sudha towards the audience, and as though addressing the people gathered there, she continued in a loud voice.

"I started my period at age twelve years, I had my baby at age twenty six years, I nursed my son for six months; and you see this man..."

Kiran pointed to Raj who was sitting next to her.

"This man is my husband. I was a virgin until I married him. Just ask him, was I or wasn't I a virgin, Raj, until our wedding night?"

Raj felt a little embarrassed. He lowered his head down and wanted Kiran to shut up and sit down, but instead, she raised her voice even higher and as if attacking Dr. Sudha, shouted,

"You doctors say that normally older women tend to get this disease. Doctor, I am less than thirty years old. Then tell me, why did *I* get this disease..., hum..., tell me why did a *much younger woman like me* get breast cancer?"

Her face had turned red with anger, and as though it was the doctor's fault that she got cancer. Kiran was yelling at Dr. Sudha angrily,

"I don't smoke, I don't drink, I don't sunbathe, nothing like that. And still I got this disease, what do you say to that doctor? What can you do about it doctor, hum… and what can I do about it?" Her whole body was trembling.

"Rani…quiet…Rani…please…" Raj was totally embarrassed to see his wife get up and yell hysterically like that at Dr. Sudha, but Kiran seemed to be totally out of control.

Kiran ignored Raj completely. She turned her attention to the people and continued her bellowing.

"And people, you know what? My cancer is at an advanced stage. It's *terminal*. Yes, it is t…e…r…m…i…n…a…l! Do you know what it means? Do you?"

And in a shrilly, almost hysterical sounding voice, she yelled,

"That means it's going to kill me soon. Yes, kill me. I'm never going to see my son go to school, not even to KG…" She stood with her hands raised over her head and started crying profusely. Raj held her hands tightly and started pulling her to take her out of the room.

'Rani… stop it, dear…please…stop it…' As he was desperately trying to calm her down, she was crying even more, like a child, with loud voice, and continuously saying, "Please God…don't take me away so soon…please…let me at least see my son go to the school… just once…God please…"

Everybody in the room was frozen stiff to see this drama. Even Dr. Sudha was confused to see Kiran, a soft spoken young woman like her, in this act. It was most unexpected.

The whole scene was very, very sad and heart wrenching.

Raj was trying to pull Kiran out of the room, but it was as if she had gained the strength of a charging bull. Anila and Malti quickly came forward to help Raj. The three of them finally managed to take Kiran out of the room. There were more than a hundred people in the room, but the silence was almost deafening.

"Is it true, doctor, what that lady just said?" Somebody broke the silence.

"Yes, unfortunately that's true. Kiran is a young woman with a toddler son, and her breast cancer has been diagnosed at an advanced stage. Unlucky for her that it's a rare kind of cancer. I feel very sorry that I cannot do anything for her..." Dr. Sudha sounded like she was getting a lump in her throat. She tried to control it and after clearing her throat, she continued,

"Unfortunately, we doctors cannot predict when a woman will develop cancer in her breast. It is only *after* she develops it that we can diagnose it. We strongly recommend all kinds of methods for early detection because that could give a chance for control. However, cancer can only be *detected* and *not predicted definitively, as yet!*"

Dr. Sudha took a few long breaths and continued.

"In a few cases, even after early detection, the disease progresses fast. In such cases, the most modern and advanced medical treatments also seem to fail. What can we doctors do? Absolutely nothing." From her voice, Dr. Sudha was sounding quite low in her spirits by now.

"But then, doctor, all those reasons you just stated..."

"Yes, and all those risk factor you discussed earlier..." a couple of women, almost simultaneously, asked Dr. Sudha.

"Those are after all, statistical data and measurements." Dr. Sudha tried to explain.

Climb to Victory Over Breast Cancer

"Data is collected only after the fact, it is analyzed only after the fact, inferences are drawn only after the fact, and medical treatments are given based solely on the values obtained only after the fact. *Only after the fact!* That seems to be the big obstacle here, but what can we do? Right now, nothing much..."

"But doctor, each person is different, isn't it?" Someone asked.

"Yes, that's true. We doctors realize that each cancer patient is unique, in the sense, different from the rest, with a different body chemistry, different mental framework, different genetic-make-up, different temperament, different situation, practically everything different, but the medical treatment that we give to all cancer patients, although somewhat customized pertaining to individual case, remains not terribly different from each other."

As Dr. Sudha went on explaining more and more, her voice started going down further and further, to a point of sounding almost apologetic. Yet, she continued,

"We really haven't fully understood what cancer is, except that it is a disease of abnormal gene function. But then, we also postulate that most of the cancers are not inherited but arise from gene mutations that a person acquires during his or her life. Scientists and medical researchers are working day and night to comprehend this disease, but so far with not much success. We cannot give any guarantees to any of our patients."

It was most unusual for Dr. Sudha, known to be a vibrant woman with a zest for life, and who would always encourage her patients for a positive attitude, to talk to people in such a depressing tone.

Even more unusual was for her to walk to her chair quietly and sit down in the middle of her session that she so loved to conduct. It was as if she herself was helpless. She was looking quite frustrated and sad.

People were looking at each other wondering if she was going to continue, or if the session was over for the day.

"Does this mean we should stop all our efforts in medical research, doctor?" One young and bright looking woman was heard asking Dr. Sudha. There was a tone of slight anger in her voice. Dr. Sudha just looked in her direction with a mild surprise, but didn't say anything.

The bright looking young woman stood up and as if addressing the entire crowd, said,

"We humans worked hard and put an end to many diseases such as diphtheria, cholera, tetanus, small pox, chicken pox, measles, by finding their vaccines. You know that all these diseases were killing thousands of people in the earlier times. But today, they are controlled through the vaccines. If some of you remember, not too long, children used to get vaccine for small pox as a part of their routine childhood immunization. My mother and father got them during their childhood. But, that is not true anymore as this disease is almost eradicated from the face of the earth today. And the credit goes to the hard work of dedicated scientists and researchers. Infections used to kill hundreds of people earlier, but today? Today when we get any infection, we right away take antibiotics to control it. Rarely you hear or see someone dying of infection today. And the credit goes to the hard work of dedicated scientists and researchers. They have continuously strived hard in the pursuit of scientific knowledge to understand the 'whys and why-not's' of diseases and have come up with a solution for the benefit of health and wellness of humans and other living beings as well."

Then this bright looking young woman walked slowly towards where Dr. Sudha was sitting. Looking at the crowd in the front, she said, "Look at the life expectancy today, people. Scientific discoveries have significantly increased the life expectancy of humans. Not too long ago, very few people survived the age of fifty years, but today? Today, people live for over seventy-five years of age. If someone dies at age fifty, we think that that's too young to die, right?" She received a few nods from the audience.

She continued,

"My friends, as recent as just in the last couple of years, when we had this horrible COVID19 virus erupted, threatening crores of people across the whole world, creating a global pandemic and taking the whole humanity for a hostage for more than two years, we did not lose hope. Scientists in many countries, researched tirelessly day and night to develop vaccines and treatments for this virus, right?"

All the people gathered there nodded in unison.

Just then, Malti and Anila entered the hall after taking care of Kiran and returned to their seats. The bright looking young woman smiled at them and walking closer to where they were sitting, continued,

"We know of diabetes, hypertension, and many such chronic diseases and their reasons for developing. We have this knowledge only because of the hard work of dedicated scientists and medical researchers. They came up with medical treatments to keep all these diseases completely under control. Thanks to them, people lead a normal and healthy life even when they have diabetes or hypertension or any such chronic disease today. Credit for all the wonderful medicines for chronic diseases goes to the hard work of dedicated scientists and medical researchers. Why can't we think along the same lines for cancer as well?"

"You are right dear, we should..." Anila said softly with a smile on her face. She was sitting very close to the speaker. All the people in the room almost clapped for this bright looking young woman for her timely 'pep' talk.

All the while that the bright looking young woman was speaking to the audience, Dr. Sudha was intently listening to her with a smile on her face. She looked as though she had taken a deep breath of fresh air and regained her energy. She stood up from her chair and walked towards that young woman.

"You know, I was hoping one of you would come up with some optimistic answers. Sometimes, I seem to get tired of carrying the torch of optimism all the time. Do you work in medical research?" She asked the young woman.

"Yes doctor. As a matter of fact, I'm a medical researcher in Oncology; I just returned after a research fellowship in one of the prominent cancer centers of Canada." The young woman answered.

"Then why don't you give some pointers about your field to our people today? You are an excellent speaker and hold a very positive outlook towards everything." Dr. Sudha was impressed with her earlier speech.

The bright, young woman readily agreed, and turning towards the people, she said,

"Dr. Sudha has just requested me to continue my talking to you all. It's my pleasure actually…" She smiled at the people and started talking,

"Cancer research is going on in every corner of the world today. Scientists are working day and night to overcome this disease. Not just overcome but to *predict* ahead of time by doing a blood test, if a woman could get breast cancer. You learnt from Dr. Sudha earlier that there are Oncogenes present in all of us. These genes can cause cancer if activated. But ladies and gentlemen, I am very happy to tell you that scientists have also found genes that stop or suppress cancer growth. These are called tumor suppressor genes."

"I call them 'Rama genes'." Dr. Sudha interjected with a smile.

"Yes, exactly, Dr. Sudha. That's a new thing…"

"And I call Oncogenes, the 'Kumbhakarna genes'…" Dr. Sudha said with a smile.

"Oh that's a very apt description, Dr. Sudha." The bright, young woman looked genuinely impressed with these befitting names from Hindu mythology to medical terms.

She continued,

"Many among us know the story of Ramayana. When the demon Kumbhakarna wakes up, that is, when the Oncogenes are activated, then our body sets out its Rama genes, that is, its tumor suppressor genes to take an aim at the Oncogenes. Many scientists are working hard to develop technology based on these 'Rama genes' of human body. A good many cancer research laboratories are focusing their attention on gene therapy as a *cure* for cancer." The moment people heard the word 'cure' for cancer, there was a light applause.

"What's gene therapy?" Someone asked.

"In one simple sentence, I would say, gene therapy is the insertion of functional genes into an individual's cells and tissues to treat a faulty hereditary disease. You all know that we are born with a specific genetic make-up, but thanks to the hard work of scientists; in gene therapy, a defective gene is replaced with a functional one. Although the technology is still in its infancy, it has been used with some success." She was eloquent in explaining gene therapy.

Then she slowly walked towards the center of the room and as though staring at the people, asked,

"Do you know that scientists are also working on finding a *vaccine* for cancer?"

Everybody in the room, including Dr. Sudha, was paying one hundred percent attention to this young woman. She continued.

"Many experts endorse the vaccine as a simple way to prevent deadly cancer. In recent years, interest in cancer vaccines has grown as researchers learn more about how the immune system can fight cancer. If they do find a vaccine for it, it could revolutionize breast cancer prevention and treatment. If vaccine is possible, and I think it will be, sooner than we think, then eradication of cancer could be achieved reasonably easily. Once its vaccine is discovered, it may become a part of the routine childhood immunization. Cancer will then be well under control, just like all those other diseases I mentioned earlier. The picture is very bright, my dear friends, very, very bright."

That young medical researcher then put her one hand on her chest where her heart was, as if to display her total respect, and said,

"Science has played a very important role in the entire history of mankind, and I assure you all, it will continue to do so in the future too..."

Then she slowly turned towards Dr. Sudha and said,

"Dr. Sudha, we now know that cancer is a gene-based disease. The situation is not that dismal or hopeless as you portrayed earlier, doctor. It is just a matter of time when we can control or cure that too. Really, just a matter of time..."

When people heard that, they started applauding this young woman whole heartedly.

"Right on..." A few said.

"That's the way it should be..." Others commented.

"Oh, that's wonderful." A few said.

"Even if it happens in our children's times that would be okay..." there was a brief mutter among a few women.

With humility and a smile on her face, she accepted their admiration and sat down. The atmosphere in the room was filled with optimism and enthusiasm. People were looking at the young woman with genuine admiration and applauding her courage and knowledge.

The happiest person in the room was Dr. Sudha. The session of that day had taken a course exactly how she wanted, in a very optimistic and positive direction.

'*Rama did kill Kumbhakarna*, after all, and not just in the story of Ramayana' she thought to herself and, with a smile that reflected total satisfaction, declared the session being adjourned for the day.

As the uphill battle towards reaching the summit was getting harder and harder, the women were getting stronger and stronger with each successful group session!

Visualization Technique

Malti had organized in her house, a new kind of session for women with breast cancer. All the arrangements were made as per the requirements of Shantabai, her psychotherapist of almost two years now. There were no charts on the walls, no slide projector, no chairs, not even bright light; there was just a thick carpet on the floor for women to sit on and, since all the drapes of the windows were drawn, only a dim light was illuminating the room. In one corner was placed a CD player, and a CD with soothing soft music, coupled with the sounds of waves was being played at a low volume. The music was filling up the room, imparting a serene touch to the atmosphere of the room.

There were ten women, all breast cancer patients, sitting on the carpet in front of Shantabai. She was sitting in her usual lotus position. Her torso was straight and shoulders drawn back but relaxed.

"We have all gathered here today for getting to know a new technique. The scientists have termed this technique '*Visualization Technique.*' It is utilizing the 'holistic approach', employed quite regularly in medical treatments, especially in the cancer treatment." Shantabai started talking to the ladies in her deep, soothing voice.

"My dear ladies, you all have heard many, many times the close relationship between our body, mind and spirit. Ample energy is created out of this relationship and that energy forms the basis of this new technique." Shantabai said.

"This technique may be new, but the concept that it is based upon, is an age-old one. The technique is founded upon the concept of a close relationship between our body, mind and spirit, which in turn, is based upon the principles of Hindu philosophy. This ancient philosophy vehemently states that the thoughts generated by our mind have a direct influence on the body. Over the centuries, Hindu philosophers tried to gain access to their inner wisdom and strength, and learn more about the 'self'! Medical researchers have utilized this intrinsic yearning of mankind to explore the 'self' for developing many techniques that would improve health and treatments for various diseases. One of these techniques that many scientists found very beneficial in medical treatments is Visualization. It is done through *visual imagery,* which means creating visual images. This technique today has an ever-expanding application in science and medicine, especially in cancer treatment."

Shantabai stopped briefly and looked at all the women. There was a total silence and they were listening to her intently.

"I know, you all are breast cancer patients. Some of you are newly diagnosed, some are undergoing treatment and some have survived it for more than a year but afraid of its recurrence. This technique will prove to be extremely beneficial to all of you, I promise you that. As I said earlier, *thoughts create certain kinds of biological effects in our bodies.* It is scientifically established now that negative thoughts create stress and anxiety. Stress and anxiety, in turn, release what the doctors call cortisones. Cortisones are degenerative stress hormones that are destructive to the body causing diseases. As against that, happy and positive thoughts release beneficial hormones such as endorphins and growth hormones, which are regenerative and healing for the body. So, as you can see, this is all in your hands, ladies, in *your own* hands! You can heal yourself by having positive thoughts and creating visual images of what you wish to see in your lives. This technique helps you keep your subconscious mind completely focused on what *you* want, and that is of course, getting well, isn't it?"

Shantabai looked around again and continued, "Human body is the most efficient machinery that Mother Nature created. If we couple our body's efficiency with this technique, utilizing visual imagery of positive things, then combating and defeating cancer is not too difficult. We want to get better and we want to heal ourselves by the power of imagery, right?" Shantabai saw everyone nodding.

"So let us now think of some positive things. Positive things are usually happy things, or such things that we like and make us feel happy. So, ladies, what happy things can we think of? What things do you all like?"

With her question, they all looked at each other for a moment. Then one woman said with a faint smile, "I like to see ocean waves."

That encouraged others.

Another woman replied, "Yes, I like a vast beach of an ocean."

A third woman said, "I like to see tall coconut trees swinging gently with the wind."

Shantabai smiled at the coincidence of all three answers focusing on only one topic, ocean beach with palm trees!

"Could that be the effect of the sound of waves from the CD?" She wondered.

"Okay then, let us start a visual imagery of what you all like. Close your eyes now and repeat after me." With her eyes closed and hands rested on her lap, Shantabai started the mantra of 'Om…' Her deep and somber voice reverberated in the room.

All the women closed their eyes too; many among them tried to sit in the same position as Shantabai, but most of them couldn't.

They all repeated after her, "Om…"

Their voices resounded in the room.

This continued for a few minutes.

As they were all chanting 'Om…' Shantabai started talking in a gentle tone, slowly and softly, one sentence after another with a few seconds gap in them.

"Now imagine, you are standing on the beach in front of
a vast ocean, its vastness extending past the horizon;
the gentle waves are approaching you, touching your
feet and ankles and receding back at precise intervals;
every time the waves recede, the sand underneath your
feet tickles the soles of your feet and makes you chuckle a bit;
the sky above is as blue as the ocean below;
there is a light wind that is gently playing with the
leaves of the palm trees that you see on the beach;
the gentle swing of the leaves is making its
silky sound that is very soothing to you;
just imagine all this, my dear ladies…"

Shantabai opened her eyes and looked at the women. They were all sitting placidly with their eyes shut. All of them were obviously visualizing this beautiful scenery. Shantabai continued, *"Imagine, a wave coming towards you, gently massaging your feet, receding back with some sand underneath your feet, thus tickling your soles and giving you pleasure…"*

She repeated this description over and over again at least twenty times, in a deep, soft voice with her usual soothing style.

The women were lost in their imagery completely by now.

"You are having an immense pleasure with
the ocean's playful waves;
while standing and enjoying this ultimate
delight, you are gazing at the horizon;
soon it turns orange red as the
Sun starts to set slowly;
the entire sky is gradually turning its color
from beautiful blue to orange red;
and so is the ocean;
you are completely immersed in this
heavenly scenery..."

Shantabai looked at all the women again. The expressions
on their faces gave her an assurance that they were imagining a
beautiful scene and soaking in the imagery.

Shantabai continued,

"You are gazing at the horizon, when suddenly
an old, ugly warship props up at the horizon;
you notice its prow and realize that it is
moving towards you and approaching you very fast;
you are confused momentarily;
you can't make up your mind if you
should get out of there or stay put;
as the warship reaches the beach, you notice
hideous looking pirates getting out of the
warship and running towards you;
you see the vicious expressions on their faces
and you want to run, but you can't;
you just cannot run;
you are stuck in the sand;
the same warm sand that was tickling your soles
and giving you pleasure is now holding you tight;
you cannot run and you have no ammunition
to fight with those pirates, you are totally helpless..."

Shantabai looked at the women again. Although their eyes were completely shut, each of them had an expression of being disturbed on their faces.

She noticed some tension as well on many faces.

She continued.

"You are frustrated;
you are scared too;
the hideous pirates are coming close to you
and you are sure they could hurt you;
but you cannot defend yourself;
you just cannot;
nor can you run for your life;
you are getting mentally prepared to surrender
to their vicious actions when suddenly you
see another ship, a clean and beautiful one,
approaching you fast;
as it reaches the beach where you are standing,
kind and gentle looking warriors jump out of
the ship and come closer to you;
you feel confident that they will rescue you and
protect you from the frightful pirates;
the kind warriors start fighting the pirates;
you feel relieved that you have help just in
time of your need;
you start encouraging the warriors and seeing
your hope and encouragement, they get stimulated
even more to give a strong fight to the pirates..."

Shantabai again looked at the women.

Most of them had an expression of release of their tension, some of them actually exhibiting an expression of relief on their faces.

She continued.

"After giving a fierce fight to those kind warriors,
the pirates finally accept a defeat and try to
run away to their warship;
the kind warriors chase the defeated pirates and
destroy their warship;
the pirates are drowned, finished,
dead and gone for good..."

Shantabai could clearly see the women imagining this scene from their facial expressions. She then advised the women to continue closing their eyes and observe carefully the faces of the kind warriors.

"Look at the kind warriors, ladies;
whom do they look like?
do they look like your own self?
do they have your faces?
perhaps they do!
Yes, they definitely do!
they are a part of you, ladies, they are your
own white blood cells, your own body's
defense mechanism!
with your hope and willpower you have
given them strength!
and the drowned pirates, that were about to attack
you, were your cancer cells..."

The moment the women heard the word cancer, they opened their eyes almost as a reflex.

Shantabai smiled at them and said, "Yes, they were your cancer cells, but they are dead and gone now. You supported your immune system with your hope and positive thinking and that provided strength to those kind and gentle but strong warriors of your body to fight and defeat the attackers, which were cancer cells, completely."

She could clearly hear many sighs of relief from the women. Each one of them had an expression, as if filled with redemption, on their faces. They looked totally happy.

Just one session of this technique, technique of Visualization to inculcate positive thinking, but it had done the trick.

She was sure, after a few sessions such as this one, the doctors would certainly find an improvement in their patients' health. This thought made her feel quite happy and satisfied.

"Ladies, now let's conclude this session."

Saying this, Shantabai closed her eyes and sitting in the same lotus position again, started uttering the mantra of 'Om…' in her deep, soothing voice.

All the women followed her, repeating the mantra after her.

Their voices resounded in the room.

Shantabai strongly felt that their voices were sounding a lot chirpier this time!

Cancer – I am its Master!

The room was filled to capacity with people. There wasn't a room even for an ant to crawl inside. Most of the family members, friends and neighbors of all the women, who were regularly partaking in these sessions based on a new concept of Visualization Technique, were present there. So were many others, who came to know about these sessions dealing with this new subject.

Initially started as a novelty and as an experiment, sessions on Visualization Technique were becoming very popular. Conducted initially only for breast cancer patients, they were gathering immense popularity among patients of other diseases and surgery as well. The enrolment was increasing day by day, and inquiries were steadily on the rise. More and more women, and sometimes men too, were expressing their desires to participate in these sessions. The sessions that were offered once every six or eight weeks initially, had their frequency increased to once every week. And yet, each one was full to its capacity every week.

The session, which was about to take place right now, was jointly organized by Anila and Malti, and jointly conducted by Dr. Sudha and Shantabai. Everyone in the room, except the participants, was curious about this new technique.

"Ladies and gentlemen," Shantabai started talking to the gathered crowd, in her usual deep, soothing voice, and everyone became attentive.

"When a patient sees the cancer cells being completely destroyed by her own immune system, she comes out of her imagery with her heart full of hope. She starts looking ahead for a brighter future. Her whole outlook to life becomes positive and that positive thought does the magic."

"But what does positive thinking have to do with cancer?" Someone from the crowd asked.

"What does it have, you ask? Almost everything." Shantabai said.

"Our immune system, let us call it the defense department of our body, gets a tremendous boost and a direct help from our positive thinking."

"Any scientific support for this thought or it's just a...?" a skeptic in the audience asked.

"Yes, there is enough medical support for this thought. A renowned cancer specialist, our own Dr. Sudha, will explain it in a scientific way." Shantabai then looked at Dr. Sudha and said,

"Dr. Sudha, perhaps your explanation may convince our audience here better." Shantabai requested Dr. Sudha with a smile.

Dr. Sudha agreed and started talking to the audience.

"When I give treatment for cancer with radiation and chemotherapy after the surgery to my patients, I insist that they all take some treatment also for their minds during and after their medical treatments. I recommend them to go see Shantabai, a psychotherapist, for such treatment."

People knew that Dr. Sudha was a bright doctor and a renowned cancer specialist. They started listening to her attentively.

"I presume that you are all familiar with the mind-body connection. I am a doctor of the *body*, I give treatment for the *body* of a patient. In my judgment, Shantabai is the doctor of the *mind*. I firmly believe that the Visualization Technique is a *technique* that is based on this beautiful mind-body connection." People were listening to Dr. Sudha with full attention.

"Someone among you asked earlier if there is any scientific support for this type of technique. The answer to that is a definite *yes*! Shantabai explained to us earlier that when the patient comes out of her imagery, she is filled with hope. Her entire thought process takes a positive direction. The medical fact is that this positive thought that arises in her mind helps her immune system tremendously. You know that our immune system is a complex network of specialized cells and organs that has evolved to defend the body against attacks by "foreign" invaders. When the system is functioning properly, it fights off the infection that is brought on the body by agents such as bacteria, viruses, fungi, and parasites. However, when our immune system does not function properly, it can unleash a torrent of diseases. These diseases could include from simple allergy or cold to cancer and other more complicated diseases."

Dr. Sudha looked around. Not a single person in that room was moving even slightly, they looked practically being still.

She continued.

"We know that biological links between the immune system and the central nervous system exist at several levels. A new field of research, known as *psycho-neuro-immunology*[10], is evolving in the recent years."

---

[10] Details given at the end of the book.

"What's that?" A few people unknowingly uttered this question.

"'Psycho-neuro-immunology' seems like a long, complicated word, but look at it this way… " Dr. Sudha realized that this is a complex word, so she tried to explain it in much simpler terms.

"In simple terms, psycho-neuro-immunology is the study of the effect of the mind on health and resistance to disease. It explores how our immune system and our brain interact with each other to influence our health. You can imagine that emotions play an important role in modulating our bodily systems, right?"

She saw a few heads nodding.

"That in turn influences our health. For example, we have heard it too many times that stress is suspected to increase our susceptibility to various infectious diseases and even cancer. Now, evidence is mounting that *the immune system and the nervous system may be intricately interconnected.*"

Dr. Sudha was expert in explaining effortlessly such a difficult topic in a relatively easy manner.

She looked at the people again, and when she noticed that they did not look confused or anything, she continued,

"My dear people, the mind-body connection is real! New medical research shows that a healthy, active brain boosts your immune system function and keeping a *positive attitude* helps keep you healthy. This is a medical fact, not fiction!"

Dr. Sudha then looked at Shantabai and said with a smile,

"And as you can see, Shantabai's sessions of Visualization Technique, a technique that generates *positive thoughts* among cancer patients, do have enough scientific support."

Dr. Sudha finished her talk and sat down.

The listeners were so thrilled to hear Dr. Sudha's beautiful and articulate explanation about the current scientific research that a few among them tried to give her an applause, but she held it back by gesturing them not to clap, for, it was more like a tutorial session than a public speech.

"You just heard Dr. Sudha explain the mind-body connection in scientific terms. You also heard from her that keeping a positive attitude does help your immune system to fight infections and even a deadly disease like cancer."

Shantabai started talking to the people.

"Now, my friends, we are going to present something totally different here. It may seem purely of entertainment to you, but it is as educational as Dr. Sudha's explanation about the medical science was. It may provoke your thoughts;, it may make you think hard; you be the judge of it."

Shantabai looked for Malti in the audience and called her to the front of the audience. She requested Malti to say a few words before they started this 'entertainment' session.

"Friends, I have been taking Shantabai's psychotherapy treatments for the last couple of years." Malti said.

Wrapped up in a beautiful, blue silk sari and wearing a light make-up and a select few ornaments, Malti looked very pleasant and dignified.

With total confidence, she started talking to the people.

"When my daughter took me to Shantabai for the first time, I gave my daughter a lot of resistance; but once I started meeting Shantabai regularly, it was almost addictive, I would say. Now, you must be wondering why I went to her for any treatment at all, in the first place. Well, my friends, I am a breast cancer survivor."

Climb to Victory Over Breast Cancer

The moment Malti said the last sentence everyone looked a little surprised, for, Malti looked too gorgeous to have survived any disease, especially a deadly disease as breast cancer.

"Before, during and even after my cancer treatment, I needed Shantabai's visits. Before, because it was Shantabai who inspired me and talked me into taking an action against the disease by starting its treatment; so I did. During the treatment, I needed her to help me give a fight to the disease *mentally*, so I did. And afterwards, which is now, I shall never let that vicious disease recur in my life." Malti looked at everyone and then asked,

"Friends, do you know how I will keep cancer out of my life forever?"

"How…" A few people said with utmost curiosity.

"I will never allow cancer to recur in my life because I *am its Master…*" Malti said emphatically and looked around.

She noticed the crowd getting a little confused with her statement. Some laughed, taking it as a joke; others looked doubtful about Malti's sanity, whispering among themselves, 'is she crazy or what ?'; a couple of them started getting ready to leave as they didn't want to waste their time in Malti's antics.

"Please come here Shantabai, and tell these people what I am saying is the truth."

Noticing such minor ripples of disagreement in the audience, Malti called Shantabai to support what she told the people.

"What Malti is saying is one hundred percent true, ladies and gentlemen, I can vouch for it." Shantabai said while trying to grab everyone's attention.

"When she first came to me with her daughter, she seemed quite skeptical. She was not even sure if she should meet me again after that first meeting. Fortunately in that first meeting

I found out that Malti had a cancerous lump in her breast, but she was reluctant to do anything about it. She wanted to die. She wanted to end her life since her life had no meaning, in her judgment. As you can imagine, I was surprised to hear that at first, but slowly and steadily, she started realizing her folly and her mistaken judgment. That's how it all started."

"This lady, who looks so good and well-collected, wanted to die?" A couple of women sitting in the front row asked with surprise.

"Yes. She wanted to die. She wanted to end her life. But look at her mental disposition now; it is totally transformed into the opposite direction. This is something you all must hear. Malti and I have prepared a brief skit, and through this skit, we can demonstrate what we meant. Would you like to watch our skit?" Shantabai asked.

The audience looked interested, including those, who were getting ready to leave. They sat down to watch the skit.

"This is Malti, she is talking on her own behalf..." Shantabai told Malti to stand on the right side, facing the audience.

"And I am Malti's cancer talking..." Shantabai herself stood on the left side, facing the audience.

The moment she said 'I'm Malti's cancer talking...' people got curious about the whole skit.

Cancer: *Do you realize I am your friend?*

Malti: *Friend? How so?*

Cancer: *Do you remember, after your husband died unexpectedly, you wanted to die too. You wanted to commit suicide but didn't have enough guts to do that, remember?*

Malti: *Yes, yes, I remember, so?*

Cancer: *So, I thought, since you want to die but you can't because you are timid to kill yourself, let me visit you. Let me, your cancer, kill you and save your trouble of committing suicide.*

Malti: *Oh I see. Hum, how thoughtful of you…*

Cancer: *Yes, very thoughtful. You felt that no one needed you any more, you thought that your life was totally empty, you felt exceptionally lonely, so I thought let me be your friend, let me be your close companion, so I developed in you…*

Malti: *But I have my three lovely children…*

Cancer: *But they were busy in their own lives. They didn't need you, that's what you used to tell yourself all the time, remember? You convinced yourself that when your husband died, everything else in your life died too, remember? You used to just sit in one room day after day, night after night, without talking to anyone, even to your children, without doing anything. You really looked like a zombie, so I thought I must help you and end this miserable life of yours. But alas! You intervened in my plan altogether.*

Malti: *Your plan, plan of what?*

Cancer: *My plan of ending your life, of course.*

Malti: *And how did I intervene in that?*

Cancer: *By going to that, that cunning, double-crossing woman…*

Malti: *Cunning woman, you mean that psychotherapist? What did she do to you?*

Cancer: *You went to that woman and she convinced you that your life is not empty at all. She convinced you that your children, all three of them, needed you, the society needed you as well, since you have so much to offer. When you were convinced of all that, the first thing you did was get rid of my roots. Ouch, how it hurt me then, you have no idea…*

Malti: *You are sick, a bloody sick devil…*

Cancer: *Oh how I loved it when you were in total despair, how you saw nothing but darkness everywhere. I was beautifully rooting in you. I loved it when you were completely distressed, full of sorrow. That made my roots stronger. You, sitting alone in the corner, feeling hopeless, provided me with ample of food for my growth. That was my nourishment.*

Malti: *You are despicable, don't talk to me.*

Cancer: *But, with that woman's psychotherapeutic treatment, you started taking interest in life, you became hopeful for life. How terrible!*

Malti: *My God, you are a monster.*

Cancer: *You call me a monster, but I played a very important role when that woman was teaching you all those things, do you realize that? I am the one who takes a lion's share in your learning the lesson of leading a good life.*

Malti: *You? You taught me a lesson? How so?*

Cancer: *Yes I did, my dear lady, believe it or not, I did. That woman taught you that if you remain hopeful, happy and if you always think positive…ouch, even saying these words gives me an ache in my groin; anyways, she said that that will make you healthier and help you fight me better. The role I played in this valuable lesson was that, it was me who demonstrated to you clearly that by you remaining positive all the time and never ever entertaining any pessimistic thought, you can develop a very strong immunity that can destroy me. It was me, the Cancer, the disease people are so scared of, who taught you this! Now you see my role? A lion's share? I ran away to make you feel as a conqueror.*

Malti: *My, my! Aren't you egotistical?*

Cancer: *You may call me egotistical, or you may call me conceited; but the truth of the matter is that, my dear lady, when someone defeats **me**, the Cancer, in the war, that someone is known to be a survivor, isn't it?"*

Malti: *Oh, my, my!*

Cancer: *I am not finished yet, my lady.*

Have you anytime heard anyone being called a 'typhoid-survivor'? Or a 'malaria-survivor'? Hum, have you? It is always a cancer-survivor!

Malti: *Yes, I do admit it, albeit grudgingly, that what you are saying is true. I am called a 'survivor' by all because of defeating you, the cancer. Hey, but you were not that easy to defeat, okay?*

Cancer: *I know that. And I must admit I had a lot of fun in giving you a fight.*

Malti: *Fun, did you say fun? How so?*

Cancer: *It was something like a gorilla-warfare between us, don't you think? There were a few times when you used to feel really depressed. Those times gave me enough nourishment to grow. I was almost sure at times that you were going to wave a white flag in our war! But then...*

Malti: *Sorry to interrupt you, Mr. Cancer, but, let me tell you something you may not know. Thinking positively all the time is very difficult, you know. It is hard to remain optimistic all the time, especially when one is going through the tough ordeal of cancer treatment.*

Cancer: *Oh I can imagine that. It must be putting a big responsibility on the patient, I mean the fighter, right?*

Malti: *Right. You got it.*

Cancer: *But then, as I was saying, in your case, that woman with her 'psycho-tools' would come on the scene and inculcate* *some 'positive poison' in you. And then, there you were, full of ammunition to give me a fierce fight. Oh how I hated those tools and that poison of positive thinking! I couldn't take it anymore. Finally, I had to accept my defeat and run away.*

Malti: *Ah ha! See...*

Cancer: *But hey, you know what? Even during my fleeing, I felt very proud of myself.*

Malti: *You felt proud? About what?*

Cancer: *That I was so successful in teaching you such a valuable lesson of life. A lesson you could learn only because of my presence in you for a short time. Something you would have never learnt otherwise. It was only with me on your mind that you made such a concerted effort the whole time to develop a positive attitude and try to remain happy, isn't it? Tell me honestly now, don't I deserve a little credit in your learning?*

Malti: *Well, yes, I suppose. You do get some credit. Ever since I have had a fight with you, Mr. Cancer, I don't take anything for granted any more. I have developed such a tremendous fighting spirit now that I can face any situation without fear. The most valuable lesson I have learnt from this war with you is about the direct correlation between beautiful, positive thoughts and physical health. Now you can never root yourself in me, and even if you do, you can never defeat me! Mr. Cancer, you may be scary as hell, but you still are in my control, because I am your Master!*

People were stunned to watch this skit and see the importance of positive thinking so beautifully demonstrated. Many got goose pimples on their bodies while watching it. It was very emotional too. A few women in the audience had tears running down their cheeks.

Shantabai, with her deep and cultured voice, was superb in acting. For Malti, it wasn't acting at all. It was her own, real-life experience, and therefore, she had poured all her emotions in the demonstration.

Anila and Dr. Sudha got up from their chairs and started applauding for Malti and Shantabai; they just couldn't control their own enthusiasm. The whole audience joined them spontaneously in their applause.

The session for that day was declared adjourned by the organizers. There was a long line up of people for registering in the forthcoming sessions on Visualization Technique.

The uphill climb was slowly, but surely, getting to be manageable with the strength of positive thoughts and a whole lot of optimism!

❐

Getting Stronger on the Climb...

"How was your breast cancer diagnosed?" One woman was asking another. They both looked like they were in their sixties.

"It was diagnosed with a mammogram." She answered.

"What's that?" The first woman asked.

"It's a kind of an X-ray photograph they take of your breasts..." The second woman tried to answer.

"But isn't X-ray used only for bones and skeletons?" The first woman asked again.

"I honestly don't know how it works." The second woman was not all that knowledgeable about mammograms, either.

"I can tell you briefly about it, if you wish..." A younger woman overheard their conversation and volunteered to join in the conversation. "A mammogram is an X-ray test of the breasts, as you said. It is used to screen for breast problems, such as a lump, and to see whether a lump is fluid-filled or a solid mass."

"What does it do exactly?" The two older women asked the younger one.

"You see, many small tumors can be seen on a mammogram before they can be felt by hand. So, a mammogram is always preferred to screen for breast cancer in women without symptoms. Early detection is always better, isn't it?" The younger woman answered.

"Is there any risk in getting a mammogram?" The first older woman asked again.

"That I really don't know." The younger woman answered.

"Oh, I know that." A fourth woman joined the group. "Mammography technique uses some kind of mild radiation. So, there is always a slight risk of damage to the breast cells or breast tissue due to low levels of radiation used for this test, isn't it? But, the risk of damage from the X-ray is very low compared to the potential benefits of the test."

"Yes, yes, that's for sure." Rest of the women agreed.

This conversation was taking place in a session that Anila, Malti, Tanuja and Sheila together had organized in the usual place, in Malti's house. They wanted to test how a forum for only women with breast cancer without any formal structure or agenda, would work?

This session for women was meant only for sharing their experiences with each other, and if possible, iron out their doubts and queries about the disease. As decided, there was no definite structure to it; the women were requested to just mingle among themselves and converse with each other.

The room was packed with women of all ages. Not all were breast cancer patients or survivors. There were a few women who themselves did not have breast cancer, but knew of someone who did, in their family and friend circles. A few women wearing black scarves on their heads were obviously undergoing chemotherapy and covering the absence of hair on their heads.

"Malti, you are so lucky," someone said when she saw Malti approaching the group.

"Lucky? How so?" Malti was unaware what was being talked about in the group.

"We were talking about the mammogram…" One woman from the group informed her.

"And, we were thinking about you, you are so lucky, you didn't have to lose your entire breast..." Another woman said to Malti.

"Oh that? Yes, that's for sure. It's my daughter who takes the credit for it. She insisted I see Dr. Sudha and that's when I had it done. The mammogram detected a tiny lump in my breast. When tested it was found to be malignant. Fortunately it was at a very early stage, so I got away with just lumpectomy." Malti said.

There was another group of women siting in a different location within the room and chatting among themselves.

"Were you there when this psychotherapist, what's her name..." One woman said to another.

"Her name is Shantabai." Another woman answered.

Both these women were very well dressed and looked like they were over sixty years of age.

"Yes, Shantabai. When she conducted a special session on a new technique called Visualization Technique, were you there?"

"Yes, I was. And it was simply fantastic. I am going to register for her sessions. I think that'll help me. Perhaps you should join it too. You know, sometimes I feel that it's *me* who invited my breast cancer."

"Why do you say that?"

"Ever since I was a little girl, I had this habit of trying to do *everything perfectly*, no short cuts. Everyone called me a 'little Miss Perfectionist.' As I grew up, that habit grew too, and before I knew it, I became an obsessive, compulsive worker."

"Yes, I believe that. I have seen your house, it's spotless, your children were always very well dressed up, and you took them to a million places to learn different things. And the meals? You always took extra efforts to prepare full, well balanced meals. Never any shortcuts, like we do. And you worked outside home on a regular job too. I often used to wonder, 'where does this woman get this much time and energy'?"

"Well, all that hit me finally. I got totally exhausted. Completely burnt out, may be. With not enough sleep and rest, my immunity started dwindling down. Dr. Sudha said that exhaustion didn't cause the cancer, but coupled with my stress, it didn't help me either. Now she has given me strict orders to take a minimum of seven hours of sleep at nights and a few minutes rest during the daytime, as a part of the medication."

"So, do you?"

"Yes, since this devil of a disease entered me..."

"That's good."

"You know, before Shantabai starts her session, she always asks women what makes them happy?"

"Really?"

"I think I am going to say, 'a comfortable bed and a soft pillow...'"

Both the women laughed at this, and then decided to register themselves for the sessions on Visualization Technique conducted by Shantabai.

"This mastectomy is so very inconvenient to me, you have no idea..."

"What do you mean, inconvenient?" A few women had formed a small group and were chatting in yet another location in the room. Most of the women in this group looked quite athletic and seemed like they were barely over forty years of age.

"You know I played badminton every evening for at least two hours before I got breast cancer, right? But since this breast surgery, I can barely play two games."

"How come?"

"I'm right handed, and guess what? I lost my breast precisely on the right side. My hand hurts like crazy when I play longer…"

"The same with me too. It's such an obstruction for me too." Another woman joined the group.

"What do you play?"

"I am an instructor for javelin throwing."

"Oh, really? That's wonderful. Were you the champion in college days?"

"Yes."

"I think I have heard about you. Oh, you were good…"

"Thank you, but not anymore. With my right breast gone to cancer, it has imposed a limit on my right hand activity. Honestly, I am not sure if I can continue my instruction in javelin throwing, anymore."

"At least, you all have vigorous games that you worry about. In my case, I am a calligraphy artist, and still I can't pursue it anymore…" Yet another woman started talking with this group.

"Your right breast too?" They asked her.

"No, it's my left one." She answered.

"Then?"

"But I'm left handed." She said.

"Oh, no…" All of them said together and laughed mildly.

"Are you women doing your arm exercises regularly?" Anila overheard their conversation and walked towards the group, asking everyone who complained about their left and right hands hurting.

"What's that?" The whole group turned to Anila.

"Soon after the mastectomy, Dr. Sudha advises all her patients to do a special exercise that she calls 'wall climbing'.

It helps muscles around the breast area to strengthen. This is how it's done."

Then Anila walked to the nearest wall and standing with her face towards the wall and feet about six inches away from the wall, she said,

"To begin this exercise, stand like this, facing the wall. Then place your hands on the wall, shoulder width apart and on the same level with each other. Slowly 'walk or crawl' your hands up the wall until you feel slight tension. Stop and hold this position for about thirty seconds." A couple of women from the group joined her and started copying her.

"Remember to breathe, ladies. Now, slowly push your hands up the wall a little bit further."

"That's good." Anila said.

Slowly, all the women in that group joined them in the exercise.

"If you can go high enough, put one hand over the other and hold. Slowly release the stretch and walk the hands down to the original position. Repeat with the other hand on the top."

"How many times do we do this exercise?" Someone asked her.

"Oh, I would say at least fifteen to twenty repeats every time and preferably two or three times per day. I did it, I still do it and that seems to help me a lot."

"Which side did you lose your breast, madam?"

"Left side." Anila answered and smiled at the group. Just then she spotted Tanuja talking to another group of women. She walked towards them and joined them in their conversation.

"Why me? I kept asking this question."

Tanuja was talking to a group of women who were around the same age as hers.

"I was angry when I was diagnosed with my breast cancer. I was on the top of my career in music and I have two young daughters; they both have aspirations of becoming musicians too. I kept wondering, 'do I have enough time to teach them music with this condition?' And this thought made me angry as hell." Tanuja said in a sad tone.

"Yes, you are right. I had exactly the same feelings. Why me? What did I do to get this horrible disease of breast cancer? And that too, so early in life? I have three young children you know. Do I have enough time to raise them now?"

The woman became a little emotional.

"Yah, same here. I have two boys, both under ten years of age. And here I am, diagnosed with this horrible disease…"

This woman also became a little emotional.

"You know, I never thought I would get cancer. I knew my next door neighbor got breast cancer. Shortly after that, I came to know that one of my cousins got it too. But I never imagined that *I could be the next victim…*" Another woman said with tears in her eyes.

There was a brief silence in the group.

"How do you handle this feeling, Anila?" Tanuja asked her as she saw her approaching the group.

Anila was known by all to be a very compassionate social worker, and considered to be the wise one by many.

"I overheard your conversation. What you ladies are discussing is one hundred percent right, actually. The first thought that comes to our mind is *'why me?'* right?" Anila asked the women in the group.

"Yes. I felt that 'someone up there' was punishing me." One woman said with a tone of distress, while looking above.

"I always questioned, 'what did I do to deserve this calamity in life'?" Another woman said, sounding a bit angry.

"Oh, I know the feeling. You are all absolutely right in feeling this way. You feel angry and you feel sad and helpless, all of that at the same time." Anila started talking.

"Believe me, I felt exactly the same way when mine was diagnosed. But then I realized, *cancer does not have its favorites. It picks up any one, unfortunately even the innocent bystanders,* if you will! There is no one invincible. When it develops in you, you have no choice but to accept it."

"Hum..." A couple of women let out an exclamation with a disconsolate tone.

"Well, you just accept it, I suppose." Tanuja said.

"Grudgingly, of course!" One woman said.

"Well, ladies, to tell you all honestly, I have adopted a bit of a philosophical attitude for that. You see, cancer creates fear among us, and that fear is fear of death; more like, fear of an early or untimely death, right? You try to learn to cope with that fear." Anila said.

"That's hard." Someone said.

"Yes, no doubt about that." Anila continued,

"But try to employ your own way for coping with it. Each person's way of coping with fear could be different. For example, Tanuja, you could start the music training for your daughters immediately, without wasting any time. That will keep you fully occupied mentally. As the goal of training them comes closer and closer, the degree of fear will automatically become lesser and lesser. The biggest advantage in all such activities would be that you will not have time to dwell on cancer or its fear. Do you agree, dear?" Tanuja nodded with her eyes full of tears and hugged Anila.

Anila continued,

"The very same thing applies to you two young mothers as well. I would say, start getting involved with your children as much as possible, in their school projects, in games they play, in everything. Read them different books. Children have an excellent memory, you know. They don't forget what they learn during their childhood. Try not to leave any 'could have's or 'should have's while raising your children, especially after diagnosis of cancer. Children are your legacy, and they will remember you all their lives if you get involved with them."

The two women were quietly listening to Anila's wisdom.

Anila felt good that her advice was proving to be quite useful to these women. She continued.

"And do get some spiritual help for yourself too. Personally for me, I believe in the concept of the Supreme Being, or God, as some call it. That faith alone can overpower the fear of death."

All the women in that group felt that they received some solace from Anila.

"And during all this time, do not forget to get proper treatment for your disease, okay?" She smiled at all of them and walked towards another group of women.

There were only three women in this group and they were all standing quietly, not talking to any one or with each other, just watching everybody in other groups.

"How is it going, ladies?" Anila inquired in an effort to get them involved in talking with each other. But instead of saying anything to her, they just shrugged their shoulders and kept quiet.

"Madam, could I ask you a personal question?" One of the three women finally opened her mouth.

"Oh, sure." Anila said.

"When your cancer was detected and you had surgery of removing your breast, did your husband move out of your bedroom, permanently?" Anila noticed that the woman who asked this question had her eyes full of tears. She could see a lot of pain in that woman. And perhaps the other two women were in great pain too; that was why they were so quiet, and not talking to anyone about anything.

What was Anila to answer to the question? Should she have told her how Manav was behaving, or how he had changed completely from his original self or that they had not had any intimate relationship, since her surgery? But she said nothing of the sort.

She just couldn't. Instead, she just smiled at them and as if she never heard the question, moved on to another group of women, who were discussing the breast removal surgery and its pro-s and con-s!

She joined the group with a question,

"Do most of you have had a surgery...?"

Most of the women nodded to her question.

"With one breast removed, does that make any of you feel a little lop-sided, with one breast gone, that is?" One woman asked the group.

"Yes, I do." Someone from the group said.

"I do too, but only after I take off my bra." Another woman said.

"What do you mean?" The first woman asked her.

"I wear a special bra. It has one cup fully padded. That way, it looks normal, and more importantly, that helps me feel good."

"You know, I am seriously thinking of reconstructive plastic surgery now. My husband keeps saying, 'it doesn't make any difference to me, one breast, two breasts', but..." some other woman started talking.

"Hey, if your husband doesn't mind it, then why are you doing it?" Someone interrupted her.

"For my sake. I can't look at myself in the mirror like this. Even during bath, I still get an eerie feeling putting soap on the empty side." That woman said and then shuddered.

"I know exactly what you mean. It's an awful feeling. All these years, you have two breasts, a nice pair, and now suddenly, there is only one..." This woman also shuddered.

"The only one seems like a lonely one..." Some other woman tried to joke.

"Plastic surgery is improved so much, there's so much advancement happening in it, I say, why not?"

"Yah, why not?" Many women agreed to the idea of having reconstructive plastic surgery for them.

"I think I'll have to have this surgery, really." One woman sounded quite serious when she talked. "My husband doesn't understand my feelings. It makes me feel incomplete, a less of a woman, when he comes to me at nighttime, if you know what I mean..."

Many among them agreed with her.

All this while, Anila was quietly listening to them, trying to grasp their feelings and emotions and assessing their marital situations and love relations; at the same time, comparing them with her own relationship with Manav. She had seen pain in the eyes of a woman earlier, who she felt definitely belonged to her own category. She was sure there were many more like her in today's forum.

'*A session for men, especially for the husbands of breast cancer victims, is an absolute must,*' she thought to herself and decided to organize one with the help from others. She continued listening to the women's talk in the same group.

The women were still busy talking about the plastic surgery.

"Hey, do you know that lady over there. She somehow looks familiar…" someone pointed to Sheila, who was helping Malti and Anila that day.

"Yes, I know her. Of course, I don't mean personally. She is one of the top models of our country, do you know that? She is pretty much in every magazine and on TV for some advertisement or another… " One woman answered.

"What is she doing here, with a perfect figure like that?"

"Well, someone told me that her breasts are not real…" One woman said while lowering her voice, as if she was sharing a big secret.

"What?"

"Um, Hum…"

"You mean she is also a breast cancer survivor?"

"Yes, she is, indirectly …" Anila informed them.

All the women, who had seen and admired Sheila in her various commercials, were stunned to get this new and unexpected piece of information about her.

"Why don't I call her here and request her to talk to you all. Would you like that?"

"Yes."

"Yah."

"Oh sure, if it's possible…"

"Would love it, really…"

The response from the women was overwhelming.

Anila decided to call Sheila and have her talk to the entire room full of women. It was Sheila's turn to address the women's forum that day.

Sheila stood in front of everybody. She was beautifully dressed up in a light blue pant suit with fine red stripes, with a bright red belt at the waist. She was wearing bright red colored, high heeled sandals and the same colored small bow in her hair. In that custom-made, designer suit with its right accessories, she was looking absolutely stunning. All the women were staring at her.

Sheila started talking directly to all the women.

"I know you are all looking at me right now, assessing everything I am wearing, right from my hair clips to my sandals. And as you are looking at me with a keen eye, I am noticing a surprise on most of your faces. Many of you, perhaps all of you, must be wondering what am *I, a model with a perfect figure*, doing here. Am I right?" She looked at all the women in the room and saw them nod.

She even heard a few of them, especially those in the front row, utter a few words to that effect.

She smiled and continued.

"The other day when I was trying on some new style of bras, I glimpsed at myself in the changing room mirror, and believe me, I did a double take. Was that gorgeous young woman with the *spectacular cleavage* really me? I wondered. It's almost ten years now, since I have had my own natural breasts removed, and replaced by these beautiful fake ones…"

The moment she said it, the whole audience felt some kind of a jolt. No one knew about it. She looked at the audience with a confident smile again and said,

"But ladies, I'm convinced that I'm the luckiest woman on Earth. I did lose my natural breasts, yes, but far from fearing that my femininity has disappeared, I feel very fortunate. Thanks to reconstructive surgery, I've attained a beautiful, permanent figure with two brand new breasts that my surgeon designed especially for my height and slim waist. Do you know why I had my natural breasts removed?" There was a pin-drop silence in the room, although almost all the women in the room were shaking their heads.

"I had my natural breasts removed because they were like two ticking time-bombs for me. It was diagnosed with the genetic testing that I'd inherited a defective cancer gene. That meant that I stood a very high, almost ninety per cent chance of developing breast cancer, compared with the average of less than ten per cent." Sheila looked at the audience again and with a serious face, continued telling her life story.

"In the village that I came from, people didn't know what cancer meant. Knowing about things like genetics or genetic history was far from imagination of these people. I had lost my mother and two elder sisters unexpectedly at their younger age, but no one knew why?" Women were getting engrossed in Sheila's personal story by now. Sheila continued telling her story.

"By some wonderful turns in my life that was purely a stroke of good luck, I left the little village permanently and moved in with Usha didi to Mumbai. Again, with sheer luck, I met Dr. Sudha at Usha didi's place. As you might know, Dr. Sudha is Usha didi's student. When Dr. Sudha came to know about my family history, she, with my request and Usha didi's consent, immediately carried out the special blood test on me. Lo and behold, I had inherited the faulty BRCA1[11] gene." Sheila looked at the audience.

---

[11] Refer to the details at the end of the book.

All the women were listening intently to her life story. A few among them nodded their heads.

"To those of you who don't, I would suggest, do talk to Dr. Sudha. She has a mastery over explaining it beautifully in layperson's terms. Anyways, when I heard this from her, my stomach lurched and I lost my control and went berserk. I knew what lay ahead of me, perhaps the same as *Ma* and my two older sisters. I was extremely stressed; I wanted some kind of assurance of not getting breast cancer. That's when I took the option of having my healthy breasts removed. I knew instantly that, a preventative mastectomy, as Dr. Sudha calls such type of surgery, would guarantee me my peace of mind. So ladies, I have had a *bilateral prophylactic mastectomy*[12], which means both breasts being surgically removed. It is also called 'preventative bilateral mastectomy'. In this procedure, you opt to surgically remove your both breasts *before* the onset of the disease. A preventative double mastectomy may sound horrific, but I felt it was the only way to be free from the curse of breast cancer. Much more importantly, that saved my life."

"But then, these beautiful breasts of yours, they look so natural too…" A few women expressed their doubts.

"They *look* natural but they are not. That's the artistic accomplishment of a wonderful plastic surgeon. He was a good friend of Dr. Sudha. The love and trust of my Usha didi for these two wonderful doctors has been incredible."

With this last sentence, Sheila got a little emotional and had to wait for a few seconds to collect her. She took a few long, deep breaths and continued.

"I took the decision of removing my natural breasts as a prevention of the disease, but the thought disturbed me too much. I started getting nightmares where I would look at my

---

[12] Refer to the details at the end of the book.

chest and it was empty. No breasts. I started becoming depressed again. Usha didi talked to Dr. Sudha again about my nightmares. That's when Dr. Sudha suggested reconstructive surgery for me, and introduced me to her surgeon friend. I was so relieved when Dr. Sudha and her surgeon friend explained to me that he would construct for me new breasts at the same time of removing my natural breasts. Living without breasts may suit some women, but not me. I was only twenty years of age then. Just imagine, a twenty year-old young woman, how would she feel losing her both breasts?"

Sheila's eyes were full with tears, so were most of the women's in the audience.

She had moved the whole audience with her personal story.

Sheila took a couple of long, breaths again and continued her story.

"The surgeon explained the entire procedure, how it's done and all that, to me. From that moment on, I started preparing myself. I was promised by Dr. Sudha that her surgeon friend was one of the finest in his field and the implants he would insert in my breasts' place would never look fake or artificial. That's exactly how it was! Not even a small scar anywhere! To this day, no one, I mean, not a single person knows my secret. You all know that I model bras too, but the most experts in that industry too, have not doubted it." Sheila looked around and said,

"I've never relied on my breasts for sex appeal or anything like that, mind you, but I realize that these fake breasts gave me my confidence and my self-esteem of being a woman. I would recommend every woman who has to undergo mastectomy for one or both breasts, this reconstructive surgery. It does improve the quality of your life."

Then giving a little lighter tone to her story, Sheila said.

"As my new fear-free life started, I changed my name from Shailender to Sheila, and dropped my last name altogether. As you all know, my fake breasts have given me a tremendous opportunity to become one of the most sought after models of our country, and have brought plenty of fame and fortune for me." With this sentence, she smiled at the audience. All the women spontaneously clapped for her speech. They instantly developed a great liking for her.

"Tell us about your operation please, Sheila." A few of them requested her.

Sheila looked at them and said, "Well, I'll tell that story some other time. Right now, we are gathered here for your 'climb to recovery', isn't it?" They all agreed and thanked her for her personal story-telling.

"I have joined this support group and have promised Dr. Sudha, as well as Anila and Malti and everyone involved, to help in whatever they need my help for. I want to make the most of my life. That's a promise to me and to you all."

In a thunder of claps, Sheila bowed politely with her slender, shapely body, to one and all. The session for that day was over with a great success. She had imparted great hope in almost all the women gathered there, The women were, indeed, getting stronger on their climb, by now!

Uphill Expedition Together with their Men...

"One very important thing we must do is, avoid the numbers game. That's one big mistake I did…" Dr. Manav Joshi was standing and talking to a group of men.

A session organized specially and only for men was going on in one of the rooms in Malti's house. Only the husbands of women with breast cancer patients were invited to attend this session. Naturally, no woman was seen anywhere in this session. Anila had arranged it with the help of her husband, Manav; and Kiran's husband, Raj, had taken special efforts to organize it and send as many invitations as they could to all the men they knew, who would be genuinely interested.

"When you had your breast cancer detected, did your husband move out of your bedroom?" A woman had asked Anila during the women's forum. Since then, that question was resonating in her ears constantly. She had clearly heard the pain in that woman's voice and seen on her face; that had never left her thought since then.

"Having a forum for only men is a must," she concluded.

With that decisive conclusion, she initiated a session, where men, the husbands of women with breast cancer would actively participate in their uphill expedition to recovery.

"What do you mean, numbers game, Dr. Joshi?" One man asked.

"I'll explain. When we went to Dr. Sudha to get my wife's reports, she told us that my wife had developed breast cancer, I was completely shocked, to a point that I lost my total sense. In that state, instead of collecting myself and supporting my wife, I, like a bloody fool, blurted out in loud voice, 'oh my God, that means my wife's days are numbered now.' To tell you all honestly, I can't even imagine what my wife must have felt when she heard me say that." Manav became a little upset and stood still for a moment.

"But fortunately for me, my wife, that's Anila as you all know, is a very strong and courageous woman. She exhibited tremendous courage and during her entire cancer treatment, gave *me* the courage to pull through her treatment." Manav stopped to wipe his brow for a few moments.

He continued, "Dr. Sudha had told me very clearly 'to take care of her', and I did; but my friends, I failed miserably in another very important area..."

"What's that?" Someone from the audience asked again.

"Dr. Sudha had also told me emphatically 'to be very supportive', but I wasn't, at all."

"Why, what did you do?" A younger looking man asked Manav.

"I... I made her feel like *less of a woman*, if you all know what I mean..."

"I know exactly what you mean, Dr. Joshi..." Another man stood up and started talking to the group.

"When my wife's breast cancer was detected, the first thing I did was, pull my bed out of our bedroom and move it to the next room. I have been sleeping there ever since then. She underwent mastectomy, a complete treatment of radiation and chemotherapy as well. It is almost two years now, but I am still sleeping in the room next to hers." The man tried to cover his face with one hand and was on the verge of crying.

"Do you know..." With quivering lips, he continued talking, "I have not seen her without her blouse yet, I simply can't...I have no guts to look at her chest..." and then he broke down completely.

The whole atmosphere in the room became quite tense for a few minutes. No one talked.

"Is it the fear that we cannot face when our women get breast cancer? Or is it something else?" Men started talking among themselves.

"It is fear of death of our spouse." Someone from the audience pulled his courage and said loudly. Men stopped immediately after hearing him.

"Yes, yes, fear of losing wife..." Some other man supported him.

"Whether it is your wife or a girlfriend, it is the fear of losing her that traumatizes us."

There was a little murmur in the room.

"Yes, but I would say, it is not just fear of losing your wife..." One man commented.

"Then, what?"

"It is also the fear of not being able to function normally." The same man answered.

"What do you mean?"

"Ever since my wife has had her surgery and lost her breast, I have not been able to 'function' as a husband, you know..."

and then with a slight hesitation, he said, "I mean I just can't 'make love' to her, I just can't, because, because…" not being able to express properly, he just stood quietly.

"Because when I see or touch the flatness of her chest, I almost immediately get something like *erectile dysfunction (ED)*. I just don't seem to…" He tried explaining.

And he had hit the nail right on its head.

He didn't even have to complete what he wanted to say when Manav got up and interrupted him.

"Yes, that's it. That's exactly it." Then he looked around and said, "I'm glad I'm not alone in this."

"You too, Dr. Joshi?" A few men, who knew Manav quite well, sounded surprised that a very-well educated person like Manav would also have this problem.

"Yes, my friends, me too. It has been more than two years now. I know very well that sexual excitation begins as a state of mind, and not body. Accordingly, I do get excited and feel like having some intimacy with my dear wife every so often. However, every time I approach her with that purpose in mind, the moment I see that part of her chest which is totally flat and bare, that's it. It is as if I instantly lose my vigor. I grow weak in my limbs, I start feeling terribly exhausted, I panic and then I have to, almost immediately, withdraw myself from the thought or action of intimacy completely."

Men were looking at each other when Manav narrated his own situation in such honest words.

"I always thought that it's the love between two people that matters the most. But now I am really confused. How is it that we tend to forget this important principle?" One man said after listening to Manav.

"Yes, now, I wonder about that too. I love my wife very much, so, her having or *not* having breasts would not carry that much importance in our 'love making'. Well, at least that's what I thought. But she lost her one breast to cancer and since then, I have lost my desire for her." Another man iterated his experience. "Honestly, it's damn confusing to me…"

"So, is it fear of losing your wife or confusion of not being able to function as a husband?" Someone asked.

"I think it is both, fear and confusion…" Someone said.

"Fear, I can understand, since it is connected directly to death by cancer; but why confusion?"

"Confusion also because, we just don't know whether she would feel good about our sexual advances or she would feel awkward about it?"

"That's exactly how my story goes too. And we both are musicians…"

Ajoy was present in the group too, and a few people recognized him.

"I fell in love with my wife way back when she was just an upcoming artist. We got married, had two beautiful girls, and now, out of nowhere, this lightening, called cancer, struck us. It's like our whole life was totally devastated. Tanuja, that's my wife, lost her both breasts."

Ajoy closed his eyes and took a deep breath to control from crying.

"I pretended to be very brave, only in front of her of course; for her sake and for the sake of my two girls. But whenever I was alone, I would cry my guts out. I was scared out of my wits, but I didn't want anyone to know that. Someone asked earlier about fear and confusion. Friends, I think I am filled with both, fear and confusion. And to add to that, my Tanuja didn't just lose her breasts, she lost her singing too with cancer." Ajoy couldn't control his emotions any more. He started crying profusely.

Some people in that room had heard of Tanuja Bose, the famous singer, and also that she had lost her singing to cancer. Now, they were witnessing her husband crying and grieving. The entire atmosphere in the room was filled with grief. No one spoke for a few minutes.

"I think, there is no single answer or solution to this problem. Each couple has a unique situation and that can be solved by that couple alone, no one else..." Raj stood up and started talking to the people.

He was also one of the helpers of this session.

"Making love is a very personal matter." He said. "My name is Raj Prakash Rao. When my wife's cancer was detected, she was only twenty eight years of age. We have one son; he was not even out of diapers when her breast cancer was detected. And that was just a few months ago."

"Oh, no...",

"Really?"

"Oh, shit man..."

Comments coming from all the men in the room were full of sympathy for Raj, although most of them were husbands of breast cancer patients.

"And as if this was not catastrophic enough, my wife's breast cancer is one of those rare kinds, which doesn't give much time to the patient for surviving..."

The moment Raj said this, everyone in the room got suddenly very quiet and serious. No one could utter a single word. Not even of sympathy. It was as though he had given them a huge electrical shock.

However, Raj stayed relatively calm and continued talking,

"But my friends, I do want to tell you all that we have forbidden her breast cancer to enter our bedroom. We make love to each other as passionately as before. Her breast cancer, bc, I call it the *bastard coward*, has no room in it." Everyone was stunned to hear his brave statement and his strong conviction behind it.

Raj did look fairly calm, at least outwardly.

"I consider this passionate activity of having an intercourse with my wife as *meditation*, that's done with a deep sense of love and affection. You all must have experienced it. Making love has a tremendous meditative quality in it. I do not wish to give it up, or have it polluted with confusion or fear. That is how I genuinely feel and that's exactly how I convinced my wife too. Thank God, she also believes in this now."

Everyone was dead silent. They looked shocked but at the same time, looked full of admiration for Raj. He kept quiet for a few moments and then continued,

"Not enough research is done in my wife's cancer case. They don't know at what stage her cancer could be, or how far treatable it is. And, therefore, they have given her only a year, or two at the most, to live…" At this point, Raj's voice started cracking up, but he still continued speaking,

"Friends, I urge you, do not waste your precious time with your wife in fear or confusion. I personally can't and don't want to! And I honestly urge you again; make the most of every single day. That's what I do!"

Raj cracked up completely and started crying silently. Many men in the room were also crying silently. There was a total absence of sound in the room for a few moments.

It was proven beyond the shadow of doubt that 'it is a *myth* that men don't cry'!

"What Mr. Rao just said makes a hell of a sense, guys. Let us not waste this precious time in futile way, like fear or confusion. My wife displayed tremendous courage when she went for her surgery. She has expressed her courage so many times afterwards too, when she would go for her chemotherapy or radiation. It was always *her* who would hold *my* hands and give *me* courage. I feel so ashamed of myself now." Some one new got some courage to stand up and speak to the group.

"Talking about feeling ashamed, do you know how I feel?" Another man stood up and asked a question to the audience. "Along with fear and confusion, I feel extremely embarrassed and awkward too." This got immediate attention from the people.

"What do you mean, embarrassed and awkward?"

"My dear people, in my case, it's *me* who has developed breast cancer, not my wife." He said with his head turned as downwards as he could. "When I went to the hospital with my wife for the treatment, most of the people including some of the hospital staff first suspected my *wife* to have breast cancer. When they came to know it was *me*, I almost saw an expression on a few of their faces as though they had seen a clown or something. And that was not the only time this happened. I get this type of experience almost all the time, when I go for my chemotherapy treatments. My wife has a problem telling anyone in our friend circle, or sometimes even in our extended family members, that *I, the husband*, has had breast cancer. My disease is as serious as women's, but we don't seem to get much sympathy from anyone…"

This man was almost on the verge of crying, but he continued,

"In my cricket club, where I was considered to be a valuable player, a couple of my own teammates made fun of me. One asked me jokingly, 'so, what size are you choosing for your reconstructive surgery? Lemons or oranges?' Immediately another answered, 'watermelons…' and they all laughed loudly.

What do I say to that? Since cancer was going to hit me anyways, I wish it was some other form of cancer…"

He cupped his mouth slightly and started crying softly.

Some men were stunned to hear all this.

They didn't know that men too can get breast cancer.

"What this gentleman said is true. Whether it is the husband or the wife, breast cancer is a *family disease*. And to do away with fear or confusion, or embarrassment, we must face this disease with courage and full family support."

"But how will we achieve this?"

"How do you handle it?"

There was a slight chaos in the room, with people asking various questions and talking among themselves.

"With communication and openness." Manav stood up and said loudly. "Communication and openness is the answer to all our questions, and also to our fear and confusion. And to our embarrassment too."

"Communication with whom?"

"Openness about what?" Some men started throwing questions.

"Communication with our partners. Openness about our own feelings and fears. Combining both, we communicate our fears and feelings, even embarrassment, to our loved ones, especially our partners, and we express frankly and openly about how and what we feel about this disease." Manav said.

There were a few questioning faces among the men.

"To explain it better…" Manav said after looking at their faces. He started talking as though he was now ready to give one of his famous lectures in his English literature class.

"Let me quote my own experience. For more than two years now, I have been carrying this intense fear within me. I don't think I'm scared of my wife's disease, *per se*, I think it has to do with that empty area on her chest when she lost her one breast to cancer and refused to undergo any reconstructive surgery. That empty spot reminds me continuously, every single day, of her getting cancer, which would surely kill her. But I have been hiding my fear all this time. And to hide it successfully, I have been pretending to read philosophy books. I thought this philosophical reading would camouflage my fears while giving me some courage to face it eventually. But alas! It did neither. My wife is a smart woman. She recognized my cowardice. She made me realize that I was only deceiving *myself, and not her.* So finally one day, with her insistence, I opened up to her completely. It felt so good, I tell you, my friends. There is nothing like complete honesty and open communication..."

Manav pulled out a handkerchief from his pocket, wiped his brow and forehead that was shining with a few sweat beads, and continued again. "Today for the first time, I felt that I am not alone, I am not the only one feeling this way. There are many among us who are going through exactly what I have been facing these last two years. I feel somewhat encouraged, even better, to see that I wasn't the only husband who was a coward."

Then Manav directed his gaze at Raj and said,

"When I heard Mr. Rao say, 'making love is a kind of meditation,' it struck my inner chord. Just like him, I also firmly believe that there is a beautiful, meditative quality in 'love making'. When he said, 'don't waste your precious time', it hit me hard as a blatant reality of my own life that I'm a husband of a cancer survivor. Therefore, my time with my wife is very precious."

Then Manav walked closer to the window and as if talking to himself, he said,

"I have already wasted enough time of our lives in futile thinking; let me not waste it any more. This is a promise to me that when I go home today, I am going to hold my Annie in my arms and tell her face to face,

> *"Let me not to the marriage of true minds,*
> *Admit impediments.*
> *Love is no love*
> *Which alters when it alteration finds.*
> *Or bends with the remover to remove.*
> *Oh no! It is an ever fixed mark.*
> *That looks on tempests and is never shaken…"*

Manav completed the recitation that came to him so very naturally. He looked around. Everyone was staring at him as if they were totally spell bound by his beautiful recitation of Shakespeare's poetry, in that passionate, resonating voice of his. He himself realized in that instance, that that was his original voice. It had come back to him.

He felt extremely elated. And totally liberated too! As though, he was set free from the captivity of some grotesque oppressor!

With deep satisfaction, Manav was about to sit down when he looked outside. Through the window, he saw Anila, standing in the corridor, looking at him, with tears running down her cheeks.

'She heard me…', he felt sure and instantly knew, things were going to be back to normal in their lives, just like they were before, before her breast cancer was diagnosed.

◻

Cancer is my teacher!

As the women were striving to climb and reach the summit of complete recovery, and as they were gaining physical and mental strength, this was the right time to inject in them strong doses of 'hope and positivity'!

And precisely for that very reason, the five women of the Support group had organized a session for discussing 'advantages of positive thinking to health'.

The number of people attending such types of tutorial sessions had gone up to phenomenal levels and a room in Malti's bungalow for such lectures was no longer sufficient. Therefore, a hall was taken for it. The main speaker for today's session was again, Shantabai, the psychotherapist; and it was going to be in the presence of Dr. Sudha.

Shantabai entered the hall and looked around. It was a big hall, packed to capacity with people, mostly women, women of all ages, shapes and sizes. They were all sitting on the floor. In one quick glance at their clothing and the gold jewelry, or lack thereof, she could assess that they were from all economic strata of the society. The hall was actually the dining area of the same community college where Dr. Manav Joshi had been teaching before his retirement. The floors were cleared off all the chairs and tables and covered with some simple, rolling-type jute mats, for sitting on the floor. This was a very popular and one of most efficient ways of accommodating a much larger audience in a smaller area.

A few men were standing around, bordering the seated crowd of women on the floor. Shantabai walked across the hall led by Anila and Malti to the far side of the hall. There was a small piece of carpet laid out on the floor, with a single microphone on a stand in the middle of it. Shantabai was requested to sit in front of the microphone, on the floor. She sat comfortably in her usual, lotus position on the floor in front of the microphone. Malti introduced Shantabai to the audience and then walked towards Anila and Dr. Sudha and sat with them, who were also sitting on the floor on the rolled mats

Shantabai cleared her throat, and dismounting the microphone from its stand and taking it in her hand, greeted the audience in her usual deep, soothing voice. She thanked them for coming all the way from various areas of the city for this lecture, and started addressing the topic of the speech.

"Today's lecture, as you all know, is arranged specifically to talk to you all about the advantages of positive thinking related to your health. And it is primarily focused on breast cancer. As you all know, I am not a doctor or a cancer specialist like Dr. Sudha, nor am I a breast cancer survivor like Malti or Anila. I am a psychotherapist. As Dr. Sudha calls me sometimes, I am a doctor of the mind!"

In spite of a big crowd, there was a pin drop silence in the hall. Dr. Sudha, Malti and Anila looked around and could actually feel the eagerness on people's faces. As organizers of this event, they felt satisfied to see the huge gathering of people there.

Shantabai started stressing the various points of positive thinking, and how helpful it can be, with narration of a few anecdotes. She was a motivational speaker and with her voice, her speech had a spell binding effect on the audience. She was riding on a high tide of emotion in her speech, intending to take everyone in the audience with her, when right in the middle of her speech, one man darted in the direction towards some woman sitting on the floor and with his hands thrown out in air, started speaking in a very loud voice in that direction. "This is exactly what I have been telling you over and over again. Don't you get it? "

As though not at all cognizant of the crowd around him, he kept on shouting out in one specific direction,

"It is *you* who has to decide to get well, it is *you* who has to take the reins of your life in your hands..."

He was emphasizing the '*you*' part of his sentences with both his voice and his right hand forefinger pointing out straight at some woman in the audience.

Shantabai looked startled. So did everybody. They all started looking, first in the direction of that man and then in the direction of his pointed finger. He was looking at a young, frail looking woman who was sitting on the floor. She looked startled too for a moment and then started to cry silently. There was a toddler sleeping soundly on her lap. The toddler also woke up and started crying with a loud sound. The whole audience was taken aback with this commotion.

Dr. Sudha looked at the man and the frail woman he was talking to. They were none other than Raj and Kiran. Dr. Sudha knew instantly what was going on. She hurriedly approached Raj and tried to take him out of the hall. Malti and Anila darted towards Kiran and helped her get up with her toddler and walk outside the hall. Amma, who was sitting next to Kiran, quietly got up and followed them too. However, just as Kiran managed to reach the door, Raj ran towards her, hugged her tightly with her crying child squished in between them, and started saying,

"Rani, this is exactly what you need to do, don't you understand? Believe in yourself, like that nice lady said, 'have faith in your doctor and the treatments.' You say you are a part of the Support group, but you are not following any of the supporting ideas yourself. Don't let the disease defeat you. Do it for me, Rani, do it for our baby, and do it soon, Rani, time is running out on us now...."

Dr. Sudha tried her best to quiet him down, but she was not successful. He had become too emotional, and obviously swept away with Shantabai's speech on positive thinking.

In utter dismay, people watched this drama for a minute or so. They were all staring at the two people, Raj and Kiran, alternately. But those two seemed totally oblivious to the surroundings and the people around them. Dr. Sudha and Anila finally managed to get this young family out of the hall and out of everyone's sight. Malti took the microphone in her hands and in a commanding voice requested everyone to be quiet, apologized to Shantabai and when everything was settled down, requested her to continue the speech.

Shantabai spoke for almost an hour after the incident. However, that scene never left her or any body's mind. What everyone had seen there was almost a dumbfounding, real life drama. It was very intense too. The whole thing had an intriguing effect on people, especially Shantabai. The lecture was over and people slowly dispersed. Dr. Sudha, Malti and Anila were also getting ready to leave the place when Shantabai approached them and requested them to brief her up with some details about this young family, and if possible, arrange to meet them in person.

"Didn't that young woman, Kiran, attend our very first meeting in the community center when we talked about organizing and starting a Cancer Support group, doctor?" Anila asked.

Dr. Sudha nodded.

"She sounded so calm and balanced at that time, didn't she?" Malti asked.

Dr. Sudha nodded again.

"Yes, she certainly did, but lately, things have gone a little haywire with her..." Dr. Sudha said.

"I was sure she would help us in this undertaking, Dr. Sudha."

"You saw that young man, he is her husband. His name is Raj Prakash Rao. He is a middle management executive in a local bank. He calls her Rani. That toddler on her lap is their only son and the older woman is his mother, they call her *Amma*. Rani is working in the same bank as a teller...."

Dr. Sudha started telling Anila, Malti and Shantabai about Kiran. She wasn't too concerned with the doctor-patient confidentiality, as those three women were her team members in the fight against breast cancer for all breast cancer patients.

After narrating Kiran's complete story to the three women, Dr. Sudha abruptly became very quiet and just took a few long breaths.

"Why, what happened doctor?" Anila asked her.

"This young woman has developed a relatively rare kind of breast cancer, called Inflammatory Breast cancer. And her cancer is fairly advanced. Not much can be done for her, really."

Dr. Sudha looked visibly upset after mentioning the disease to Shantabai, Anila and Malti, which disturbed those three women too.

Dr. Sudha took a few long and deep breaths again, and said,

"She is my patient, but it is always at Raj's insistence that Kiran reluctantly comes to me for some consultation. It is also at his insistence, that she joined our group, but her heart is not in it, I can see that very clearly. And amazing as it may sound but she has refused to take any of my treatment for her cancer. According to him, her interest is somewhere else since the diagnosis of the disease..."

"Where?" All three of them inquired.

"Well, it's a life-changing medical diagnosis for them, right? So I advised her to quit her job and focus completely on the treatment of cancer. She doesn't want to do either of them, though. According to Raj, she is completely changed since the diagnosis of the disease. Cancer has damaged her sense of self. She has denied herself a normal life as a wife or a mother. She feels hopeless, and feels her life is finished already...."

When Dr. Sudha was telling them all this, Malti remembered her own days after Manubhai's demise in a flash of that second. And so did Shantabai, remembering Malti's state of mind at that time. They both exchanged glances at each other for a second and quickly turned towards what the doctor was saying.

"It has already killed all her dreams, I can see that. Do you all recall her tantrums a few days ago in one of our sessions?" Dr. Sudha asked them. They all nodded.

"Yes, yes, I remember them very well. Kiran kept on yelling about her young age and called you a liar. She even questioned your medical expertise when you said breast cancer is primarily an older age disease." Anila said.

"Yes, and another myth she firmly believes in is that breast cancer happens to women who are not virgins on their wedding nights..."

Dr. Sudha said.

"What?" All three of them exclaimed.

"Yes. That's why she was stressing that point on that day as well, do you remember?" Dr. Sudha asked.

"Yes, I remember." Shantabai said.

"How ignorant! Who told her all this nonsense…?" Anila asked, not directing it at any one specifically.

"That must be the figment of her own imagination, obviously. Nowhere is it written in literature or said by any doctor or a scientist." Dr. Sudha said.

"I think that sometime, somewhere, if somebody writes something about breast cancer and something about multiple sex partners in the same context, especially in the Western countries, then that can be totally misunderstood by some people…" Shantabai said.

"In the Eastern countries." Anila joined Shantabai in completing what she was saying.

"That's so true." Malti said.

"Being a virgin on the wedding night has absolutely nothing to do with getting this disease, I tell her all the time, but she doesn't believe me." Dr. Sudha continued.

"Not just that, every time I say something to her about the treatment for cancer, she ignores me completely and pulls this tantrum of crying and yelling loudly. Fortunately, Raj is very sensible; he is not giving up so easily."

"Oh, Good for him." Anila said.

"As of late, Kiran has taken up a totally different activity for herself, I was told by Raj." Dr. Sudha said with a very serious face.

"What kind of activity?" All three of them asked almost simultaneously.

"She wants Raj, her husband, to meet some girl of *her* choice from their native town in Karnataka, and marry her."

"What?" All of them almost screamed as though struck with lightening.

"Yes. Kiran feels that by arranging a girl, who would be a good wife to Raj, a good mother to her son, and a good daughter-in-law to her mother-in-law, she could die in peace." Dr. Sudha said.

"Oh my God, ..., really?" The three women almost didn't believe Dr. Sudha.

"Yes, really. That's true. I couldn't believe it either. When I heard it for the first time, I was thunderstruck, just like you three are right now. 'Is she for real?' I kept on wondering, but I know her mental condition now. She's making a big fuss about her medical condition now. She says all the time that that's going to kill her shortly. I understand her frustration. I just can't imagine what her husband must be going through. He complains all the time to me about this stupid activity of his wife finding a girl for him, but he is afraid that she would become hysterical. As it is, she complains to him that he is not giving her a few good and happy last months of her life by denying participating in this activity. I can see he loves her very much but he can't do anything anymore."

Anila, Malti and Shantabai were quiet for a few seconds, looking very serious and sad. "What about her mother-in-law? Kiran seemed quite attached to her when I took her out of the hall..." Anila asked.

"Well, the mother-in-law sympathizes with her completely, but apparently, advises Raj to do what his wife wishes to do." Dr. Sudha informed.

"What do you mean?" They all asked the doctor.

"I mean, that old woman, although she loves Kiran, is quite willing and actually helping her find a suitable girl from Karnataka for Raj."

"Oh my God!" Malti said.

"Unbelievable, really. We need to do something for this young woman, and soon. We need to put some sense in her." Anila said.

"I think I can work on her. Dr. Sudha. Please give me that assignment. I will try to work on her..." Shantabai looked like she was ready to take upon the challenge; a big challenge of putting some sense into Kiran's head.

"Shantabai, you will be facing an uphill battle, you realize that, right? Kiran is convinced that her cancer is going to kill her very soon. She is ignoring everyone's requests, everyone's advice, refusing to take medical treatment as well. She insists that she will die in peace only if she accomplishes this mission of finding a girl for her husband and therefore she is focusing all her energies on it. She is actually in a rush to do this." Dr. Sudha warned Shantabai.

"Dr. Sudha, I want to start my psychotherapy work on this woman right away. I don't think we should let her waste her precious time in all this nonsense." Shantabai seemed confident. She was determined to work on Kiran's psychology.

"My best wishes to you, Shantabai, remember this patient is a case of *total absence of hope, coupled with grotesque ignorance, the most dreadful combination for cancer patients.* She does not seem to realize the seriousness of her disease, nor does she understand the emergency of medical help for her wellbeing. She seems completely oblivious to the crisis in her life."

Dr. Sudha warned Shantabai, but deep down, she felt happy for Kiran and confident in Shantabai's skills. All of them left with heavy hearts for Kiran.

"Om..."

The *mantra* in Shantabai's deep and soothing voice resounded in the room. She was sitting in her usual lotus position with her eyes closed. In front of her, sitting on the floor were Malti, Anila, Raj and Kiran. It was with great difficulty that Raj was able to convince Kiran to visit Shantabai; she finally agreed. That was a good start. Malti and Anila volunteered to help Shantabai in Kiran's case.

"Kindly repeat after me, everybody…" Shantabai said. Malti and Anila started repeating after her, and in a few minutes, Raj joined them too. But Kiran kept quiet. She looked a little apprehensive, a little timid too. There were only four of them in the room at the time. That's how it was purposely arranged.

"This is how we start the Visualization Technique, in a completely serene atmosphere, with this mantra, as it has a tremendous meditative quality." Shantabai explained to Raj and Kiran, and started reciting the mantra again. Malti, Anila and Raj repeated after her again. Kiran listened to them, but still looked reluctant to participate in the process.

"Would you like to try reciting Om, Kiran?" Shantabai asked her directly, but she shook her head.

"It might make you feel better, just try it for a minute…"

Shantabai insisted but Kiran shook her head vigorously this time, indicating she was not at all interested in participating in any of that.

Ignoring her reluctance to join them, Shantabai still continued reciting the mantra and the other three people kept on repeating after her, all of them with their eyes closed. During the recitation, Shantabai momentarily opened her eyes for a quick glance at Kiran. She was looking at her wristwatch, obviously checking the time. That gave a clear indication to Shantabai that Kiran was totally disinterested in trying out the new technique or even being there. She closed her eyes again and while reciting the mantra, decided to try a different route to get Kiran involved in the process.

"Malti, would you kindly assume Kiran's role now?" Shantabai stopped reciting and gently asked Malti.

Malti was ready, she nodded willingly. But hearing her own name, Kiran looked a little startled. Raj looked a little confused too. Malti got up and stood on the right side of the room, facing Anila, Raj and Kiran.

"And I will assume the role of Kiran's Cancer. The Cancer will be talking to Kiran now…" Shantabai got up and stood on the left side of the room, facing Anila, Raj and Kiran.

The moment she said 'Kiran's Cancer…' Kiran got even a bigger jolt. She looked quite curious and started watching the two women, standing in front of her, with keen eyes.

Malti, in Kiran's role, started talking to Shantabai, who had assumed the role of Kiran's Cancer.

Malti in Kiran's Role: *I am soon going to die.*

Cancer: *That's what you have been saying since the day of your diagnosis. Ever since then, you are behaving as though you have been my prey, and it's only a matter of short time before you die. You just can't think of anything else, anything except your death, can you?*

Malti in Kiran's Role: *No, that's not true. I'm going to die very soon, that's for sure, but my death is not the only thing on my mind. There is another thought that's been on my mind too, a very important one.*

Cancer: *What's that?*

Malti in Kiran's Role: *I am looking for a good woman, who would be a good wife for my Raj and a loving mother to my Kittu.*

Malti and Shantabai glanced at Raj and Kiran; they both looked disturbed, but did not get up and leave. 'The drama could continue', they thought and quickly assumed their roles again.

Cancer: *What? What are you saying?*

Malti in Kiran's Role: *That's right. Ever since you imposed your presence in my life and invaded my body, I can't think of anything else. I have made it my mission, you know, and I'm trying very hard to attain it.*

Cancer: *I see. So, since I invaded your life, as you put it, you accepted immediately that you are going to die. Is that it? You don't want to give me a fight, you don't want to defeat me, you don't want to even try to win over me, is that it? This reminds me of someone who had the same defeatist attitude just like you. She was also waiting for her death, same like you. She didn't love her husband and she didn't love her child either.*

Malti in Kiran's Role: *You arrogant scoundrel, what nonsense are you talking?*

Cancer: *Hey, there's no need to swear at me, okay? I am saying what I am noticing. You really don't love your husband and your son; otherwise, you wouldn't wait for your death like this. You would try every which way to make sure that you live as long as possible for them.*

Malti in Kiran's Role: *Oh ho, ho…! What a gem of wisdom? How pretentious of you? First you invade my life, attack me brutally and get ready to kill me, then you become judgmental; you question my love for my dear husband and son; and as if that is not bad enough, you pretend to teach me words of wisdom in that condescending tone of yours.*

Cancer: *Okay, in that case let me ask you directly, do you love your husband?*

Malti in Kiran's Role: *Of course I do! What kind of stupid question is this? You have no idea how much I love my Raj.*

Cancer: *And how about your son?*

Malti in Kiran's Role: *Another foolish question! Of course I love my son. Kittu is our love child. We call him the blossoming of our love, mine and Raj's.*

Cancer: *In that case, you silly woman, when you have two such loving people in your life, how is it that you are waiting for your death? I know I am growing in you, but why aren't you giving me a fight? Why not? You call me foolish, but look who really is behaving foolishly? You know fully well who my real enemies are, they are my victim's self-confidence, my victim's faith in her healthy and loving family support, my victim's friends and their loving support; these are all my bitter enemies. These enemies build up my victim's positive attitude. And that is my most fierce enemy! I always wish to live and grow in my victim's body, but with a healthy attitude, my victim can certainly overpower my wish. Positive attitude is very vital, my dear woman. Wake up now, come out of that jungle of hopeless, dismal thoughts .....*

Malti in Kiran's Role: *Stop it, stop right this minute. I am appalled at your series of accusations. You accuse me of feeling hopeless, you accuse me of not having a positive attitude, but have you looked at yourself anytime? Have you assessed yourself? If not, let me tell you, Mr. Cancer Know-it all! You are one of the deadliest cancers of all types of breast cancers. Once you get into some one's body, you don't give that person any chance. It is you who made me feel this way. It is you who made me feel hopeless. What's more, you didn't give me even a simple indication of your presence and development in me.*

Cancer: *Well, yes, as you put it, I am one of the deadly ones; and you are right, I didn't give you even a simple indication of my development. Both these accusations are true, but then, the only answer I have for both your accusations is, 'it is your fate'!*

Malti in Kiran's Role: *Oh, so now you are blaming my fate, is it?*

Cancer: *Yes, it is your fate. Let me tell you something that I have observed with you humans. Most of you humans believe that every human life is controlled by two major factors. The first and the foremost is fate and the second is the genetic make-up. No one can alter or run away from these two controlling factors, according to your belief, isn't it?*

Malti in Kiran's Role: *So, what you are saying is - it's my own fate that was responsible for you, a deadly cancer, developing in me, is that it?*

Cancer: *Well, yes, but let me also tell you something very important; I'm sure you will be happy to hear it.*

Malti in Kiran's Role: *And what's that?*

Cancer: *Although fate and genetic structure are not in your hands, since these are God-given certainties of your life, as you humans put it, you still have one very, very powerful tool in your own hands. And that is your own 'Free Will'. My dear woman, free will is also a fact of human life, and most of you believe in it. You can utilize this tool to overpower or at least to modify many turns of your life dictated by fate or anything else. In your case, fate and genes dictated my presence, a deadly cancer in you, agreed; but with your own free will, you can take the best medical treatment, employ the best possible therapy, utilize your family support to the best level and with all such positive steps, defeat me completely."*

Malti in Kiran's Role: *Hmm...*

Cancer: *Honestly, in whom I could enter and develop is really not in my hands, do you know that? But when I enter and develop in anyone, I very earnestly try to teach them this valuable lesson of positive steps and defeat me. And I have noticed that most of them do learn this lesson from me very quickly.*

Malti in Kiran's Role: *You said, 'most of them'; does that mean not all of them?*

Cancer: *That's right; no, not all of them. Occasionally, I do come across an odd one, like...*

Malti in Kiran's Role: *Like me?*

Cancer: *Well, yes, like you. But then, fortunately such odd ball person also eventually comes around on the right track; perhaps they have their friends and family members to help them learn this lesson.*

Malti and Shantabai both looked at Kiran momentarily. Noticing that she was totally engrossed in their presentation, they continued with it.

Malti in Kiran's Role: *My, my, aren't you sounding totally pedantic now; and quite conceited too, I might say?*

Cancer: *Probably, yes.*

Malti in Kiran's Role: *Then tell me this, Mr. Schoolmaster, supposing I do learn this valuable lesson from you and give you a fight and win over, as you put it, death is still inevitable for me, isn't it?*

Cancer: *Oh, ho, ho...now look who is pretending to be a great philosopher? My dear woman, this is the most profound, age-old statement. There is nothing new in it. Death is inevitable to all mortals! Anyone born, is sure to die, then how can you avoid it? You obviously didn't get my point. The point I'm trying to make here is that, those in whom I enter and develop, they realize 'the mortality of their life' instantly. With my advent, it suddenly dawns upon them that there's definitely an end to their life. Their life is not endless or eternal. It is almost as if they wake up with a jolt from a deep sleep, deep sleep of total ignorance, shall we say...*

Climb to Victory Over Breast Cancer

Malti in Kiran's Role: *Hum…*

Cancer: *Hey, can I share a secret with you?*

Malti in Kiran's Role: *What's that?*

Cancer: *These humans, who wake up instantly from their deep sleep, which is because of me of course…*

Malti in Kiran's Role: *Of course…I get it.*

Cancer: *They start living their life fully and beautifully; it almost amuses me to see that change in them. Suddenly, they try to live every moment of their life. And as I said earlier, that's solely because of this realization of mortality of life that 'I teach them'. On one hand, they give me a fight with all possible ammunition, and on the other, they try to fulfill all their desires. Those, who love nature, go for nature hikes; those, who love painting, do painting; those, who love to travel, go on site-seeing journeys; and so on. They refuse to postpone anything anymore. It's so amusing to me, I tell you.*

Malti in Kiran's Role: *Amusing? Why do you find it amusing?*

Cancer: *Well, whenever I see them busy in all such activities, I just laugh to myself with amusement. I really find it funny and equally perplexing as to; why does this, supposedly the most intelligent species of the universe, need someone like me, a deadly disease, to realize that they are all mortals? Why? Don't they know the simple Truth of the universe that any life that is born is sure to die too, sometime? Don't they?*

Malti in Kiran's Role: *Well, yes, they do, actually.*

Cancer: *Then why do they realize it only after they come face to face with me, the Cancer? As soon as I enter their body, why do they behave as though suddenly some alarm clock just went on and woke them up? Hmm, why? Am I some kind of an alarm that they need?*

Malti in Kiran's Role: *Well, I don't know about that, but what you say is certainly something to ponder upon.*

Cancer: *Honestly, you humans crack me up! You need me to teach you this basic thing of life. Ha, ha, ha!*

Malti in Kiran's Role: *Don't get so amused at our folly. Now, tell me one more thing, Mr. Alarm clock, what if your alarm doesn't sound at all?*

Cancer: *There you go again, talking negatively. Do I end anyone's life instantly? Do I? Don't I give some time to every person for a fight? Don't I? I am not that cruel, you know. In many, many instances I give plenty of time to all my hosts to give me a fair fight. Many do, but a few don't. To those who don't, I want to tell them over and over again, 'come-on people, don't despair, don't give up, fight with me', stressing upon the fact that, fighting is something totally in their hands, and their hands alone, not in mine.*

The dialogue between Shantabai and Malti was barely over when Raj turned to Kiran and holding her tightly in his arms, said, "Rani, did you hear that? Did you hear that Rani? It's all in your hands and your hands alone darling…"

His eyes were full of tears, ready to overflow anytime. And so were Kiran's.

They both stood there in a close hug, with tears running down their cheeks continuously for a few minutes, while Anila, Malti and Shantabai watched them silently, hoping this presentation had achieved some success and Kiran was inspired to change her reluctance and negative attitude towards her cancer treatment.

☐

Taking hundreds like them on the Climb to Victory

Today the five women - Anila, Tanuja, Malti and Kiran, four breast cancer survivors and Sheila, a victim of preventative double mastectomy at a young age of twenty years - are sitting on Malti's patio and discussing their recent past. Each one of them has her own distinct story and each one has faced her own uphill battle while reaching the summit of recovery with success. In attaining the goal, all of them have gained tremendous strength, that of positivity and optimism. And with these 'power tools' they have started doing gigantic efforts for creating a Support Group for as many breast cancer survivors as possible!

They are joined by Dr. Sudha and Shantabai as well.

"First of all, I express my heartfelt kudos to all of you, my dear friends; you have worked tirelessly for the past so many months, to spread awareness of breast cancer among people." Dr. Sudha looks at them while talking and notices a distinct smile on their faces, a smile expressing joy of accomplishment.

"This indeed was a very difficult task. I am happy that we could get Shantabai involved too in our task."

"Mind you, this certainly is not the end, but a *beginning,* I might add. There are all those people out there, who need to be aware of this deadly disease. As I always say, *ignorance about this disease is deadlier than the disease itself.* It generates fear, which in turn slaughters hope, and then the whole scenario turns ugly, not just for the breast cancer patient but for her whole family."

"Well, that was the reason we held all those fora; for families, for teenagers, even for the husbands alone." Anila says. "Malti volunteering her bungalow has been a big boon. That was why we could conduct all those various events for different groups." She further adds.

"Yes, I agree. However, now that hundreds of people are responding to our efforts of inculcating awareness with some necessary medical and scientific information about breast cancer, I think we need a place even bigger than Malti's bungalow. What do you all say?" Dr. Sudha asks them all.

"Yes, we are on an excellent track for all this work; it is gaining good momentum, so it does need a much larger space." Malti agrees.

"We also need at least one large room that is totally dedicated to conducting the Visualization Technique on patients." Shantabai says.

"And not just a large room, but a large room with all the proper amenities to provide right atmosphere for conducting this technique." Kiran says, with a bit of sheepish smile.

Everyone looks at her and smiles, for, they all know that she was the most reluctant of all to participate in this technique, but afterwards, was very much enthusiastic in attending it.

"How are you feeling, Kiran?" Anila asks her.

"I'm feeling very weak with all this medication, but my husband is very happy that I'm undergoing proper treatment; he is also happy that I meet you all and help you occasionally." Kiran answers matter-of-factly.

"Take lots of rest, dear, and continue visiting us only when you can, okay?" What else could Anila say to her?

"How are you spending your time besides the treatment and visits to Shantabai?" Malti asks her with total compassion in her voice.

"Actually, I have started reading children's books and then trying to enact each story for my son. That keeps me mentally occupied and my son loves it. He giggles a lot whenever I enact a story; that makes me forget all my pain and misery." Everyone is happy to hear Kiran's honest reply.

"You do like the 'enacting' part of our work too, don't you, dear?" Dr. Sudha asks her.

Kiran nods heartily.

"Talking about enacting, I think the enacting that Shantabai and Malti have been doing – Shantabai taking the role of 'cancer' and conversing with Malti as the cancer patient - is simply phenomenal." Anila says and everyone claps gently for them.

"I wish to give kudos to Sheila too; she is one fine inspiration to many women with her personal story. You see, people have a hard time believing that beautiful, successful women could also have medical problems, isn't it?" Dr. Sudha says, giving Sheila a very appreciative look.

"Yes, very true." Malti says.

"People tend to forget that beautiful, successful models are also normal human beings like them, with all kinds of physical and mental problems, right?"

Sheila states seriously and everyone nods.

Their discussion continues at length about how a larger space could be acquired for their work, preferably annexed to the existing Cancer Center of the city, so that the work of awareness of breast cancer could be done on a much larger scale, right there on the premises of the medical treatment, when Malti suddenly looks at Dr. Sudha and poses a question.

"Dr. Sudha, I have never asked you one question that has been on my mind ever since I got involved in conducting the 'women's' fora and what I noticed in them." Malti asks.

"What is it, Malti?"

"Technically, cancer to any part of the body is bad, and if it is terminal, it could kill the person, right? But I noticed that when a woman is diagnosed especially with *breast cancer*, it is very frightening to her; cancer of her breast is devastating to her. Why is that?"

"A good question, Malti. I also want to know, Dr. Sudha. What is it about *breast cancer* that frightens a woman the most?" Anila says.

"I agree totally. When I was to undergo surgery and lose my breast, I was completely devastated. I am a singer, so I should be more concerned about a throat cancer, but I felt completely destroyed when I found out that it was *breast cancer*. I don't understand this." Tanuja says, although there has been a limit on her singing career because of her breast cancer.

"Yes, yes. Even I was devastated when I had that stupid bilateral preventative mastectomy. There is no exception to this. Why?" Sheila says, although she is reaping the profits of her new 'figure' that she has gained after the plastic surgery.

"Yes, ladies, I am listening to you all and I agree totally to what you are saying. This question had turned into a puzzle for me too for some time. I was thinking constantly about this puzzle when one day the answer came to me, almost as a revelation." Dr. Sudha focuses her look on all of them, one by one, while talking.

"The answer entails significance of two factors in a woman's life. They are, a woman's attitude towards her breasts and secondly, their importance to her own identity as a woman. And the reason for the significance of these two factors, according to my judgment of course is; a woman goes through many roles in her life; that of a daughter, a sister, a friend, a neighbor, a wife or a lover and a mother.

Of all these roles, she adores and enjoys two roles the most, that of a wife or a lover and that of a mother! And both these roles have a very close relationship with her breasts. Her two breasts, that give her a satiated feeling of utmost erotic pleasures in romantic love-making with her partner, also give her the maximum pleasure of total contentment and the utmost maternal pleasures when she nurses her infant. There is that special relationship she has with her breasts. And when this very part of her body is attacked by cancer, it seems as if a tornado has hit her and shaken her whole being from inside out."

All the women are listening to Dr. Sudha intently.

"I have noticed this fact not just here in India, but also in Canada when I was working there. I have seen that a woman's whole emotional equilibrium is lost due to this disease, be that a woman in a country of openness and freedom like Canada or of old traditions and customs, like India. Not just that, I could safely infer that for a woman of any age, young or old, breast cancer stirs her completely emotionally."

"Could it also be the fear of loss of self-esteem and femininity, Dr. Sudha?" Sheila asks.

"Oh, absolutely, Sheila. In your case, you were afraid that after the bilateral surgery, no one will marry you and you could never have children, right? You see ladies, the incapability of fulfilling the accustomed roles that women feel, and that coupled with possible end of life in sight, causes acute mental anguish."

Dr. Sudha is trying to answer all their questions and they look satisfied with her explanation.

"I am so very happy that Dr. Sudha is also integrating psychotherapy as an important part of cancer treatment, especially the visualization technique." Shantabai looks at Dr. Sudha, and says further, "When a doctor, a cancer specialist like her promotes the fact that *'the body-mind connection is real'*, people believe it." Shantabai compliments Dr. Sudha.

In turn, she thanks Shantabai heartily.

All five women listen to both Dr. Sudha and Shantabai with dedicated attention.

"Now, as I express my sincere thanks to all of you wonderful ladies for this meeting. I also extend my profound compliments to all of you – Anila, Malti, Tanuja, Kiran and Sheila. You all have climbed to the summit of recovery with your tremendous efforts in your uphill battle.

I realize that each one of you has a summit with a definition of its own; however, the fact is that *you did reach it.* I feel very, very proud of you all, indeed!"

**

It has been almost five years now.

After climbing to 'the summit of victory' over their malady of breast cancer, the five women did not sit quietly. They initiated to create, with full zest, a Support Group for women with breast cancer with the help of Dr. Sudha and Shantabai.

And the idea has caught on, blossoming into a phenomenon!

Each Cancer Centre of the country has assigned a special area solely dedicated to conducting 'Group Therapy' for all cancer patients, especially breast cancer patients.

The awareness about this disease is spreading in leaps and bounds across the country; *it is no longer a 'taboo'*!

People are supporting the cause wholeheartedly and families of the breast cancer patients understand fully what a woman goes through when victimized by this deadly disease. They are genuinely thankful to these five women - Anila, Tanuja, Malti, Kiran and Sheila – for their 'Himalayan' efforts for bringing the intricate scientific knowledge of this disease into their homes, thereby eradicating ignorance altogether. The 'everyday', simple women of yesterday have become their heroes today!

Anila

"Annie, I will be back at the usual time…"

Manav enters the veranda twirling his car keys in his hand. He is all ready to go to the club for playing his favorite sport of badminton.

He is dressed up meticulously in white shorts, white tee-shirt, white socks and white wrist band on his right hand.

Anila is sitting in the veranda with her mobile phone, ready to make a few important calls.

"Okay dear, don't be late, I'll be waiting for you for dinner?" Anila says.

"Annie, do you want me to pick up something on my way home?" Manav asks while putting on his white canvas shoes.

"No, it's okay." Anila answers.

"Alright then, see you later, my sweet Annie. " Manav picks up his racket and leaves.

Manav is in a great mood; he has been requested to join the college as a Professor Emeritus in the department of English.

And he is going to, for that's his passion, and not just profession.

Things are back to the very same as *before!*

Manav usually walks in, after the games, with Jasmine flowers in his hands.

He loves to put them in her hair himself.

Anila loves it too.

She is the backbone of the 'Support Group' and is super busy with the Support Centre activities.

She is ready to accomplish a huge mound of work right now, so that hundreds of women like her will also be on their climb to victory!

Tanuja

"...kaun karat tori binati piyarava..."

A young singer of classical music, barely twenty years of age, is sitting in the singer's specific pose on the stage and singing. Clad in a bright pink sari and a matching blouse, which makes her youthful looks even more charming, she is stringing a Tambura gently with her fingers. With her eyes closed, she looks totally engrossed in her singing.

The hall is packed to capacity with music connoisseurs and everyone in the audience is swaying with her music, the whole audience looking like a meadow swayed by gentle wind.

'So young and yet such a Mastery in classical music...' Many people in the audience clearly have this expression on their faces.

Yes, this is Sangeeta, Tanuja's first born child. With this concert, she is fulfilling her mother's dream of seeing the daughter sing in front of a knowledgeable audience someday. That day has arrived today; and her dream is being materialized.

Sangeeta opens her eyes momentarily and looks at the audience and smiles. Then her gaze moves to the very first row and fixes on one person, Tanuja Bose. She is sitting on a soft cushioned chair, wrapped up in a *Pashmina* shawl(spun from cashmere wools). Sangeeta smiles again and closes her eyes, ready to resume her singing again. In that brief moment, she has read the expressions on her mother's face, expression of satisfaction and extreme joy.

This is all the result of a strong determination coupled with tremendous hard work of Sangeeta, Shruti, Ajoy and most importantly Tanuja, the breast cancer survivor. With Dr. Sudha's help in medical treatment, Shantabai's help in developing psychological strength, and with the help and encouragement of her own family and friends like Anila, Malti and others in the Support group, she has been able to achieve what she had otherwise imagined to be impossible.

Tanuja is sure that her daughter would be the nightingale of the country of tomorrow, as she was, of yesterday!

Tanuja is listening to Sangeeta and while doing so, continuously shedding tears. They are tears of contentment, of pride, of fruition, and above all, tears of extreme happiness; she did climb the difficult mountain and reached the summit of recovery of her breast cancer and now, she is standing tall among many like her, rejoicing the victory after the climb!

Malti

"*Ma*, did you get the list for the party completed?" Kirti is sitting on the patio and asking her mother with a shout as Malti is sitting in her bedroom, preparing the list.

"I'm almost done dear…" Malti answers from her bedroom, but Kirti can't hear her.

"Go to your grandmother's room and see if she has finished her list. Run…" Kirti tells her three year old son.

The little boy runs towards Malti's bedroom and hollers for his grandmother.

Malti gets up from her table, walks towards the door, picks him up and starts kissing his cheeks and hugging him. Just then, his little cousin also comes running towards them. Malti picks her up too. Malti loves the fact that they need their grandmother much more than they need their mother.

Just then, the telephone rings. Malti takes the telephone and starts talking and discussing something. After a few minutes, she hangs up.

"Is everything okay, *Ma*?" Kirti asks.

"Yes, yes. I have given my house for all the activities of the Support group until we find a much larger space within the local Cancer Centre."

"Really, *Ma*?" Aarti asks.

"Yes, really…" Malti says with full conviction.

"That's commendable, *Ma*."

Both her daughters look very much impressed with Malti's generosity.

"Honestly, *Ma*, we don't know what we could have done without you when we got married and when we had our babies. Really, *Ma*." Kirti tells Malti with a genuine feeling of appreciation.

"My dear daughters, I am so glad you both feel that way. Believe me, I need you too very badly, even more than you think."

They both know how Malti's need '*to be needed*' was costing her, her own life; they also know how her climb to recovery had started with total reluctance, but then, they saw how Malti reached the summit of recovery, after all, and now?

Now, she is helping many, many women like herself , to be with her on the climb to victory!

Sheila

"Okay, so you have lost your hair due to chemotherapy. But that does not mean you should hide away from the world until your hair grows back..." Sheila is talking to a small group of women in one of the sessions.

Since the day Sheila talked openly about herself, her experiences and her life story in the 'Women's Forum', she has instantly become very popular among all the members of the Support Group. That includes men as well.

"But Sheila, it is almost impossible for me to go out like this..." One woman takes off the black scarf from her head and complains while patting her hairless head with her hand.

"Yah... I wear a nice sari and a matching blouse, I wear nice bangles and then tie this ugly black scarf on my head. I can't do that..." A second woman says.

"The black scarf looks kind of repulsive, you know..." Another woman says and the rest of the women agree with her.

"Listen, going out without a scarf is impossible, and wearing a black scarf may be repulsive too; but is that the only way you can cover your heads? With a black scarf?" Sheila asks them.

"Then what do you do?" Sheila has become an expert for all the questions and tips relating to beauty for breast cancer victims.

"You may want to change the color of the scarf sometimes, matching your dresses, saris, or whatever you are wearing. There are beautiful scarves available in all kinds of material like silk, tissue, fine cotton, etc. in the market. Go to the shopping places, look for the ones you like and buy them."

The women listen to her intently.

"There is another alternative too. You could use wigs." Sheila suggests.

"Oh, but the wigs are very expensive."

"Yah, they are kind of pricy..." Many women complain.

"As it is, a lot of money has been spent in my medical treatment; if I start spending for wigs and all such things, it would be almost impossible for me to make the ends meet, Sheila." One woman says.

"Who is going to look at us any way?" Another woman asks a genuine question.

"I'll be happy if my *husband* looks at me..." A third woman says with a slight complaining tone in her voice.

"Yah, we are not models..." Some of the women laugh. However, there is an undercurrent of a bit of a sarcasm coupled with a bit of sorrow in their laughter. At least, Sheila feels it that way.

"Ladies, ladies, you don't have to be a model to want to look good. It is not necessary that you should be in the fashion industry or some such field and then only you are permitted to take care of yourself and look good. Let's assume that no one looks at you, not even your husbands, but *you do*. Don't you? Aren't *you* important to *yourself?*"

Then she walks towards the window and as if looking outside and talking to the trees, says,

"It took nerves of steel for me to come to that decision of surgically removing both my natural breasts. That was the only viable option for me to live free of fear of getting breast cancer."

She then turns towards the women and looking at them face to face, says,

"But then I told myself, *'what didn't kill me made me stronger!'* After I got the reconstructive surgery and saw that my new breasts added a big plus to my figure, I didn't just stop there. I started working hard to get every inch of my body beautiful."

She puts on a big smile and says, "Ladies, I owe it to me, the *new me*, just as you owe it to the *new you - the brave survivors of breast cancer!*"

"But Sheila…" Someone is about to ask her something. "I know, I know. You are going to say, 'we are not models.' And I know you are not, but does that mean you neglect how you look? Neglect your *desire* to look good? Aren't *you living* still?"

Then she walks closer towards them and says, "You are women; you *want* to look good, because, when you look good, you *feel* good too. And…" Sheila gives herself a few seconds to look at all the women and then says,

"…that's one more sure way of showing your family, friends, and the whole world that *you have beaten your cancer!*"

Anila and Dr. Sudha always thought that Sheila added that extra pizzazz to the work of building a Support group; therefore, she was taken in as a core group member and was assigned a special title that Anila thought of - 'Patient Advocate' of the Support group!

And she has been fulfilling her role simply beautifully!

She is helping the women bring back their self-esteem; more importantly, she is encouraging them to look beautiful even during the dreadful climb to victory!

Kiran

"Kittu, what do you want for a snack in your recess time, son?" Raj is asking Kittu as he is getting ready for his school in the morning. *Amma* is helping him with his clothes, but he seems to be more interested in looking at the pictures of bears in the book.

"Krishnadev, get ready fast, dear..." *Amma* keeps on saying and he is co-operating reluctantly.

Finally when he is ready, *Amma* and he come out of his room.

"Come on, let's go..." Raj Prakash puts some snack in Kittu's little backpack and holds his hand to go out.

"Wait Papa, I want to say 'bye' to mummy." He runs towards his mother.

Kiran is sitting in an armchair, looking very frail and weak, all wrapped up in a woolen shawl, but she has a bright smile on her face.

"Come here, my Kittu..." She says, extending her hands to her son.

He practically buries himself in her arms.

"Have a good day, okay love! I will be waiting for you to come home and tell me everything about your school."

He pulls himself out of her arms and picking up the backpack, which is a blue colored bag with a huge picture of a teddy bear on it that Kiran herself had picked up for him, he just nods hard and runs to his father.

Raj says 'good bye' to Kiran and *Amma*, and they set out to walk to Kittu's school.

Kittu's school is at a walking distance from their house.

This has been their daily schedule; every morning Kiran gives her son a big bear hug before he goes to school and in the afternoon, she slowly walks to the balcony with *Amma*'s help and sees her son walk towards home from school.

With Dr. Sudha's excellent cancer treatment, which Kiran was finally convinced to take, and with Shantabai's psychotherapy, she could give a fierce fight to her rare type of breast cancer.

Her cancer has entered the terminal stage. She has been in this battle for almost six years now. Her surviving five years longer than what is recorded for such a deadly disease, has been commended in the entire medical community.

The happiest thing is that every single day, for more than two years now, she sees her son leave for school, and receives him after school; something that she very much desired for, but never expected.

"Daddy, do you know the story of a huge bear that mummy told me?"

Raj just shook his head.

"I will tell you that story tonight. It's so funny…"

Kittu starts talking about the story and chuckling to himself intermittently. He is telling his father how his mother, while pretending to be the big bear, has even acted up some of that part of the story.

As they approach the school, Raj gives a 'goodbye' hug to his son; Kittu starts walking towards his school through the yard.

He turns and looks back at his father one more time and waves at him with a smile. Raj waves back and stares at his little figure walking away.

"Did you hear it, Rani?" In his mind, Raj is talking to his beloved wife, Kiran, while looking at Kittu walking to the school.

"Kittu says that he will tell me the same story that you told him, and enact it too, the way you did for him. This is exactly what I was telling you, and fortunately, you cooperated. You took medical treatment to defeat your breast cancer with a positive attitude, and see; instead of just one year, you already have almost six full years with me and your son."

Raj's monologue within his mind with his wife is going on, on a full speed.

"Rani, you are now carved in our son's memory permanently; we'll be talking about you all the time. And that way, you will be *with me all the time.*"

Intense emotions overpower Raj.

He continues, "Rani, you *won the battle!* You really did. You may not be on the top of the mountain, but whatever climb you could do, that has achieved our goal, and that to me is 'victory'; I am so very proud of you, my darling wife!"

He quickly wipes his eyes and starts walking fast towards his bank.

———————

Climb to Victory Over Breast Cancer

About Kumbhakarna

One of the two prominent epics in India, named Ramayana, entails a story of a prince named Rama and a demon named Ravana, who was a king of Lanka. When Rama's wife, Sita, was kidnapped by Ravana, Rama declared a war against Ravana and defeated him. In that war, Ravana's younger brother, named Kumbhakarna, himself a vicious demon, helped Ravana fight against Rama.

The characteristic of Kumbhakarna was that he slept all the time, and therefore unlike all other demons, harmed no one. In the entire story of Ramayana, he woke up only once to help Ravana fight the war against Rama.

Otherwise known to be a harmless demon, as soon as Kumbhakarna woke up from his deep sleep, his demonic actions started and he killed many people.

Ever since then, the name Kumbhakarna has been synonymous with sleeping endlessly, but doing demonic actions, if awakened!

Hence, the advice to all - 'Never wake up Kumbhakarna!

About Rama

In the epic Ramayana, the story tells us that when Kumbhakarna woke up from his deep sleep, he started destroying and destructing everything, and killing people. No one could conquer him. Finally, Rama took an aim with his bow and arrow, and with *just one arrow*, killed the demon.

Scientific Information
(Pertaining to the five cases discussed in this book)

What is Cancer?

Cancer is not one disease. The word "cancer" actually refers to **a** collection of **more than 100** different **diseases,** with wide-ranging **and** varied characteristics that may call for wide-ranging **and** varied treatments. However, it is a fact that it is *a disease that is resulted from uncontrolled growth and division of abnormal cells in the body.*

Cells in the body normally divide (reproduce) only when new cells are needed. Sometimes cells divide for no reason, creating a mass of tissue called a tumor. Tumors can be benign (non cancerous) or malignant (cancerous).

In most of the cancers, a tissue cell becomes abnormal and reproduces without control or order, forming a malignant tumor. Cancer cells can break off from the original tumor, travel to other parts of the body, and form new tumors. This process is called metastasis. Metastasis is a late stage of cancer.

Cancer is a Genetic Disease

Oncologists and Researchers have firmly stated now that *Cancer is a genetic disease, caused by abnormal gene function.*

It is caused by changes in genes that control the way cells grow and multiply. It is basically a disease of uncontrolled cell division that is caused by abnormal function of genes in the patient's body. It is this abnormal gene function that impacts the cancer cells to behave differently than the normal cells in the patient's body.

General Information about the science of Genetics

Genetics is the study of how living things receive common traits from previous generations. Our bodies are made up of trillions of cells grouped to form tissues and organs. In each cell, there is present a molecule called DNA[13]. These traits are described by the genetic information carried by DNA. The instructions for constructing and operating an organism are contained in the organism's DNA. Every living thing on earth has DNA in its cells.

A gene is a hereditary unit consisting of DNA that occupies a specific spot on a chromosome and determines the characteristic in an organism.

Genes are passed on from parent to child and are an important part of what determines the physical appearance and also behavior.

What are Genes?

Genes are segments of DNA that contain instructions on how to make the proteins the body needs in order to function. They govern hereditary traits, such as skin color, hair color, eye color, bone and facial structures and height, as well as susceptibility (meaning likelihood of being affected) to certain diseases, such as cancer.

---

[13] Deoxyribonucleic acid

Genes also tell the cells when to grow, work, divide and die. Normally, our cells follow these instructions and we stay healthy. The genes that one is born with, are in every cell of one's body.

We now understand that genes serve two major roles in cancer: some contribute to the development of cancer and others stop cancer from developing or growing.

Genes that can cause cancer are called Oncogenes. Genes that stop or suppress cancer growth are called *tumor suppressor genes* (TSG).

Even if a person is born with healthy genes, some of them can become changed (mutated) over the course of his or her life. This explains why most cancers are not inherited but arise from gene mutations a person acquires during life. The older a person gets, the more gene mutations that person may accumulate. This is why cancer risk increases with age. In contrast, cancers that are due to heredity tend to occur earlier in life than cancers of the same type that are not due to heredity. Only about 5% to 10% of all cancers are due to heredity. *It is important to note that the cancer itself is not inherited, but the abnormal gene that could cause the cancer is what is inherited.*

What is Breast Cancer?

A breast is made up of three main parts: lobules, ducts, and connective tissue. The lobules are the glands that produce milk, the ducts are tubes that carry milk to the nipple, and the connective tissue (which consists of fibrous and fatty tissue) surrounds and holds everything together. Breast cancer can begin in any of these different parts of the breast, but most breast cancers are known to begin in the ducts or the lobules.

When the cancer cells begin in the ducts and then grow outside the ducts into other parts of the breast tissue, it is called *Invasive ductal carcinoma*. Also, when the cancer cells begin in the lobules and then spread from the lobules to the breast tissues, it is called *Invasive lobular carcinoma*. These invasive cancer cells can also spread to other parts of the body. One of the uncommon types of breast cancer includes inflammatory Breast Cancer (IBC)[14].

Where does Breast Cancer form?

Breast cancers may develop in the glandular tissue of the breast, specifically in the milk ducts and the milk lobules. These ducts and lobules are located in all parts of the breast tissue, including tissue just under the skin. The breast tissue extends from the collarbone to the lower rib margin, and from the middle of the chest, around the side and under the arm.

In a mastectomy[15], it is necessary to remove tissue from just beneath the skin down to the chest wall and around the borders of the chest. However, even with very thorough and delicate surgical techniques, it is impossible to remove every milk duct and lobule, given the extent of the breast tissue and the location of these glands just beneath the skin.

What are the symptoms of Breast Cancer?

Breast cancer can have different symptoms for different people. Most don't notice any signs at all. The most common symptom is a lump in the breast or armpit. Other symptoms include skin changes, pain, a nipple that pulls inward, and unusual discharge from your nipple.

---

[14] Information about IBC is given later in this chapter.
[15] Surgery to remove the breast is called a mastectomy.

Common Symptoms of Breast cancer include:

- A lump in the breast or underarm that doesn't go away. This is often the first symptom of breast cancer. The doctor can usually see a lump on a mammogram long before a woman can see or feel it.

- Swelling in the armpit or near your collarbone. This could mean **breast cancer** has spread to **lymph nodes** in that area. Swelling may start before a woman can feel a lump.

- A woman must inform the doctor as soon as she notices it.

- Pain and tenderness, although lumps don't usually hurt. Some may cause a prickly feeling.

- A flat or indented area on the **breast** that could happen because of a tumor.

- **Breast changes** such as a difference in the size, contour, texture, or temperature of the breast.

- Changes in the nipple, as stated below:
    1. Pulls inward
    2. Is dimpled
    3. Burns
    4. Itches
    5. Develops sores

- Unusual Nipple Discharge. It could be clear, bloody, or of another color.

- A marble-like area under the skin that feels different from any other part of either breast.

How is Breast Cancer diagnosed?

The following tests and procedures are generally used to diagnose breast cancer.

They are:

- **Breast exam.** The doctor will check both the breasts and the lymph nodes in the woman's armpit, feeling for any lumps or other abnormalities.

- **Mammogram.** A mammogram is an X-ray of the breast. Mammograms are commonly used to screen for breast cancer. If an abnormality is detected on a screening mammogram, the doctor may recommend a diagnostic mammogram to further evaluate that abnormality.

- **Breast ultrasound.** Ultrasound uses sound waves to produce images of structures deep within the body. Ultrasound may be used to determine whether a new breast lump is a solid mass or a fluid-filled cyst.

- **Removing a sample of breast cells for testing (biopsy).** A biopsy is the only definitive way to make a diagnosis of breast cancer. During a biopsy, your doctor uses a specialized needle device guided by X-ray or another imaging test to extract a core of tissue from the suspicious area. Often, a small metal marker is left at the site within your breast so the area can be easily identified on future imaging tests. Biopsy samples are sent to a laboratory for analysis where experts determine whether the cells are cancerous. A biopsy sample is also analyzed to determine the type of cells involved in the breast cancer, the aggressiveness (grade) of the cancer, and whether the cancer cells have hormone receptors or other receptors that may influence your treatment options.

- **Breast magnetic resonance imaging (MRI).** An MRI machine uses a magnet and radio waves to create pictures of the interior of your breast. Before a breast MRI, you receive an injection of dye. Unlike other types of imaging tests, an MRI doesn't use radiation to create the images.

Other tests and procedures may be used depending on the patient's situation.

Staging of Breast Cancer

The extent of cancer is called Staging; it classifies a cancer based on how much cancer there is in the body and where it is when first diagnosed. Information from various tests is used to find out what part of the breast has cancer, the size of the tumor, whether the cancer has spread from where it first started and where the cancer has spread.

Classification or staging of Cancer describes the severity of an individual's cancer. Knowing a cancer's stage helps the doctor develop a treatment plan and estimate the likely outcome or course of the disease and also the chance of recovery or recurrence.

For breast cancer, there are 5 stages – stage 0 followed by stages 1 to 4. Often the stages 1 to 4 are written as the Roman numerals I, II, III and IV. Generally, the higher the stage number, the more the cancer has spread.

Therefore, 0 indicates cancer that is non-invasive or contained within the milk ducts and Stage IV breast cancer, also called metastatic breast cancer, indicates cancer that has spread to other areas of the body.

Stage III breast cancer is locally advanced. Stage IV breast cancer is cancer that has spread to other organs. Once the doctors have diagnosed the patient's breast cancer, they work to establish the extent (stage) of the patient's cancer.

Tests and procedures used to stage the breast cancer may include the following:

- Blood tests, such as a complete blood count

- Mammogram of the other breast to look for signs of cancer
- Breast MRI
- Bone scan
- Computerized tomography (CT) scan
- Positron emission tomography (PET) scan

Not all patients need all of the above tests and procedures. The doctor selects the appropriate tests based on specific circumstances, and new symptoms if any, that the patient may be experiencing.

In most of the cases, the patient's healthcare team / doctors team uses the stage of the breast cancer to plan treatment and estimate the outcome (the patient's prognosis).

What is the Treatment for Breast Cancer?

When a woman is diagnosed with breast cancer, the healthcare team will create a treatment plan just for her. It will be based on her health and specific information about her cancer. When deciding which treatments to offer, her healthcare team will consider the following:

- her overall health
- the stage of her cancer
- if she has reached menopause
- the hormone receptor status of the cancer
- the HER2[16] status of her cancer
- the risk that the cancer will come back, or recur (for early stage breast cancers)

---

[16] HER2- Human Epidermal growth factor Receptor 2 – this is a protein that promotes the breast cancer cells to grow and multiply.

Climb to Victory Over Breast Cancer

What is Fine Needle Biopsy?[17]

A biopsy is a procedure to remove a piece of tissue or a sample of cells from the body so that it can be tested in a laboratory. A Needle biopsy is a general term that is often used to describe inserting a special needle through the skin to collect cells from a suspicious area.

The doctor marks the precise area where the local anesthesia is administered, to numb the area being biopsied to minimize the pain. A sharp hollow needle is pierced into the numb area, to withdraw some fluid into it. It is then spread it onto a couple of glass slides for microscope examination. The slides are then stained sent to a laboratory for analysis. The sample may be chemically treated or frozen and sliced into very thin sections. The sections are placed on glass slides, stained to enhance contrast and studied under a microscope.

The biopsy results help the doctor determine whether the cells are cancerous. If the cells are cancerous, the results can tell *where* the cancer originated —the type of cancer.

A biopsy also helps the doctor determine how aggressive the patient's cancer is — the cancer's grade. The grade is sometimes expressed as a number on a scale of 1 to 4 and is determined by how cancer cells look under the microscope.

Low-grade (grade I) cancers are generally the least aggressive and high-grade (grade IV) cancers are generally the most aggressive. This information may help guide treatment options.

Just like with all **cancers**, an early diagnosis of breast cancer may help increase a woman's survival rate. According to the American Cancer Society, women with localized breast cancer — where it has not spread to any other part of the body — have a 99% chance of living for at least five years after diagnosis.

---

[17] This is discussed through the characters, named Tanuja, Malti and Kiran in this book.

The latest fast and reliable method of diagnosis

There may be nothing more vital for the thousands of patients left worried and wondering following an abnormal screening mammography or clinical breast examination. However, scientists have a *developed a blood test* that may soon provide exactly that[18]. The test screens blood samples for evidence of the disease, quickly providing an answer that previously meant waiting for diagnostic mammograms, ultrasounds and biopsies.

Breast Cancer and Heredity[19]

The greatest risk factor for breast cancer is heredity—having a mother, aunt, sister, or daughter who has breast cancer. A woman is at even greater risk if her relative developed breast cancer before age 40.

Most of the time, different types of cancer that occur, are linked with common family habits such as cigarette smoking, which can damage the genes in the lungs, throat, mouth, and several other organs. However, studies have shown that certain cancers can occur to excess in some families. For example, a woman whose mother, sister, or daughter (first-degree relatives) has had breast cancer, she is about twice as likely to develop breast cancer as a woman whose close female relatives have not had breast cancer.

What is the Breast Cancer gene?

Each cell in your body carries about 100,000 genes. Genes control how the cell functions, such as telling it when to divide and when to grow. About 5-10% of all breast cancers are due

---

[18] Initially developed through a research program at the University of Calgary, Alberta, Canada, this test promises a great hope.

[19] This is discussed through the character, named Sheila in this book.

to Genetic reasons. Genes that can cause cancer are called Oncogenes[20], and genes that stop or suppress cancer growth are called *tumor suppressor genes* (TSG)[21].

For unknown reasons, a gene within a cell can become faulty, change how the cell works, and cause abnormal cells to grow uncontrolled. More than one faulty gene has been found in women with breast cancer.

A parent can pass on a copy of a faulty gene to his or her children. If a person inherits a faulty gene found to cause breast cancer, he/she has a much higher risk of developing breast cancer.

BRCA1 and BRCA2[22]

These are tumor suppressor genes, which mean that when they function normally, they keep cells from growing rapidly, thereby, tumors from forming.

These are the two best-known breast cancer susceptibility genes. Individuals who carry an inherited mutation in the breast cancer, *BRCA1* and *BRCA2* genes have a significant risk of developing breast and ovarian cancer over the course of their lifetime. Mutations of the BRCA1 gene are linked to breast and ovarian cancer. BRCA2 gene mutations are related to a higher risk of breast cancer, as well as pancreatic and ovarian cancer, in both men and women. Scientists have demonstrated that mutations of BRCA1 and BRCA2 give rise to increased risk of breast cancer. If a woman is tested positive for either BRCA1 or BRCA2 mutation, she is at high risk for breast and ovarian cancer, including other cancers like colorectal cancer. There is a 50% risk of genetically transmitting

---

[20] I have named them as *Kumbhakarna* in this book.

[21] I have named them as *Rama* in this book.

[22] This is discussed through the character, named Sheila in this book.

the mutation from the parent to the children. However, it is observed that only about 5% breast cancers belong to this category where a specific genetic mutation can be identified. Apart from identifiable genetic mutation that increases the risk of breast cancer, presence of a family member with breast cancer would increase the risk of development of breast cancer in a woman. Unlike patients who are carriers of well-recognized genetic mutations like BRCA1 or BRCA2, these women do not have any evidence of genetic alterations that would increase the risk of breast cancer. The increased breast cancer risk in this group of women may be related to a group of genes rather than a single gene mutation.

These genetic alterations as a group may have increased predisposition to development of breast cancer. It is also difficult to separate environmental factors in these patients. The role of environmental factors is difficult to quantify in this situation and how much of this increased risk is caused by common environmental factors is difficult to judge.

Could Breast Cancer be *predicted* ahead of its diagnosis?

Breast cancer is generally diagnosed when a patient reports having some kind of symptoms of the condition and/or the cancer is found during an exam and imaging tests, such as a mammogram, ultrasound, or MRI.

However, recent studies show that *blood proteins change up to two years before* a woman's breast cancer diagnosis.

Therefore, there is a reason to believe that scientists can develop these findings into an *early-detection blood test* for women at high risk for developing breast cancer.

What are the risk factors of Breast Cancer for a woman?

If you are a woman, you are at risk. (Men can also develop breast cancer, but this is rare.) You may be more likely to develop breast cancer if you have one or more risk factors, but risk factors do not cause breast cancer. However, not having a risk factor does not mean that you will not get breast cancer.

In many cases, it's not known why a woman develops breast cancer. In fact, 70 percent of all women with breast cancer have no known risk factor.

The greatest risk factor of breast cancer for a woman is heredity—having a mother, aunt, sister, or daughter who has breast cancer. A woman is at even greater risk if her relative developed breast cancer before age 40.

A woman's risk for breast cancer also increases as she grows older. Just to quote the observation: A woman who is 35 years old has a 1-in-622 chance of developing breast cancer, yet a woman who is 60 years old has a 1-in-24 chance of developing breast cancer.

Other risk factors include:

- Having cancer in one breast (more likely to develop cancer in the other breast)
- Late menopause (after age 55)
- Getting your period early in life (before age 12)
- Having your first child after age 30
- Never giving birth
- Being obese after menopause
- Taking hormone replacement therapy (HRT)

Race (breast cancer occurs more frequently in Caucasian women than in Hispanic, Asian, or African-American women)

Do most women with Breast Cancer have a family history of the disease?

No. Women with a family history of breast cancer account for only 20-30% of all women with the disease. If a woman has a relative who has breast cancer, she has an increased risk. She should keep a careful watch of her breast health. Still, 75% of women with a family history of breast cancer will not develop the disease.

Women without a family history of breast cancer are also at risk of developing breast cancer, especially if they are over age 60.

Fibroadenoma[23]

A fibroadenoma is a solid breast lump. This breast lump is not cancer. A fibroadenoma happens most often between ages 15 and 35. But it can be found at any age in anyone who has periods. Fibroadenoma are common breast lumps.

Does having a benign breast condition mean having a higher risk?

Benign breast conditions mean breast conditions that are not cancerous, meaning, breast that have cysts or lumps. A typical example of a solid breast lump is fibroadenoma. This breast lump is usually not cancer and they are found in women at any age or in women who have periods. They rarely increase the risk of breast cancer. Some women have a condition called hyperplasia which means excessive cell growth. This condition, otherwise benign, is known to increase the risk only slightly.

---

[23] This is discussed through the character, named Anila, in this book.

Climb to Victory Over Breast Cancer

What are the ways one can protect from Breast Cancer?

- Examine your breasts each month
- Get a mammogram, especially after age 40
- Have your breast examined by a health care provider/ doctor at least once a year.

Is Stress related to Breast Cancer?[24]

Scientists have found that stress doubles a woman's risk of developing breast cancer. The reason that is given for this link is that if someone is excessively stressed, they may suppress their immune system with stress, and that may affect the hormonal balance in the breast. That may be the link between stress and breast cancer. Recently, scientists have found that excessive stress doubles a woman's risk of developing breast cancer.

Breast cancer is an extremely complex disease and it is difficult to pin-point one single risk factor, such as a stressful period in one's life, being directly linked with the disease developing. Further research is needed before any direct association between stress and increased breast cancer risk is confirmed. Having stated that, however, it has been observed that women diagnosed with metastasized breast cancer, who have endured previous traumatic or stressful events, see their cancer *recur* nearly twice as fast as other women.

What is Metastatic Breast Cancer?

Metastatic breast cancer occurs when the cancer spreads from the breast to another part of the body. Symptoms and treatment for this stage of breast cancer are different to those

---

[24] This is discussed through the character of Malti, in this book.

of the earlier stages. Doctors may also refer to metastatic breast cancer as advanced breast cancer or stage IV breast cancer.

For example, when the breast cancer spreads to the lungs, it is termed as breast cancer with *lung metastasis*. Here, the patient has persistent cough, shortness of breath, difficulty in breathing, wheezing, and coughing up blood, clearly pointing to the cancerous breast cells spreading to the lungs[25].

Prognostic value of depression and anxiety on breast cancer occurrence, recurrence and mortality

Depression and anxiety[26] are common comorbidities in breast cancer patients. Whether depression and anxiety are associated with breast cancer progression or mortality is not yet clear.

Independent studies show that depression is associated with a 24% increase in the risk of cancer recurrence, where the mean age of patients is less than 60 years. These studies assessed depression *before* the breast cancer diagnosis, and also *after* the breast cancer diagnosis.

The results showed that the prognostic impact of the depression was significant when depression was assessed *after* the breast cancer diagnosis.

Thus the above results confirm that depression is associated with a 17% increase in the risk of cancer *recurrence.*

In summary, the analysis confirms that depression, anxiety, and the combination of both are associated with increased recurrence and all-cause mortality in patients with breast cancer.

---

[25] This is discussed through the character of Tanuja in this book.
[26] This is discussed through the character of Malti in this book.

Climb to Victory Over Breast Cancer

What is Breast Conserving Therapy (BCT)[27]?

If breast cancer is detected in its early stage, doctors usually advice the Breast conserving therapy (BCT). This Therapy consists of removal of the lump from the breast, termed as *lumpectomy*, and a portion of the surrounding tissue.

Lumpectomy, followed by radiation and hormone therapy, is considered to be a safe, effective treatment for non-hereditary or sporadic forms of early breast cancer. However, for hereditary breast cancers, the use of BCT is controversial due to conflicting data about increased risk of recurrence in the treated breast and development of new tumors in the untreated breast.

Researchers, having performed a retrospective study evaluating over 16,000 women with early stage breast cancer have discovered that women electing BCT had the highest survival rate.

What is Inflammatory Breast Cancer (IBC)[28]?

Inflammatory breast cancer is a rare but very aggressive and invasive type of breast cancer in which the cancer cells block the lymph vessels in the skin of the breast. This type of breast cancer is called "inflammatory" because the breast often looks swollen and red, or "inflamed." It is unique because it does not present itself with a lump and therefore often is not detected by mammography or ultrasound.

Inflammatory breast cancer causes breast changes in the nipple and surrounding areas. Other symptoms include rapid increase in breast size, redness, persistent itching, skin hot to the touch. IBC often initially resembles metastasis, and is sometimes misdiagnosed as an insect bite.

---

[27] This is discussed through the character of Malti in this book.
[28] This is discussed through the character of Kiran, in this book.

Thankfully, IBC accounts for less than 5 percent of all breast cancer cases in the world. It tends to be diagnosed in younger women compared to non-IBC breast cancer. It occurs more frequently at a younger age in most of the women. Like the other types of breast cancer, IBC can occur in men too, but usually at an older age than in women. Inflammatory breast cancer is considered to be a locally advanced cancer — meaning it has spread from its point of origin to nearby tissue and possibly to nearby lymph nodes.

Some studies have shown that there is an association between family history of breast cancer and IBC, but more studies are needed to draw firm conclusions.

Inflammatory breast cancer is defined histologically by the presence of cancer cells in the sub- dermal lymphatic on skin biopsy. Diagnosis is done with an MRI or biopsy.

What are the symptoms of IBC?

Inflammatory breast cancer doesn't commonly form a lump, as occurs with other forms of breast cancer. Instead, signs and symptoms of inflammatory breast cancer include:

- Rapid change in the appearance of one breast, over the course of several weeks - redness, swelling, and warmth in the breast, often without a distinct lump in the breast.
- Thickness, heaviness or visible enlargement of one breast.
- Discoloration, giving the breast a red, purple, pink or bruised appearance.
- Unusual warmth of the affected breast.
- Dimpling or ridges on the skin of the affected breast, similar to an orange peel - the skin has ridges or appears pitted, which is caused by a buildup of fluid and swelling in the breast.

Climb to Victory Over Breast Cancer

- Tenderness, pain or aching.

- Enlarged lymph nodes under the arm, above the collarbone or below the collarbone.

- Flattening or turning inward of the nipple – appears inverted (facing inward).

These symptoms usually develop quickly, over a period of weeks or months. Swollen **lymph nodes** may also be present under the arm, above the collarbone, or in both places. However, it is important to note that these symptoms may also be signs of other conditions such as infection, injury, or other types of cancer.

How is IBC diagnosed?

Diagnosis of IBC is based primarily on the results of a doctor's **clinical** examination. Biopsy, mammogram, and breast **ultrasound** are used to confirm the diagnosis. IBC is classified as either stage IIIB or **stage IV breast cancer**.

Stage III breast cancer is locally advanced. Stage IV breast cancer is cancer that has spread to other organs. IBC tends to grow rapidly, and the physical appearance of the breast of patients with IBC is different from that of patients with other stage III breast cancers. IBC is an especially aggressive, locally advanced breast cancer.

All invasive breast cancers should be tested for HER2 either on the biopsy sample or when the tumor is removed with surgery.

How is IBC treated?

Immediately after the surgery to remove the breast (mastectomy), the following treatment consisting of chemotherapy, targeted therapy, surgery, radiation therapy and hormonal therapy, is used to treat IBC. Patients may also receive supportive care to help manage the side effects of cancer and its treatment. Chemotherapy is generally the first treatment for patients with IBC. Chemotherapy is systemic treatment which means that it affects cells throughout the body. The purpose of chemotherapy is to control or kill cancer cells, including those that may have spread to other parts of the body.

After chemotherapy, patients with IBC may undergo surgery and radiation therapy to the chest wall. Both radiation and surgery are local treatments that affect only cells in the tumor and its immediately surrounding area. The purpose of surgery is to remove the tumor from the body, while the purpose of radiation therapy is to destroy remaining cancer cells.

Breast Cancer Preventative Mastectomy[29]

In hopes of avoiding future disease, some women at very high risk of developing breast cancer elect to have both breasts surgically removed, a procedure called *bilateral prophylactic mastectomy*. A recent study suggests that bilateral prophylactic mastectomy reduces the risk of breast cancer by at least 95 percent in women who have a deleterious (disease-causing) mutation in the *BRCA1* gene or the *BRCA2* gene and by up to 90 percent in women who have a strong family history of breast cancer.

Here, the surgery aims to remove all breast tissue that potentially could develop breast cancer. Preventive breast cancer surgery also may be considered if a woman has already had breast cancer and is therefore at increased risk for developing the disease again in either breast.

---

[29] This is discussed through the character of Sheila, in this book.

Who should have bilateral prophylactic mastectomy?

Does this mean that every patient should consider breast cancer prevention surgery? The answer is clearly '*No*'. The decision to proceed with prophylactic mastectomy is an individual decision. Such factors are only an estimation of individual breast cancer risk, the ability to monitor the patient for early breast cancer and, most importantly, the patient's concerns and feelings need to be considered in making this decision.

According to the scientists and doctors, only those women who are at very high risk of breast cancer should consider surgery. This includes women with one or more of the following risk factors:

- Presence of mutated BRCA genes.
- Previous cancer in one breast and a strong family history of breast cancer.
- History of lobular carcinoma in situ (LCIS)[30].

Appropriate genetic and psychological counseling is strongly recommended before the prophylactic mastectomy, to discuss the psychosocial impacts of the procedure.

General Information about Puberty and Normal Breast Development among females[31]

Puberty refers to the process of physical changes by which a child's body becomes an adult's body, capable of reproduction. Puberty is initiated by hormone signals from the brain to the gonads (ovaries in females and testes in males). In response, the gonads produce a variety of hormones that stimulate the growth,

---

[30] LCIS is an uncommon condition in which abnormal cells form in the milk glands (lobules) in the breast.

[31] This is discussed through the character of Tanuja in this book.

function, or transformation of brain, bones, muscle, skin breasts and reproductive organs.

Growth accelerates in the first half of puberty and stops at the completion of puberty. Before puberty, body differences between boys and girls are almost entirely restricted to the genital organs.

During puberty, major differences of size, shape, composition, and function develop in many body structures and systems. The most obvious of these are referred to as secondary sex characteristics. In a strict sense, the term *puberty* refers to the bodily changes of sexual maturation rather than the psychosocial and cultural aspects of adolescent development.

Adolescence is the period of psychological and social transition between childhood and adulthood. Adolescence largely overlaps the period of puberty, but its boundaries are less precisely defined and it refers as much to the psychosocial and cultural characteristics of development during the teen years as to the physical changes of puberty.

What is Normal Breast Development?

Breast development is a vital part of puberty in the human females. Unlike other mammals, however, human females are the only ones who develop full breasts long before they are needed to nurse their offspring.

Breast development occurs in distinct stages, first before birth, during fetal development, with a thickening in the chest area called the mammary ridge or milk line. By the time a female infant is born, a nipple and the beginnings of the milk-duct system have formed.

Breast development occurs again at puberty and during the childbearing years. Changes also occur to the breasts during menstruation and when a woman reaches menopause.

Breast development is one of the most visible signs of puberty in girls. Some develop breasts as early as eight years and in some, there is a delayed development. However, as the estrogen hormone is secreted, it starts to signal the body to store fat tissues in the chest area which leads to the breast development. It is a continuous process and doesn't t happen in a couple of days. In fact, the process starts in the womb and continues till adulthood. But during puberty, the changes are felt and observed the most. Girls have to go through five stages of breast development before they attain full shape and size of the breast.

Following are the FIVE stages of Breast Development in girls. They are as follows:

Stage 1

The first stage of development is the preadolescent stage where the nipples or papilla starts to get elevated from the chest level. However, breast tissues are not formed at this time. So, the breast is still flat with the nipples just come out visibly. This can happen anywhere between age 8 to 13 depending on the genetic make-up of the person.

Stage 2

In the second stage of breast development, milk ducts and fat tissues are formed which makes the breasts to slightly rise above the nipple area. This stage involves the formation of the breast bud which elevates the nipples as well as develops a small mound of breast tissue along with enlargement of the diameter of the areola. The average age of girls at this time might be around 11 years.

Stage 3

The third stage of breast development is actually a continuation of the second stage where the breasts keep growing in size and so does the areola. There is still no contouring of the breasts which means they lack the round shape of the fully matured breasts and are usually conical in shape. The areola appears to look darker and puffier. On an average, a girl reaches this phase at around 12.5 years of age.

Stage 4

The fourth stage is the transitory stage between the third and fifth stage where the breasts and areola continue to grow along with the nipples. As the nipples and areola start to project out, it completes the fourth stage of development. It is during this time when a girl also faces hormonal changes and experiences her first period. As the body starts secreting estrogen fat tissues get deposited in the breast area making it grow further. While estrogen initiates fat storage in the breast area, progesterone another hormone which is secreted during menstruation leads to the development of milk glands in the milk ducts. On an average, a girl might be 13 or 14 years when she reaches this stage.

Stage 5

It takes around four to five years to reach this stage on an average from stage 1. This stage is marked with proper contouring of breasts and it starts to look more mature with the areola covering the tip of the breasts and the nipples getting erect. The breasts still keep growing and give the womanly curves that are unique to every girl. While this stage might make one's breasts look fully mature but they grow and change in shape once again during pregnancy triggered by the hormonal changes that happen during that phase.

Every girl grows at her own pace, but what one should know that if the first stage of breast development doesn't happen at around age 14 years, it is better to go to a doctor to get checked.

The breasts are usually fully mature by age 18. When fully mature, the secondary mound underneath the areola has blended in with the surrounding rounded breast shape. The nipples project outward. Milk glands and ducts fully develop. (They don't start producing milk until the baby is born to the female.)

Breast changes continue to occur over the lifespan, with lobes, or small subdivisions of breast tissue, developing first. Mammary glands develop next, and consist of 15-24 lobes. Mammary glands are influenced by hormones activated in puberty. Shrinkage of the milk ducts, called Involution, is the final major change that occurs within the breast tissue. Involution typically begins around the age of 35.

The duct system also begins to grow. Usually, the onset of these breast changes is also accompanied by the appearance of pubic hair and hair under the arms. The maturing of the breasts begins with the formation of secretory glands at the end of the milk ducts. The breasts and duct system continue to grow and mature with the development of many glands and lobules.

Open, relaxed and comfortable communication is the most important thing one can do for the child during puberty. It could be done between the young girls and their parents or between young girls and a doctor[32]. A child who is not comfortable talking to adults will act according to whatever is suggested by her biological impulses, her peers or the media and culture around her. Young girls want their mothers to be their main source of information about puberty. They appreciate a mother's stories of her own experiences.

---

[32] This is discussed through the characters of Tanuja's daughters – Sangeeta and Shruti, and Dr. Sudha in this book.

You can help your child by opening discussions from an early age and making them fun and pleasant. Do not tell your child she is a woman because she is menstruating. A 10 year old who's wearing a bra and a maxi pad needs to know she is still a child, or else she might be unfairly shoved into adult specific pressures that she is not psychologically prepared for, and might be forced to miss out on crucial developmental stages.

What is Hormonal Evolution?

Cells of multi cellular organisms need to communicate with each other to regulate their development and organize growth and cell division. Hormones contribute to these processes by acting as messengers between cells, telling them what's happening elsewhere in the body and how they should respond.

A hormone is a chemical messenger that carries a signal from one cell (or group of cells) to another. All multi-cellular organisms produce hormones, and they are often transported in the blood.

What is Contact Inhibition Theory?[33]

Contact inhibition is the natural process of arresting cell growth when two or more cells come into contact with each other. Oncologists use this property to distinguish between normal and cancerous cells. Cancer cells ignore signals that should cause them to stop dividing.

For instance, when normal cells grown in a dish in a laboratory are crowded, they no longer divide. Cancer cells, in contrast, keep dividing and pile on top of each other in lumpy layers. The environment in a laboratory dish is different from the environment in the human body, but scientists think that

---

[33] This theory is discussed by the character, named Dr. Sudha, in this book.

the loss of **contact inhibition** mechanism in laboratory dish grown cancer cells reflects the very same - loss of **contact inhibition** mechanism that normally maintains tissue balance in the human body.

When used in the context of reproduction of living cells, the phrase 'cell growth' is shorthand for the idea of growth in cell **population** by means of cell reproduction.

During cell reproduction, one cell, also called the 'mother' cell, divides to produce two daughter cells.

Cancerous cells typically lose this property and thus grow in an uncontrolled manner even when in contact with the neighboring cells. In brief, it is momentary stopping of cell growth and reproduction when it runs into another cell.

What is Gene Therapy?[34]

The definition of Gene therapy is to treat or stop a disease by inserting of genes into an individual's cells. Genes that don't work properly can cause disease. Gene therapy replaces such faulty gene or adds a new gene in an attempt to cure disease or improve your body's ability to fight disease.

Gene therapy holds promise for treating a wide range of diseases, such as cancer, cystic fibrosis, heart disease, diabetes, hemophilia and AIDS. This therapy entails replacing or fixing mutated genes and /or making the diseased cells more evident to the body's immune system,

Although the technology is still in its infancy state, it holds a promise for treating a wide range of diseases, including cancer. Researchers are still studying how and when to use gene therapy. Currently, it is available only as part of a clinical trial.

---

[34] Gene Therapy is discussed by the character named Dr. Sudha, in this book, with reference to Oncogenes and Tumor Suppressor Genes (TSG).

Is there a Vaccine for Breast Cancer?

Vaccines Could Revolutionize Breast Cancer Prevention and Treatment.

In recent years, interest in cancer vaccines has grown as researchers learn more about how the immune system can fight cancer. Studies have shown that engaging the immune system to fight cancer has a lot fewer side effects than chemotherapy or radiation therapy or surgery. There are some cancers, where, it was noted that chemotherapy never worked. But now the immunotherapy is working, and it's really kind of opened the door to a lot of new treatments for patients who didn't have any good treatments available.

Cancer vaccines can be used alongside other promising new treatments which also harness the immune system.

There are many breast cancer vaccines currently undergoing testing, including more than a dozen that target HER2. While most of the vaccines are intended as treatments, some teams of scientists are studying how they can be used for prevention as well.

Creating a preventive vaccine for people at high risk of certain cancers can be more challenging, because scientists must be sure the vaccine is entirely safe before immunizing healthy individuals.

Visualization Technique[35]

Over the centuries, human beings have developed many techniques to gain access to their inner wisdom and improve learning. Especially practiced in the older cultures of world, this theory holds true even in today's technological times, in the modern world. One technique that many people have found very beneficial is to have an imaginary guide that they can call on for advice and insight.

---

[35] This Technique is discussed and conducted in a workshop by the character of Shantabai, in this book.

Visualization is a technique for creating images, diagrams, or some kind of animation to communicate a message. Visualization through visual imagery has been an effective way to communicate both abstract and concrete ideas since the dawn of man.

Visualization today has an ever-expanding application in science, education, engineering (e.g. product visualization), medicine, etc.

Guided health imagery, a technique to help patients relax their muscles and open their minds to images of health and healthy living, has long been used to help surgery and cancer patients, as well as for reducing pain and reversing negative thoughts resulting from traumatic events

It is well known that the quality of thoughts create certain kinds of biological effects. For example it is well known, and scientifically established, that negative thoughts create stress and in turn this releases stress hormones in the body (cortisone). Cortisone is a degenerative hormone and is destructive in the body causing illness and disease. By contrast, positive, happy thoughts do the opposite. They release beneficial hormones such as: beta endorphins and human growth hormone, within the body, which are regenerative and healing to the body.

Creating visual images that you can refer to, or see in passing during your day is a good way of keeping your **subconscious mind** more focussed on your intentions (in this case to get well).

Using the visualization technique does not mean you do not attend to proper eating, rest, and using medicines that are appropriate for you (only you know what those are), but by using these techniques you will drastically improve your body's ability to realize itself to full health sooner.

Body-Mind connection

A new field of research, known as psycho-neuro-immunology, is exploring how the immune system and the brain may interact to influence health. For years stress has been suspected of increasing susceptibility to various infectious diseases or cancer. Now evidence is mounting that the immune system and the nervous system may be inextricably interconnected.

Biological links between the immune system and the central nervous system exist at several levels.

"Instinctively we have known for a long time that how we think affects how we feel. This new field explains the scientific understanding of how psychology and physical body processes interact. What we are discovering is that there is a bi-directional conversation happening between the body and the mind, meaning that the body can affect the thoughts we have, while our thoughts can also affect our physical bodies through the <u>immune, hormone and neurological systems.</u> The image that is emerging is of closely interlocked systems facilitating a two-way flow of information, primarily through the language of hormones. Immune cells, it has been suggested, may function in a sensory capacity, detecting the arrival of foreign invaders and relaying chemical signals to alert the brain. The brain, for its part, may send signals that guide the traffic of cells through the lymphoid organs.

The body-mind connection is real. New research shows that disorders in the immune system can cause disease; and a healthy and active brain boosts the immune system function well. It helps keep a person healthy. In brief, keeping a positive attitude is vital to the well-being of a human being.

To summarize - in mind-body medicine, the mind and body are not seen as two separately functioning entities, but as **one** functioning unit. The mind and emotions are viewed as influencing the body, and the body, in turn, influences the mind and emotions.

Climb to Victory Over Breast Cancer